Neutral Grounds

JIFFY KATE

Neutral Grounds (French Quarter Novel)

Jiffy Kate Books, LLC, *www.jiffykate.com*

Editing by Nichole Strauss, *Insight Editing*
Cover Design and Formatting by Juliana Cabrera, *Jersey Girl Design*
Proofreading by Janice Owen
Cover Model: Tommy Pearce
Cover Photo by Michelle Lancaster (http://www.michellelancaster.com/)

First Printing, October 2019
Printed in the United States of America

Books by Jiffy Kate

Finding Focus Series (Complete)
Finding Focus
Chasing Castles
Fighting Fire
Taming Trouble

French Quarter Novels (All Stand-alones)
Blue Bayou
Come Again
Neutral Grounds

Table 10 (parts 1-3)

Turn of Fate
(previously titled The Other One)

Watch and See

The Rookie and The Rockstar

Stud Muffin
(Donner Bakery #2 for Smartypants Romance)

Whoever said being in love is easy

was a lying bastard.

TWO YEARS AGO

Shep

"BOARDWALK FOR *TWO THOUSAND* DOLLARS? FUCK me, I'm out." Maverick throws his fake money at me then unceremoniously finishes his drink.

"That just leaves you and me, sweets." I waggle my eyebrows at my beautiful opponent only to be flipped off in return.

Rude.

"Get him, CeCe. Don't let this prick win!" Carys shouts and I flinch just a bit at her words.

Again, rude.

"Sorry, Shep," Carys says sheepishly. "I just get really competitive when I drink. I don't actually think you're a prick, I promise." She gives me a friendly smile, her head tilting just enough to show how tipsy she is, even though she's been out of the game for quite a while.

"It's fine, Carys," I assure her. And it is fine because she's just being nice. I am a prick.

A prick with a heart, but a prick just the same.

CeCe, my current adversary—Carys's best friend whom I only met one day ago when I let Maverick drag my ass to New Orleans so he could get his girl—sips her drink while waiting for my next move. She's been watching me all night and I fucking love it. She also doesn't seem to mind my eyes being on her the entire evening either, when they're not on my growing fake bank account, of course.

Priorities.

CeCe and I have an odd relationship. Actually, *relationship* isn't the correct word but I can't think of another way to describe us after the many shots and drinks I've consumed while playing this game. Who knew playing Drunk Monopoly could be so much fun?

I guess *acquaintance* is how I'd describe us. We only know each other because our best friends are in love. If it weren't for Maverick and Carys, we'd be complete strangers. I'd still think she's the hottest woman I've ever seen, but that's beside the point. I'm fairly sure CeCe doesn't do one-night stands and I'm even more certain I'm not her type.

What a shame.

I roll the dice and move the top hat game piece I was assigned, landing on Tennessee Avenue.

Shit.

"Pay up, sucker!" CeCe demands, sticking her open palm out to me.

I hand over nine hundred and fifty dollars, watching as she adds the bills to her huge stack.

"How do you have so much money?" I ask. "I own the most expensive properties in the game."

"Oh, Shep…silly, sexy, Shep," she sing-songs. "Silly, sexy, smart-yet-stupid, Shep. It's not about how expensive the property is; it's about how often someone lands on it. Owning the red and orange properties will almost always give you a win. The dark blues? Well, the odds are against you, my friend." She snorts and it's oddly attractive.

I already had a semi from our witty banter, but after that little explanation, I have a full-on erection. Her beauty is a natural turn-on but knowing she has brains, too, just upped the ante. Big time.

Wait, did she just say I was sexy?

"Did you just say I'm sexy?"

Her eyes flash to mine while her cheeks turn a delicious shade of pink. How far does that blush go? I shamelessly let my eyes wander down to her tits. They'd definitely be a handful, if not more.

"What?" she asks, feigning ignorance, but we both know CeCe Calhoun is anything but. Clearing her throat, she cocks her head. "I…I think the liquor is getting to me. What I meant to say was silly, *stupid*, Shep." Her coy smile is enough to make me hard, but then she bites down on that plump bottom lip and I'm a goner.

"I have an idea," I say, deciding to let her off the hook for her slip-up, for now.

"What?" CeCe eyes me warily and it makes me want to laugh but I manage to hold it in.

"Let's make the game interesting," I suggest.

"You mean more interesting than having to take a drink for nearly every step of this game?"

Oh, yeah, Drunk Monopoly is a beast, and even if you win the game, you'll more than likely lose to your alcohol of choice. That Jose Cuervo is a sore winner, for sure, trust me.

"I believe you and I are evenly matched in this game, so it only makes sense that we should make the stakes higher."

"We're not playing with real money, Shep."

"That's not what I mean," I say, rolling my eyes at her absurd assumption. I have more than enough money. Why would I want hers?

"Then what do you want?" CeCe sits up straight and looks me dead in the eyes. She's challenging me and it makes me want to sweep this fucking Monopoly board in the floor and fuck her right here on this table…all night long, not caring if Carys and Maverick are still in the room.

I return her gaze and hold it, simply wanting to see how long she lasts. Only after I hear Maverick mutter "for fuck's sake" under his breath do I finally answer.

"A kiss."

The laughter that erupts out of CeCe is surprising, but I don't let it affect my composure.

"And, what do I get if *I* win?" she asks.

"What do you want?"

"The empty space next to Neutral Grounds."

What the hell? This girl doesn't pull any punches, she goes right for what she wants. How the hell did she know I own that property?

I hear a throat clearing, followed by a chair scraping against the floor that brings my attention to Maverick. "Come on, Mess, let's leave these two to their *game*." He grabs Carys's hand and practically pulls her out of her chair.

Fucker.

"But I want to see who wins." Her voice is whiny and tipsy.

"I was thinking we'd play our own game," he mutters. "Strip Monopoly." That's all Carys needs to hear as she lets Mav lead her down the hallway to their bedroom.

"Y'all keep it down. We don't want to hear any live porn action," I grumble.

CeCe laughs, waving as Carys blows a kiss to her friend over her shoulder.

It was only an hour ago that the four of us left the lobby of the hotel and retired to Carys's apartment for a nightcap. What was supposed to be a drink between friends escalated to shots over a fucking board game.

"You looked surprised by my answer," CeCe says, bringing my attention back to her. "I've wanted that space for years, so I make it my business to know everything about it. Imagine my surprise when I was told who the new owner is."

"I have plans for that space," I tell her, thinking back to when I purchased it only a few months ago. Funny thing about that is it was long before I knew Maverick would be coming here to stay. I saw it in a stack of listings, various properties in the French Quarter area for sale, but one of the few that had potential. And quite honestly, I bought it because I knew Spencer Kensington was looking for properties in the same area and I would rather have it and sit on it for years, letting it rot, before I let him get his hands on it. Sure, it sounds juvenile and petty, but I don't mind stooping to his level to beat him at his own game. "But," I continue, holding CeCe's gaze and trying not to get lost in her big brown eyes. It must be the whiskey. "If it's what you want to win, I guess I could give it up."

Lies. There's no way in hell I'll let her win, but I can let her think she's winning so I can get what I want. "Just know, if I win, our kiss has to be fucking spectacular to even come close to being comparable to real estate."

"My kisses are always spectacular, don't worry."

Fuck, now my dick feels like a brick. I couldn't hide this erection if I wanted to, which I don't. I want CeCe to know what she does to me.

"How about we end the game right now and count our money," I suggest, not wanting to prolong this any further. "Biggest bank wins."

"You're on," she says. Her eyebrow rising in challenge and I fucking love it.

She starts counting her fake bills, which turns out to be more difficult than you'd think. I get distracted watching her separate them by denomination, the tip of her tongue poking out between her full, pink lips. I want to suck that tongue into my mouth and taste her.

When she's done, she looks at me with hazy eyes and a very confident smile. It's the smile that does things to my insides—weird and new things, but things I must ignore.

"Two thousand, eight hundred and fifty-two dollars. What'd you end up with?"

I've been keeping a running tally in my brain for the entire game, so I don't really need to recount my stack to know she has more money than I do. I'm not afraid to lose a silly board game. I'm not even afraid to lose to CeCe Calhoun. It's not about winning or losing tonight; it's about getting that kiss I was promised.

I want it. I want her. But just for tonight.

So, I do something I'm not very proud of. I slide three five-hundred-dollar Monopoly bills out from under my thigh, the same ones that have been hiding there since the game began, and add them to my stack.

"Sorry, babe. Looks like I got you by seven hundred dollars. Congrats on a great game, though."

Glancing up, I catch sight of those big, brown eyes and the way they go a little wider when they realize I'm serious. *Yeah, CeCe, I always collect on my debts, so pay up.* When she swallows hard, my dick twitches in my pants and my fingers itch to touch her.

It's been a while since I've fucked anyone. Relationships aren't my thing and I'm not interested in making my life messy with females who get attached. Co-workers are off-limits. People who are after my family fortune are way the fuck off-limits. So, my options are limited.

A woman I met in a hotel lobby in San Francisco.

The lady who shared an Uber with me in Chicago.

Hot, red-headed bartender in New York.

She was the last one, over a month ago, but now I have my sights set on the delicious brown-eyed, brown-haired beauty across from me. I shouldn't. My best friend is in love with her best friend. She's too closely connected and if things work out between Maverick and Carys, I'll be forced to see her again. It's not my style. She's not my style, but fuck if I don't want her more than anything I've wanted in a long damn time. Which is all the more reason I need to fuck her. She'll mess with my head if I don't. I'll always wonder.

What does she taste like?

What does she sound like when she comes?

What face does she make when she's at the peak of ecstasy?

"You want to kiss me?" she asks, her voice coming out slow and breathy, a hint of disbelief.

I can't help being intrigued by her. In one breath, she's confident and sure of herself. In the next, there's a bit of self-doubt, just enough to keep her feeling real and honest. She doesn't come off like a girl who'd be up for a one-night stand, but the way her tongue darts out to wet those fucking lips, I know there's more to CeCe Calhoun than what you see on the surface.

Standing from the chair, I let it screech against the floor as I walk around the table and brace my arms on either side of her. "We have a deal."

"Yeah," she agrees, leaning back a little due to my proximity, but her eyes are still drinking me in. Her smidge of self-doubt is mixed with lust and desire.

"We're both business people, right?" I ask, letting my voice drop as my mouth lingers near her ear. "I don't know about you, CeCe, but I never go back on a deal."

"N—no…me neither."

"Good."

The second my lips brush her cheek, I hear the inhale of breath and then her hands come up to grip my shoulders. *Oh, yeah, she wants this.*

1

2 YEARS LATER

Shep

"**Fucking hell, it's hot. How did I manage to** forget how hot it gets down here? And, who the fuck thought it'd be a good time to move?" I glare at my best friend and business partner—who might be demoted to ex status after today—as I carry another box inside my new townhouse. "Oh, that's right, you."

He smirks. "If you think it's hot now, just wait until August," he calls back as he turns to retrieve more of my shit from the moving truck. "Your balls will be melting down your legs!"

I meet him at the back of the truck and take the box from him. "That's a lovely visual, Mav, but that won't be me. I'll be locked away with my new, high-powered air conditioner until December."

"Such a fucking spoiled brat," he mutters to himself, making me chuckle. We've always given each other shit for being rich kids, but we'd never let anyone else talk about the other that way. "No worries. New Orleans will fix you right up."

Maverick pulls out a handkerchief from his back pocket and

wipes his brow before heading back into the truck to grab more of my belongings.

"You sound like such a local when you say shit like that." I say it like it's a bad thing but, deep down I know it's not. I also have a feeling he's right, but I won't be admitting that any time soon.

"I know. Ain't it great?" he counters with a shit-eating grin on his face.

Smug bastard.

Don't get me wrong, I'm happy Maverick has settled in here as well as he has. Thrilled, even. He's living his best life in The Big Easy and it shows. I've never seen him happier and more content. Our business is doing very well and the hotel he helps run, the Blue Bayou, has been booming for the last year or so. And, as if that weren't enough, the poor sap is in love. Like, completely smitten, head over heels in love. I don't envy him that, though. He can have his real-life fairytale and I'll gladly stick to the single life, thank you very much.

That's another bonus to living in a new city, fresh fish. Particularly, ones who don't know me from Adam and couldn't care less my last name is Rhys-Jones.

We finish unloading the truck and spend the next half hour soaking up that a/c I mentioned earlier while downing a few bottles of water.

"I still can't believe you didn't hire a moving company. It's very *un-Sheplike* of you." Maverick tosses his empty water bottle in a bin by the back door then pulls a beer for each of us from the cooler he brought with him.

"Come on, I'm not completely incapable of doing things on my own…or with the help of my best friend." I take a swig of the cold beer, enjoying the crisp flavor on my tongue more than the water I'd just finished. "Besides, I only brought the necessities. This place came fully furnished, so I left everything else back in Dallas."

"Ahh, so you're keeping your house on standby in case New Orleans doesn't work out? That, my friend, is *very* Sheplike."

"Fuck off, man. You know I have to keep my options open."

"Oh, believe me, I do. But, in case you were curious, there's nothing wrong with settling down. It's pretty great, actually. You should give it a try sometime, especially since you have a big milestone coming up."

"Why must everyone harp on the fact I'm turning thirty?" I ask, tossing my empty can into the trash. "You're sounding like my mother."

"Fuck," Maverick mutters. "Sorry, man. You know I don't want to be classified with her."

"I mean, age is just a number, right?" I ask him, kicking my feet out and relaxing back on the oversized leather couch. "I just don't get why everyone is so hung up on it. What, do my priorities automatically change overnight when I turn thirty? If that's the case, no wonder people dread it so much. I like my priorities right where they are and I'm nowhere near ready for them to change, regardless of my age."

"Well, you are Shepard Rhys-Jones," Mav says with a matter-of-fact tone. "We all know the rules don't apply to you."

I really hate it when he patronizes me, and normally, I'd throw a punch to his arm or gut to drive that fact home, but I let it slide since he did just help me unload all my boxes off the moving truck. Just because he's a whole six months older than I am, Maverick likes to think he knows more about life and shit but he's wrong.

And I look forward to proving that fact.

"So, how big of a celebration are we doing this year, Shep? Thirty is a pretty big milestone, or so I hear." Carys laughs and pinches Maverick on his side, causing him to jump back with a surprised yelp.

"You little..." he starts and reaches out to grab her around her waist and pulls her to him, eliciting a laugh from Carys. I pretend to hate it, but deep down, I'm mesmerized by it.

For my entire life, I've always looked at relationships from a business standpoint. My parents married because the Rhys's and Jones's wanted to form a partnership, hence the hyphenated last name. Fucking pretentious bastards.

It was part of the deal when they married that each family would be equally represented.

All of my parents' friends have similar relationships, most marrying for status—mergers and acquisitions. I'm not sure what my grandparents' relationships were like because my maternal grandparents died before I was born and my paternal grandmother died shortly after. So, I've only ever known my father's father. He spent his days in an office and his nights in his study. But I'm assuming they were similar people, my parents being products of their upbringing. That's how it is in the circle we're from.

Rich breeds rich.

Entitled breeds entitled.

Silver spoons breed fucking silver spoons.

Except for me and Maverick. Back in school, we gravitated toward each other, seeing in the other something we identified with, an intense desire to be our own people, regardless of what was expected of us. Sure, we followed in our parents' footsteps for the most part, but we always knew when the time was right, we'd break free from the roles we'd been born into and find our own path.

I'm glad Maverick is finally on his.

And me, well, I'm getting there.

"So, your birthday," Carys says, pulling me out of my thoughts. "What are we going to do?"

I shrug. "I just want to drink and see something naked."

"Did someone say naked?" Jules, the guy who helps out at the hotel walks by as we're hanging out in the courtyard of the Blue Bayou, raising his well-groomed eyebrows in interest.

"No," I tell him pointedly. I already know what his suggestion will be and the one drunken night I experienced at Revelry is enough to last the rest of my life. About a year ago, after mine and Maverick's first big sale, they talked me into it.

I regretted it for three days.

I think I was drunk for two of those.

"Come Again?" Carys suggests, smiling over at Maverick. "Maybe we can do the cooking school thing before we go next door for drinks." She gets more excited with each word. "And invite CeCe." She jumps up and down and my stomach drops at the mention of CeCe.

The ring of my cell phone saves me from giving away the emotions that get stirred up every time she's mentioned or comes around.

"Hello?" I say, placing the phone to my ear and walking off to have some privacy.

"Shepard." My mother's voice sounds off, which is completely uncharacteristic. She rarely shows emotion or a chink in her well-dressed, high-end armor. "I have some…news."

After a brief pause, she continues. "Your grandfather has passed. The funeral will be Sunday, so you'll need to cut your little vacation short and come home." She clears her throat, bringing back the bravado and smooth outer shell I'm used to getting from my mother. "We'll have the reading of the will the following day."

My chest feels a little tight at her news but not sad like I should be after hearing that my grandfather passed. Like everything else in my life, this just feels like a business transaction—something that has to be done and there's an order to it.

"I'll catch the next available flight out," I tell her, ending the call.

"Where the hell are you going?" Maverick asks, making me jump a little before turning around to face him. "You just got here."

"Dallas," I inform him. "My grandfather died."

When the words come out of my mouth, they take a shape and form I wasn't expecting. There's a sense of loss left with their departure—*his* departure. We weren't close in the conventional sense of the word. He was always so serious and driven, just like my father. But he was never unkind. He sent me to summer camp and made sure I played sports. Back then, I felt like it was because he wanted me to be well-rounded and primed to take over the family business. But through the years, I got the feeling he was living vicariously through me in a way, giving me experiences and freedoms, he never had.

And now he's gone.

Maverick's hand comes down on my shoulder and grips tightly.

"I'm sorry, man."

"Thanks, but you know there's no need for sentimental condolences," I say, shrugging him off. "This will go down like every other life event in the Rhys-Jones family—a business deal. We'll show up, wear our black, shake hands with people who don't give a shit about anything except how much money we have, and we'll go our separate ways."

"Yeah, but still—"

"But, nothing, Mav," I interrupt. "I'm fine, really. Not all grandfathers are nice and loving like yours was, unfortunately. I'm more upset I have to be back in Dallas so soon. Speaking of, I guess I should go back to my place and make my travel arrangements." I walk toward the door and slide my sunglasses over my eyes. "I'll talk to you before I leave. See ya, Carys."

I give them a small wave before pushing my way out into the sultry New Orleans afternoon.

CeCe

"THANKS, JIM," I CALL OUT OVER MY SHOULDER TO the older man who delivers my mail. Just like everyone else in the French Quarter, he's like family.

"Got something for you to sign today," he says, catching me off guard. I expected him to be halfway out the door like usual. He's always walking around like a man on a mission, worse than the speed walkers who make laps around the square for exercise.

Finishing up the drink I was making, I hand it over to the customer. "Enjoy," I tell her. "Come back and see us." As I walk over to where Jim is standing by the counter, I wipe my hands off on my apron and catch a glimpse of the envelope.

Nothing good ever comes in a registered envelope. Taxes, past due bills, notices—those are the sorts of things people pay extra money to make sure you see them and pay attention.

"Sign here," he instructs, sliding a card across the counter.

"Thanks," I say absentmindedly as I take the envelope and begin reading the return address.

Laughlin Law.

Huh, never heard of them.

Grabbing a butter knife from the silverware caddy on the counter, I make quick work of opening the envelope. As I unfold the paper, my eyes are already scanning the letter.

Miss Cecelia Calhoun,

I'm writing you on behalf of my client, Theodore Duval.

At the first line, my heart is already beating faster in my chest. Theodore Duval was my uncle. He died five years ago.

Mr. Duval is contesting the will left by his father, Theodore Duval, Sr.

Wait. What?

I start back at the beginning, reading the first few sentences again, making sure I'm understanding them correctly. *Theodore Duval, Sr.?* I'm guessing that's my Uncle Teddy. But who is this *Mr. Duval? A junior? Which would make him what, my cousin? Why have I never heard of him?* My mind is spinning as the door chimes.

"Be right with you," I mumble, unable to tear my eyes away from the crisp white paper in my hands.

Working on autopilot, with my mind on the letter, I make a few drinks and serve some desserts, thankful it's the middle of the day and between rush hours. I tend to the customers, forcing small talk when necessary and smiling when appropriate. But the second the last one leaves, I walk over to the phone that still hangs on the wall, dialing the only person who might have an idea what this is all about.

"Hey, baby," my mama's familiar voice greets on the other end of the line.

"Hey," I say, unfolding the letter and scanning it again, hoping this isn't what I think it is, but how could it—

"I know this isn't a casual call, you never call during the day…so, what's going on?"

She's always been perceptive and reads me like the back of her hand. "I got a weird letter today…registered mail. I had to sign for it and everything."

"Okay," she drawls. "Who's it from?"

"A Mr. Laughlin..." I say, pausing to swallow down the unease creeping up my throat, "on behalf of his client...Mr. Theodore Duval."

There's a long, uninterrupted silence before my mama finally breaks it by clearing her voice. "Come again?"

"Theodore...Duval," I repeat. "How can Uncle Teddy send a letter from the grave?"

"He can't," she says as she releases a huff of displeasure.

"What's this about?" I ask. "It says Mr. Theodore Duval is contesting Theodore Duval, Sr.'s will...that's a lot of Theodores. I only know about one."

"Well, I'll be damned."

I don't like the sound of that.

"Mama?" I ask, a warning in my tone, one I don't usually take with her, but I don't like the sound of this one bit. I don't like the sound of anything that threatens me or my business, and in turn, my family's well-being. "What is this about?"

Her deep sigh is enough to make me want to crawl through the phone and demand answers. "Mama."

"Well," she begins, hesitant and like she's still trying to wrap her head around the information I've given her. "There was a rumor floating around when I was younger, too young to be involved in adult conversation. Your Uncle Teddy had moved to New Orleans and met a girl. Supposedly, they had some kind of whirlwind romance, but when her rich daddy found out she was with a shop owner from New Orleans, he demanded she come back home."

She breaks for another sigh and I brace myself on the counter.

"Anyway, I remember them talking about her being pregnant and that was really why her father made her come home. Your Aunt Irene and Grandma were talking at the kitchen table one day. I'd just come from school and overheard them whispering. Mama said something about the girl's family probably forcing her to *take care of it*...Now I know they were probably talking about her getting an abortion. I think that's what everyone assumed. Uncle Teddy never spoke about her again…or the baby. But…"

This time, the pause takes up the span of a minute, at least, or maybe that's just how it feels because all of a sudden, I feel like my life is hanging on her unspoken words.

"But what, Mama? Just spit it out."

"When I went to the reading of the will," she begins again, taking small breaks to think as she speaks. "There was a letter with it…it was an old will…not even that official—something your Uncle Teddy had written up years ago, probably sometime after Mama and Daddy died, leaving just a few of us left. It said he left everything to his next of kin, which everyone in the room that day assumed was me, after his brothers and sisters died, that only left me…and you and Rory. He'd never married…never had any children…at least, that's what everyone assumed."

That statement makes me think of what my old history teacher used to tell us.

"You know what you get when you assume, right?" I deadpan, knowing she'll get the reference.

Her laugh holds no humor as she says, "You make an ass out of you and me."

"So, what you're saying," I continue, "is that Uncle Teddy left the building and business to his next of kin, which *could be* Theodore Duval…*junior*." I just go ahead and connect the dots and rip the bandage off. It's better to know what we're dealing with than to sweep it under the rug and pretend like it doesn't exist.

"I wish I had better news for you," she adds. "I… I just never… you have to know if I ever thought this was a possibility, I would've told you. Please know I didn't keep this from you intentionally. No one ever spoke about the relationship or the baby. It was just one of those things that wasn't brought up around the dinner table, like politics and religion."

I sigh, rubbing my forehead as I scan the space around me—everything in this shop feels like a part of me.

Ever since the day I started working for Uncle Teddy, I just felt like I belonged here. I picked up the business in no time. He'd always joke that I could run it better than him. After I'd been here a year, I started in on him about opening up a coffee bar. He was hesitant, but I assured him he'd never have to run it, just help me get it off the ground.

That's how we worked—he kept the day-to-day, tried-and-true portion of Neutral Grounds going and I added in new life, bringing in fresh concepts. Sure, I never made it to business school, but I got plenty of on-the-job training. My years working with Uncle Teddy were like an apprenticeship. He taught me everything I needed to know and then some.

Which is why, when he died five years ago and left everything to my mother, it didn't feel strange in the least. She deeded everything over to me and I send her money every month and help pay for my younger sister's college tuition. It's how this family works.

"What are we going to do?" This time, when my mama speaks, it sounds too small and too timid.

I straighten my back and take a deep breath, wiping back the stray strands of hair off my face. "I don't know, but I'll figure it out." I have to. That's my job in the Calhoun family. I take one for the team—like skipping college to work and help support my mother and sister. After my dad left when I was ten, my mama worked two jobs, leaving Rory and me home by ourselves a lot. When I graduated, I didn't want Rory to be alone while I was off at college and Mama was at work, so I decided to get a job. Mama quit her nighttime cleaning job and started working at the school cafeteria. It wasn't much, but between what she made and what I sent home, it was enough to pay the mortgage and get Rory through school.

"We're going to be okay," I assure her.

When the door chimes, I wipe an unexpected tear off my cheek. I don't cry. Cecilia Louise Calhoun holds her shit together. "Gotta go, Mama. I've got a customer."

She quickly says bye and hangs up, but I can tell she's worried.

That makes two of us.

Shep

AS MY DRIVER PULLS UP IN FRONT OF MY FAMILY'S estate, I already feel the air around me change, and it's not just the climate. The small sense of ease I'd started to feel after being in New Orleans for only a short period of time is gone and in its place is the rigidness of formality.

There's no warm greeting.

No mourning family gathered.

When I step inside the large foyer, I'm met with silence.

If I had to guess, my mother is playing bridge with the ladies. It is Tuesday, after all. And my father is at the office. Business doesn't even pause for death. If anything, it's moving at a faster rate, as everyone makes sure every "i" is dotted and every "t" is crossed.

"Mr. Shepard," a familiar voice greets.

Glancing up, I smile. "Maggie."

"We were expecting you later today. Dinner won't be served until six."

"I got an earlier flight."

She immediately goes into action. "Let me take your bag."

"It's fine," I tell her, hoisting my duffle higher on my shoulder. "I've got it."

"Can I get you something? A drink, perhaps?"

Sighing, I actually think about turning around and calling my driver, asking him to come back. Staying at my empty house would be better than being here. Shit, a hotel would even be better. But it's only for a couple of days. "A drink would be great," I say, smiling a genuine smile.

After I put my bag in my old room, in the west wing—yeah, the house has fucking wings—I make my way back down the stairs and partake of the drink Maggie offered, knowing I'll need the amber liquid to make it through the next forty-eight hours.

Thankfully, Maggie is great at small talk and taking my mind off of things, so the hours pass swiftly and before I know it, my parents are home and I'm once again regretting not staying in a fucking hotel. We eat in relative silence, except for my mother, who talks incessantly about a woman she'd like me to take to dinner.

Such a nice girl.

She went to Rice.

The way she says *Rice* makes it sound exotic.

Her father owns the firm…

And that's when I really tune her out. I don't give two shits about who her father is or isn't. I know exactly who she is without even knowing her damn name. A fucking Real Housewives of Dallas wannabe. She's looking for a man her parents approve of and someone who can give her the life she's accustomed to. It's not about love or attraction. In twenty-five years, she'll be my mother.

"Samuel Shepard Jones was a well-respected man," the minister begins. The church is over-packed, full of people I don't know or wish I didn't. Except Maverick. He showed up this morning, against my wishes. Fucker never listens.

"The size of this congregation today shows how much," he continues.

I slide my eyes down the pew toward my mother and father who are both sitting stoically in their seats. Typically, at a funeral, at least those closest to the deceased are crying, or at least wiping away a rogue tear. But every eye in the place is dry. I want to scoff at the words of the minister as he makes my grandfather out to be some kind of saint, but of course, I don't. Instead, I fall in line and assume the same expression as my parents, pretending to listen as we wait for Samuel Shepard Jones' final transaction.

After the funeral, everyone makes their way past the casket, offering us condolences as they pass. When a tall redhead walks up, I can tell by the slight smile on her ruby lips she's not here for condolences.

"Shepard," my mother says quietly, reaching out and clasping the hands of the woman, like they're old friends. "This is Felicity Crawford, the one I was telling you about at dinner last night."

"Hello, Shep," Felicity says, stretching her slender, well-manicured hand in my direction. "I believe you were in the same fraternity as my brother, Foster."

Trying to hide the disgust, I plaster on a fake smile. "Yeah, Foster," I tell her, shaking her hand quickly and then dropping it, stopping myself before I can wipe my palm on the leg of my pants. Foster Crawford is one of the most pretentious assholes I've ever had the displeasure of knowing. He sexually assaulted a girl during our sophomore year in college and his daddy bought his way out of it. Just the thought of him makes my stomach roll.

"Daddy would love to meet you," Felicity continues, oblivious to the fact I'd rather poke my own eyeballs out before I meet her daddy. "We'd love to have all of you over for dinner tomorrow night. It's the least we can do in your time of need."

My throat hurts from holding back my honest reactions. *Fuck no*, I don't want to have dinner with her and her family. And *our time of need*? Are you fucking kidding me?

"I'm sorry," I say, a smidge too abruptly if the side glare I get from my mother is any indication. "I'll be leaving tomorrow to head back to New Orleans."

When my mother speaks again, I can hear the eye-roll in her tone. "Shep has recently bought a bachelor pad in New Orleans…boys." She and Felicity share a knowing laugh. "We'll set something up soon."

After air kisses and empty promises, Felicity walks away, but not before she brushes the sleeve of my suit jacket, gripping my wrist slightly to get my attention.

This time, I do wipe off her touch.

"Dinner," my mother instructs. "Tomorrow night. You'll be there."

Smiling, I grit out, "No, I won't."

"You will," she sing-songs. "The reading of the will is tomorrow at five. If you want your inheritance, you'll be there."

Fuck.

As we drive to the attorney's office, I try not to think about the will.

Ever since my mother mentioned it at the funeral, a small ember has been burning—a taste of freedom. But I'm trying not to get my hopes up.

I'm sure he left me something. How much is the part I don't know. We never discussed it. He always assumed I'd be groomed to take over the family business and that one day the Rhys-Jones empire would be mine, but since I parted ways recently, my future has been less predictable. I'm not sure what will happen today.

He could've completely written me out of everything for all I know.

That thought doesn't scare me as much as it used to or as much as it probably should.

I'm not destitute by any means, but since putting the family business on the back burner to make a go of things with Maverick, I've been living off my savings. Most of the profit Maverick and I bring in goes back into our business. Give us another couple of years and we'll be much more comfortable, but building a business from the ground up takes time and money.

The cash flow from an inheritance would help tremendously. A total fucking game changer. The best part is, I'd finally be able to completely separate myself from working for my father and live the life I choose, instead of the one I was born into.

Regardless of what Maverick thinks, blazing my own path is a lot more important to me these days than what kind of car I drive or how big my house is. He loves giving me a hard time about my expensive tastes, but just because I like nice things doesn't mean I'm afraid of going after what I want.

Maybe one of these days, I'll confide in him just how much his own escape from Dallas high society two years ago led to my own. He, also, had an inheritance to help him out but he's made investments, not only in our business, but in Carys's and he gets stretched thin at times. It's my turn to pony up. We're both equal partners in every way but a little extra money in the bank would be nice.

So, yeah, I'd fucking love to claim my inheritance.

The room the receptionist escorts us into is just as stifling as the company I'm keeping.

My father takes a seat at the far end of the large mahogany table and my mother sits to his left. I take the seat across from him. He doesn't make eye contact, merely pulls out his phone and begins typing away furiously—answering emails, returning messages…who the fuck knows. He could be playing Candy Crush. Anything to keep from engaging with me these days.

I went against the grain…went my own way…turned down the chance at running the family business…which is all a big *fuck you* in his eyes. He can't fathom why I wouldn't want to be him one day.

My mother cuts her eyes to my father and then over to me. She probably wants to say something, anything to break the tension that's settled over the room, but she won't. That's not her place. She's there to look pretty and play the part. She's there not because my father is madly in love with her, but because her last name is Rhys. Her family had something my father's family wanted—real estate, properties.

When I was younger, I deluded myself into thinking we were a real family, but it didn't take long to figure out that was only true in public. According to the world, the who's who of Highland Park, we were Phillip, Jane, and Shepard Rhys-Jones. The perfect family. But in private, we were Phillip the business owner, who slept with countless women, and Jane the socialite, who screwed the pros at the country club. And Shepard, the son who saw everything.

Which is exactly why I'll never marry.

It's one business transaction I have no desire to complete.

"Sorry to keep you waiting," Mr. Hall says, wiping back a wisp of grey hair from his forehead. He quickly takes a seat at the head of the table, between me and my father. "Let's get right to it, shall we?"

"Yes," my father says, pocketing his phone and clasping his hands in front of him on the sleek table. "Let's make this quick. I don't have all day."

"Yes, sir." Even though Mr. Hall has at least twenty years on my father, he cowers down to him like everyone else. Opening his briefcase, he extracts a stack of papers. "The three of you have been asked to come here today per Mr. Jones' final requests." He lays a set of papers in front of each of us. "Mr. Jones was very clear that he wanted you all here...together."

I don't miss my father's annoyed expression. "Well, let's get to it." He checks the time on his watch before clasping his hands back together. I'm surprised he isn't tapping his fingers on the table, which is what he usually does when he feels like someone is wasting his time. It's like an audible reminder that his minutes count more than yours.

For the first time since my grandfather's death, a wave of sadness washes over me. This is it. This is all that's left of him—his legacy—the two of us sitting at this table. Well, three counting my mother...and four, I guess, if you count the money, which is an entity in itself and all anyone really cares about.

Mr. Hall begins to read through the will and I start to wonder why we couldn't have just been sent copies to read in our own time? Why would my grandfather want us all together for this?

"I appoint Clarence M. Hall of Barrows, Morrell, and Hall to be Executor of this Will and Trustee of my Estate."

When my father lets out a disgruntled sigh, Mr. Hall pauses and clears his throat, adjusting the wire-rimmed glasses perched on his nose.

"Continue," my father instructs briskly, waving a hand in the air as he reclines in his seat, apparently put out with the idea of his father leaving someone besides him in charge of his affairs.

"Yes, right," Mr. Hall says, shifting the papers as he continues. "In the event that the said Clarence Hall should predecease me or die within a period of thirty days following my death, or without having proved this my Will, or be unwilling or unable to act for any reason whatsoever, I entrust his colleague, Donald Barrows, with said duties."

I have to fight back the smirk that's trying to force its way on my face. It's not the time or place for feeling such mirth, but I do. Maybe it's displaced sadness or some shit like that, but I'm taking entirely too much pleasure in seeing my father rebuffed from his own father's will.

"For fuck's sake," he mutters under his breath.

"Phillip," my mother chastises. As much as I'm sure she's unhappy my father is not in charge, she cares even more about public appearances. It's one thing to show your true feelings in private, but never with an audience. If you're a Rhys-Jones, you always save face.

Mr. Hall keeps reading and it's as if he's trying to get through the rest of the will as fast as possible, probably ready to be done with this and send us all on our merry way.

"I revoke all prior wills and codicils."

At that statement, my father sits up a little straighter and leans over the table, resting on his elbows. I have to admit, I listen a little closer too. This could be it, the part where he disowns me for walking away. Briefly, I let my eyes flicker across to my father, wondering if I am written out, will he do the same? He's one of those men who thinks everyone should make his own way in the world, unless you're Phillip Jones, and in that case, you want your cake and eat it too.

"I give free of debts, testamentary, funeral expenses and liabilities of any kind to my Trustee on behalf of the named beneficiaries herein," Mr. Hall pauses, clearing his throat and adjusting his glasses once again, what I'm picking up as his nervous tick. "One hundred million dollars to my grandson, Shepard Rhys-Jones."

My father grunts and shifts in his seat, but I don't move an inch.

I'm still trying to register what Mr. Hall just said and I'd like him to repeat himself, but before I can say a word, he holds a finger up in the air to stop me. "There is one stipulation," he says, making brief eye contact with me before turning his gaze back to the document. "Monies will be paid upon the one-year anniversary of his…marriage."

What?

"Marriage," Mr. Hall repeats.

I must have said that out loud, but seriously, what the fuck? "Marriage?" I ask again. The starched white shirt and navy-blue tie around my neck suddenly feel too tight. Running a finger between the material and the skin on my neck, I'm now the one clearing my throat.

"That's correct," Mr. Hall confirms.

Before I can ask any other questions, my father interrupts. "What about the rest?"

"The rest," Mr. Hall says, turning back to the will. "After payment of my just debts, testamentary, funeral expenses and taxes or duties payable as a result of my death, I give my entire remaining estate not previously disposed of under any prior clause to my Trustee on behalf of Mercy House."

"That can't be right," my father insists, the legs of his chair scraping the floor as he quickly stands, towering over Mr. Hall. "There's no way in hell that senile old man left hundreds of millions of dollars to a fucking charity!"

Clearing his throat again, the older man squares his shoulders and faces my father. I have to give him props, most men would cower, but he stands his ground, backed by an official document. "That's exactly what he did," Mr. Hall says, flipping my father's copy of the will to the page where the declarations are made. "You can read it here for yourself."

My father continues to rant but I tune him out because all I can hear in my head is one word, playing over and over on repeat.

Marriage.

CeCe

"Welcome to Neutral Grounds," I call out over my shoulder, preoccupied with making a fresh pot of cold brew, trying to keep my mind off of the letter that's been giving me nightmares for the past few days.

"Yes, I'd like a soy, non-fat, two-pump, sugar-free latte with half French vanilla and half cinnamon—"

I roll my eyes and hear Carys laugh behind me. "Would you like an extra shot of bullshit to go with that?" I know my customers, and customers who are also one of my best friends, I know them even better. Coffee says a lot about a person and Carys is definitely not high-maintenance. A hot mess? Yes. But not high-maintenance.

"Well, maybe just an iced coffee with cream for now…I'll come back for the other later."

Giving her a side-eye, I walk over and fill up a cup with ice and then coffee, before topping it off with half-and-half. The good stuff. Just like Carys. When I hand it to her, I can't hold back the sigh as I lean against the counter. Her familiar face and warm smile are just what I needed.

"That's a heavy sigh…what's up?" she asks, matching my pose.

Carys is the one person I know I can talk to about this and she'll totally get it. Our businesses are a huge part of us. They support our families and run thick in our veins. It's all we know. She'll get it, and yet, I hesitate to confide in her because I don't want to even speak it out loud. It was bad enough telling Jules about it, but I had to. I needed legal counsel and he's the only almost-lawyer I know. The best part is he's free.

"Have you talked to Jules?" I ask, feeling her out to see if my current dilemma is the purpose of her visit. Maybe Jules has already spilled the tea.

She shrugs. "Yeah, he worked the overnight shift last night. I saw him this morning."

The way she nonchalantly begins to pilfer through the baked goods on the counter lets me know he hasn't mentioned the letter or Theodore Duval, Jr. If he had, her expression-filled face would be giving her away. When I don't say anything for a few seconds, she holds me with her blue eyes. "What?"

Instead of saying anything, I reach under the counter and pull out the folded paper, handing it across the counter to her.

"What's this?"

"Just read it."

After she unfolds it, she quickly scans the letter. I watch as her brows furrow in confusion and then her eyes go wide in shock.

"What the hell?" she asks, reflecting my initial response. "Is this for real?"

"As a heart attack."

We both grimace, because that's how my Uncle Teddy died. Even five years later, it's still too soon.

"What are you going to do? He can't do that, right? Take the shop… there's got to be some sort of clause or stipulation…time constraint?" I can see the wheels in her head turning as she speaks, letting her thoughts tumble out. "What did Jules say? You called him, right?"

"Yes," I say, groaning and massaging my temples. "I called him. He has a copy of the letter and he's looking into it. He said we'd have to respond to the letter ASAP and in the meantime, he's looking into the validity of the will and time limits on contesting it."

"Validity? What do you mean?"

Biting down on my bottom lip, I cringe a little, hating this part. "Well, the will was handwritten, something Uncle Teddy wrote a few years before he died. It wasn't notarized or anything, but it had his signature and was dated. Apparently, that's good enough in the State of Louisiana, but there's a chance if this guy—*Theodore*—knows that, he'll use it against me…or my mother. Since she deeded everything over to me, I don't even know what they'll do with that. It feels messy and confusing and completely above my pay grade. I literally feel like crying at the drop of a hat and you know I'm not a crier."

"What can I do?" she asks, reaching across the counter and gathering my hands in hers.

Bringing my head up, I open my eyes to see the sincerity on her face I knew would be there. Carys has always been such a great friend and I know she'd do anything in her power to help me and I'd do the same for her, but I'm not sure anyone can help me out of this one.

Except Uncle Teddy, but unless the court will accept Miss Betty channeling my dead uncle as a witness, I potentially could be screwed.

"I don't know," I tell her honestly. "Jules is going to do what he can, but he's not an actual lawyer…yet, so he can only get me so far. I don't have the money to fight something like this."

"You can't let this guy win," she says earnestly, squeezing tighter on my hands, forcing me to look her square in the eyes. "What would you do without this place…what would this place do without you?" Adamantly, she begins shaking her head. "No, I don't accept this. We'll figure this out…we have to."

She's right. I know she is. I just don't know where I'm going to get the money to fight it. Between keeping the shop running, sending my mama money, and paying Rory's tuition, I'm strapped pretty tight. I have a little in savings, but that's the only safety net I have.

"I know what you need," Carys says, her tone brightening and her smile coming back. "Shep will be back in town tonight and it's his thirtieth birthday. Mav and I want to surprise him with a few friends at Come Again."

"No."

Without breaking stride, she ignores my refusal and continues. "Just a few drinks and Sarah is making some finger foods."

"No."

"We thought we could meet around eight. Since it's a weekday night, Shaw said we could have the back table and stay as long as we want. He offered to shut it down for us, but I thought that as long as we have a table to ourselves, we should be good."

When she finally stops, I'm staring at her with an eyebrow quirked. She knows there's no way in hell I'm going to a party for Shep. Carys knows everything. She knows about the weekend we spent together and how amazing it was and the fact he ghosted me. Like, poof, gone.

I swear, it's like he erased me from his memory. Even when we're forced to be in the same room, his eyes always skip over me. He's only spoken to me a few times, when he has to. I'm constantly feeling self-conscious, like maybe I smell…or maybe I was a really terrible lay. He seemed to enjoy it at the time, but what if he was pretending?

My battered psyche doesn't need that kind of abuse tonight. All the second-guessing and self-doubt? No, thank you.

"Please come," Carys begs, turning the puppy dog eyes on me. "And not even for Shep. We'll just pretend like he's not there. Come because you need a night out and Avery will be there. We can drink on her behalf and commiserate together. It'll be good for you."

"Sarah's cooking?" I ask, feeling weak and in need of carbs to mask my anguish.

Her smile grows and she nods her head. "Yeah, crab cakes, mini muffulettas, shrimp po'boys…bread pudding with rum sauce…"

"Are you trying to seduce me or talk me into a party?"

"Both," she replies, waggling her eyebrows. "I mean, you haven't been laid in like, what? Two years. You're basically a virgin again."

"You whore," I whisper-yell.

Carys's smile turns into a smirk. "Proud of it."

After a few seconds, the door chimes and a new customer walks in, ending our impromptu therapy session. "So, you'll come?" she asks, hopefully.

I smile at the man and woman walking up to the counter and greet them, but Carys is persistent and she doesn't take no for an answer.

"His grandfather just died," she whispers, pulling out the big guns.

I didn't know that and now I feel bad. Even though Shep did me wrong, I would never wish any ill will toward him. Actually, the thought of him in pain or mourning makes me sad, which is ridiculous. I should relish in his pain…maybe have a voodoo doll fashioned after him and use it as a pincushion. But instead, I feel for him and in a moment of weakness, I cave.

"Fine, I'll be there."

Carys claps her hands and if it weren't for the customers, she probably would've jumped up and down. "Yay, okay, it'll be great. I'll see you tonight."

Somehow, a few minutes in Carys's presence and I feel lighter than I have in days.

Shep

"REALLY, MAN, WE DON'T HAVE TO DO ANYTHING. IT'S just a birthday and we can celebrate anytime. Isn't that what being in New Orleans is all about?"

"True," Maverick agrees, "but it's not just any birthday; it's a big one. You're fucking thirty! Plus, I know being back in Dallas was shit and I have no doubt you need to blow off some serious steam."

That would be the understatement of the year.

"Okay, fine. One drink. We can do something bigger later, if you want, but for tonight, I'm taking it easy. You know, because I'm so old and mature now," I say with a wink.

"What the fuck ever, man." Mav claps his hand on my shoulder as he opens the door to Come Again, letting me enter first.

"Surprise!"

For a second I worry I'm having a stroke. Not that I've ever experienced one before but it's the only explanation my brain can come up with. For one thing, Come Again is dark inside. If you didn't already know it was open, you'd probably pass it by. Sometimes I wonder if Shaw, the owner, even wants customers.

Second, there are more people screaming *surprise* at me than I know here, which is a very odd feeling. I'm sure those I don't know are customers just being nice, but still…weird. And third, I've never had a surprise party thrown for me before and I honestly don't know how to react.

I'm quite sure I'm mastering the deer in the headlights look, though.

Once my eyes have adjusted to my surroundings, I give my best friend a look that hopefully conveys "thank you" in addition to "I'm going to kick your ass for this". He just laughs and nods his head as if to say "you can fucking try."

One drink will not be enough tonight, I can already tell.

Managing to plaster on what, I hope, looks like a genuine smile, I give the crowd a wave before Maverick ushers me to the small group of people who actually know who the hell I am. Carys is here, of course, along with Jules and…low and behold, the Ice Queen, herself, CeCe Calhoun.

Holy fucking hell.

She must've been told this party was for my funeral because there's no way she's actually here to celebrate my birth. The woman hates me and for good reason, too. I'm sure she assumes I feel the same about her, but she'd be wrong. She just doesn't need to know that.

Both Carys and Jules greet me with warm hugs and birthday wishes, but all I get from CeCe is a mock "cheers" motion with her shot glass that is immediately emptied down her throat. I watch as she throws her head back, elongating that graceful neck of hers, and making me wish—not for the first time—for a repeat of the weekend we spent together almost two years ago.

Clearing my throat, I tell the group I'm heading to the bar to see what's on tap.

"Happy birthday, Shep!" I'm greeted by Avery, Shaw's fiancé, who stops wiping down the bar to focus on me. "What can I get you?" She places her hands on her stomach—her very round stomach—and I'm reminded she's pregnant. Very pregnant, in fact.

"Thanks, I'll just have a local dark beer but I can wait for someone else to pour it. Or I can pour it myself, if you'd like. You shouldn't be pouring my beer in your, uh, condition." I wave my hand in the general direction of her belly. I'm not sure why I'm acting so weird about this. I know she should be able to work whenever and wherever she wants but it just feels wrong somehow.

Avery laughs but when Shaw walks behind her, I see him nod his head at me while murmuring, "I knew I liked this one." This causes her to roll her eyes and place her hands where her hips would normally be.

"Are you saying, just because I'm pregnant, I can't pour a beer?"

The corner of Shaw's mouth quirks up slightly and I can tell he's amused by her challenge. "No, my love. You can do anything you want. I'm simply appreciative of Shepard's manners, that's all." He kisses the tip of her nose and rubs his hand across her stomach before walking off, leaving his wife a virtual pile of goo.

That's a man who knows what he's doing, to be sure, and as much as I've come to know and respect Shaw O'Sullivan, I still feel strange about witnessing their interaction. I'm not used to most forms of affection, public or otherwise, and I find myself caught between wanting to observe the moment closely and wanting to run far, far away.

As soon as my beer is in my hand, I dip my head in appreciation and leave.

Walking back over to the table, my mood immediately takes a sharp right turn. There's a spread of food fit for a king and the rich aroma is taking over this corner of the bar, making my mouth water and making me forget all about the stupid surprise party.

Now, this is something I can appreciate.

"Did Sarah do this?" I ask no one in particular, zoning in on small white bowls full of what looks like crawfish etouffee. I may not be a local just yet, but I know my Cajun food.

"She sure did. Dig in!" Carys answers.

Sarah is Shaw's sister who runs the cooking school next door. I've had her cooking before and it's one of my favorite things about this city. Truthfully, you can't go wrong anywhere you eat down here but Sarah's food is...special.

There's a smorgasbord of fried seafood and finger foods and I waste no time piling it all on my plate, along with the crawfish etouffee. I'll worry about calories and cholesterol tomorrow. This is nothing a little gym time won't fix. I'm willing to put in a few extra hours for a few minutes of buttery bliss.

"Save some room for the bread pudding," CeCe warns. I don't know what shocks me more, the fact there's bread pudding for dessert or that CeCe actually spoke to me. I look at her then back at my plate before reluctantly putting one of my muffulettas back on its tray. I don't miss the smirk that crosses her face either.

There are some days when I think it's a shame CeCe and I have the relationship we do, or *don't* have, I guess I should say. We're different in a lot of ways but, deep down, I think we're more similar than either of us would like to admit. Other days, I think our time together ended exactly the way it was supposed to. Unfortunately, it causes our forced time together now to be awkward and strained. There's no getting around it with her being best friends with my best friend's...person.

Who knows? Maybe now that I'm here permanently, we'll get over it and forge some sort of friend status. I've never been friends with anyone I've slept with in the past, but I guess there's a first time for everything. I've also never fucked someone who was a permanent fixture in my life. Probably should've thought that one through a little better, but what can I say? My dick doesn't take those sorts of things into consideration and he wanted her, plain and simple.

If I'm being honest with myself, I don't regret my weekend with her. It was hands down the most intense sex of my life. We locked ourselves away in my hotel room and didn't surface until I was forced to leave and fly back to Dallas. Thank God. Because if I'm still being honest with myself, if I hadn't had business to attend to, I might've never left.

Every time I see her, I can hear her moans of pleasure and taste the memory of her on my tongue. And then I want to fucking kick myself in the balls for it, because that's not me.

But I do wonder if CeCe ever thinks about it. The way her eyes narrow and her smile fades every time she sees me, I'd guess it's a time she'd rather forget.

As the night moves on, the customers thin out, leaving our small group with a bit more privacy. Shaw has assured us we can stay as long as we'd like and since the drinks are still flowing, we take him up on his generosity.

"How's your family doing?" Carys asks, catching me off guard. It takes me a second to realize she's asking about how my family is dealing with their grief over my grandfather dying.

"They're fine, same as always," I say, shrugging my shoulders. I can tell my answer isn't exactly what Carys was expecting by the confused look she gives Maverick. Surely, he's explained to her the Rhys-Jones's don't grieve or experience any other emotions normal people do.

Although, they were quite angry after the reading of the will.

"You know what, that's incorrect," I start, feeling the half a dozen beers loosening up my words and making them spill out of my mouth. "When I left Dallas, my parents were experiencing something completely brand new to them: their asses being handed to them."

Maverick cocks an eyebrow at me, setting his glass on the table. "What the hell happened? I've been meaning to ask how everything went after the funeral."

"It was… fucking awesome," I tell him truthfully, shaking my head at the absurdity of it all. I still can't believe how it all went down. "It was almost like one of those dramatic scenes from a movie with everyone hanging on the words of a dead man." My mind wanders back to that room and the words of my grandfather's lawyer. Absentmindedly, I tell him, "They received absolutely nothing."

"You're shitting me?" Maverick deadpans, pushing back from the table a little as he tilts his head, like he didn't hear me right.

"Nothing," I repeat, letting it sink in.

Everyone at our table has expressions that match Mav's and I can't help but laugh. It's not the first time I've thought about it since it happened, but it is the first time I've said it out loud.

I've thought a lot about my inheritance and subsequent demands in order to collect it, but I haven't truly let it all sink in.

My mother and father were completely left out of the old man's will.

The alcohol is definitely helping.

"Absolutely nothing," I repeat, before continuing my story, addressing everyone but Maverick, because he already knows this shit. "My grandfather was rich. I mean, motherfucking rich. The bastard was worth hundreds of millions of dollars and he left it all to two people."

I'm quite enjoying telling this story in such a dramatic fashion, so I let my audience simmer a bit while I finish my drink.

"Shepard Rhys-Jones, you better finish your story right this second. I feel like I'm watching one of my Bravo shows and we just went to a commercial break!" This comes from Jules, who truly looks distraught but yet ready to soak up any theatrics I let loose.

"He left me one hundred million dollars, with conditions, of course…" I hear a variety of gasps and choking sounds and one very clear "holy shit" from CeCe's direction. "And the rest is for my grandfather's lawyer, the executor of his will and trust, and he's to distribute the remaining millions to various charities, per his specific instructions. It's quite the scandal, I tell you. Or, it would be if anyone knew, so y'all better keep this among us. I'd hate for rumors about my family to be spread."

I bust out laughing, not only at what I thought was a hilarious joke but also, at the expressions on everyone's faces. I understand it's hard for some people to wrap their heads around that amount of money, but if they really think I care about my family's reputation, they're mistaken.

Maverick is the first one to speak. "Wait. Back up. What the fuck did your father do? Did your mother pass out?"

"She very nearly did. She was so distraught, she canceled the dinner she'd had planned with some society skank and her family, which was a huge relief to me. As for my father, he immediately called his lawyers to see about contesting the will but we were all assured it's very legal and *very* set in stone. I'm sure he's still trying to figure out some kind of loophole, though. He'll never accept this."

"Damn, I kinda wish I could've seen that."

"You and all of Dallas society, I'm sure."

"Who was the skank?" he asks, the only person at the table who's moved past the one hundred million dollars portion of the story.

"Foster Crawford's sister, Felicity. Can you believe that shit?" Like me, Maverick hated Foster while we were in school.

"Fuck that. I'm glad you were able to dodge that bullet."

"Enough about the skank," Jules finally says, shaking his head like he's clearing a magic eight ball. "Tell us what you're planning on doing with all that money!" He looks so excited; I almost feel bad about disappointing him with my answer.

"I'm not taking the money."

"What?!" Everyone at the table reacts in unison.

"I'm not taking it."

"Why the hell not?" Carys asks, eyes wide and mouth hanging open in shock.

"Because I have to be married for a year before I can touch it and since I never plan on getting married, I will never get the money."

I've thought about it a lot since the reading of the will and I'm at peace with my decision. It sucks big time that I won't be able to help our business out with the extra cash but marriage is a hard limit for me. Besides, who would I marry anyway? No way will I legally attach myself to any of the women my mother constantly throws at me. Not for all of my grandfather's money, would I do that.

"Well, honey, I'd love to help you out and marry you just to see the look on your parents' faces but I don't know if my reputation could handle it. Sorry, but you're a little too straight for me to pull off, so to speak." Jules winks at me.

I laugh but thank him for his thoughtfulness.

"Wow, that's a crazy situation but I'm proud of you for sticking to your guns," Maverick tells me and I know he means it. He'd never guilt me into doing anything shady for any reason, even if it would mean helping our business.

Shrugging, I reply, "Thanks. In a way, I get to help my grandfather stick it to my parents by not taking the money, so I'm good with it."

"I'll marry you."

I assume my ears are playing tricks on me. Surely, I imagined those words floating across the table in my direction. There's no way that just happened, so I pretend I didn't hear it.

Our table goes completely quiet, so when the words are spoken again, this time stronger and a bit louder, I have no choice but to acknowledge them. Turning toward CeCe, who up until this moment has remained absolutely quiet, I quirk an eyebrow at her, daring her to repeat it a third time.

"I will," she says with a nod. "I'll marry you."

CeCe

What did I do?

What did I fucking do last night?

I stick my face under the showerhead, hoping the water pelts me hard enough to knock some clarity into my brain. When I woke up this morning, I thought me offering myself to be Shep's wife was a dream. A very bad dream. But the more I let the events of last night sink in, the more I'm afraid it really happened.

I don't remember a lot, except for tequila.

The first thing I did when I walked into Come Again was demand a shot. If I was going to have to be there for Shepard Rhys-Jones's birthday, then I was going to need alcohol. I should've known better. That delicious agave nectar has been the cause of many bad decisions. At least I'm predictable.

Good ol' predictable, dependable CeCe.

What the fuck did I do?

I take that thought with me as I finish up in the shower and then get out to dry off—me, tequila, Shep, his sad ass story, my ridiculous offer. As I dry my hair, I let my imagination run wild for a brief second, thinking about what it would be like to be married to someone like Shepard Rhys-Jones. I wouldn't have to worry about this long-lost cousin of mine trying to take my business away, for one. I mean, Shep is rich, which means *I'd* be rich, too, and so I'd be able to pay this Theo guy off. Isn't that what people with money do? Use it as a power source? I wouldn't know because I've never had any.

One area I don't have to use my imagination for is the sex. I already know how amazing sex with Shep is, even though I try very hard not to think about it. When you're ghosted immediately after the best sex of your life, it kinda puts a damper on those particular memories. It also affects any follow-up relationships or possible sexy times with other men, which is just super for me. He probably had no problem falling into bed with other women and he made it perfectly clear I wasn't anything special to him.

So, why in the hell did I offer to marry him?

The simple answer is, I wanted to help him. After all the anger I have felt toward him—which, let's be honest, was mostly my pride being butt-hurt—deep down inside, it bothered me to see him upset.

Ultimately, though, my offer was shut down the second the words flew out of my mouth. Not by Shep. He looked too stunned to reply, so Maverick and Carys quickly jumped in, blamed everything on tequila, and took us home. Separately.

And, now, here I am, opening Neutral Grounds for the day and praying no one remembers the conversation that brought our evening to an abrupt end.

Of course, he's here.

Of fucking course.

The morning had been going well. The usual crowd of customers all came and went without any peep from Shep but as soon as the rush left, he swept in like a tailored-suit-wearing superhero. But more like an anti-hero, because he doesn't save the day, he ruins them. The casual saunter and relaxed expression make me think he planned the whole thing, which wouldn't surprise me in the least.

And, as luck would have it, my morning helper, Paige, just stepped out for a break, leaving me with nowhere to hide and no excuses to make.

"Morning" is his simple greeting, straight to the point, just like he is.

I admit, his voice does sound sexy, a little rough around the edges still from sleep, like this was the first time he's spoken today. It kinda reminds me of our weekend together…

No. Stop that, Cecilia Louise.

Do not go there.

"For you, maybe," I quip, trying to gain some ground with a smart remark. "For people with regular jobs, it's almost noon." Giving him a tight smile, I ask, "Would you like a coffee?"

"Yeah, that'd be great. Iced, please."

He's ignoring my saltiness and using his manners. That means he wants something and I'm really hoping it's just the coffee. Maybe a scone?

My stomach feels a little woozy as I turn around and fill a cup with ice and then pour the dark, delicious liquid gold over it, leaving a small amount of room for cream. The entire half a minute, I wish I had a mirror to see what Shep is doing.

Is he checking me out?

Looking at my ass?

Or is he feeling just as out of sorts as I am? Maybe the coolness is a facade?

Turning back around, I plaster a smile on my face as I hand him his drink, without a scone, and he slides his money across the counter, then puts his change in the tip jar. His eyes don't leave me as he takes a sip and I get the distinct but weird feeling he's examining me. Trying to figure me out too? Maybe. Trying to find the right words to apologize for his behavior the last two years? Doubtful.

"So, about last night…" he starts.

Shit, shit, shit.

Do I play dumb and say I don't know what he's talking about? Blame it all on the tequila? Assume he's asking about the awful, yet, hot Rob Lowe movie from the 80's?

"Yeah! Last night was fun. Did you have a good birthday?" So, I'm going with the playing dumb version, obviously.

"It was fine, thanks, but that's not what I want to talk to you about."

Alright, here we go. Let's just see what he has to say. I'm sure he only wants to thank me for my thoughtfulness and assure me he doesn't want or *need* to marry me. Now that I think about it, it *is* pretty presumptuous for me to think he wants to take me up on my stupid offer. I'm sure he has countless women to choose from, should he choose to marry anyone. There's no way in hell I'm at the top of that list. That's preposterous. Me? Of all people.

"Oh? What did you want to talk about?" I ask, holding on to the dumb card for dear life.

Am I really twirling my hair right now?

What the hell is wrong with me?

I continue twirling my hair until it's ready to be wrapped up in a hair-tie, securing the bun I *absolutely* meant to create to get the hair out of my face. Not to be confused with a similar action intended to be used as a flirtation device.

Nope, not here.

Not me.

"Is there somewhere we can sit and speak more privately?" he asks, motioning over to the empty tables near the windows.

Just as I'm getting ready to make an excuse that I need to stay behind the bar, Paige comes in and washes her hands, ready to get back to work. *Perfect timing, as always.*

"Sure," I concede, realizing I have no cards left and nowhere to run. "Let's go over there." I lead him to two plush chairs in the back corner of the shop, plopping into one while he gracefully sits in the other. An instant yet perfect example of how different we are.

"Do you remember me telling the group last night about my

grandfather's will?"

"Uh, vaguely. I was drinking pretty heavily… so I might've missed some details." *Lies.* I pick at the imaginary thread on my apron, unable to look him in the eye.

"Right," he says, clearing his throat. It's obvious he doesn't believe me but he continues to let me play my game, which is noble of him, I guess. Or humiliating. Let's stick with noble, for now.

"Well, I'd had a little too much to drink as well and made some details of the will public that probably should've stayed private."

Oh, so that's what this is about. Shep just wants to make sure I don't spill the beans on his unfortunate situation. Well, no problem there, buddy, the people I'd spill to were already at the table.

It dawns on me that he suddenly looks…nervous. Anxious, perhaps. Although he's maintaining some intense eye contact, his fingers won't stop moving. They go from tapping the side of his cup to the arm of the chair and back and, if I'm not mistaken, his toe is tapping. I don't think I've ever seen him look anything less than one hundred percent calm, cool, and collected. He almost seems human.

"No worries," I assure him, still hating his discomfort. "Your secret is safe with me, Shep."

"Secret?" he asks, confused until realization dawns. "Oh, I'm not worried about you repeating what you heard last night, CeCe." He pauses for a moment before continuing. "I'm wondering if your offer still stands."

What?

"Um, uh, um," is all I manage to get out while I not-so-discreetly look for a hole in the ground to swallow me up.

There's no way I heard him right.

No way.

"You seemed pretty sure of yourself last night," he states, sitting up a little straighter, his expression turning serious but still so poised and controlled and entirely too beautiful for one man. "But I'm guessing, in the light of day and with less alcohol, you've changed your mind?" His words come out so polished, almost regal. Why does he have to be so proper all the time? I wish he'd loosen up and stay that way for a while.

I stop mentally freaking out for a second and look at him. *Really* look at him. Besides how absolutely gorgeous the man is, he looks troubled and, dare I say, insecure. My heart instantly goes out to him like it did last night and I let out a deep breath.

I'm such a sucker for a lost boy.

"Would it help you? You know, if I haven't changed my mind…if the offer still stands?"

"Immensely," he replies, a little too eager for Shepard Rhys-Jones, at least the version he allows everyone else to see, which intrigues me. "Just hear me out." And, now, I have a very alert and perky Shep in front of me.

Dear Lord, what have I done?

"As I said last night, I am to inherit one hundred million dollars after I've been married for a year. If you agree to marry me, once I've received the money, on our one-year anniversary, I'll give you five percent…free and clear."

Five percent?

Of ONE HUNDRED MILLION DOLLARS?

I'm not a math whiz, but that's…*five million dollars.*

Must. Not. Faint.

Stay focused, CeCe.

I clear my throat and try to keep my voice steady. "Five percent," I repeat. "That's very… generous of you."

He waves his hand in front of him like I just thanked him for holding a door open for me. How can he think that much money isn't a big deal? It's a huge fucking deal. "I'll gladly pay it, if you agree to help me out."

"What do you get out of this agreement?" Because there has to be some kind of catch, right? "Besides a hundred million…minus five percent? Don't you have enough money already? Why would you marry someone…" I almost say *someone like me* but stop myself. "Why…" I stumble over what I'm trying to say and decide to be direct and to-the-point, like Shep. "Why would you marry someone for money?"

"Freedom."

His answer is swift and easy and when he speaks it, it's as if the air he exhaled took all his troubles away with it. It's also bullshit.

"How can getting married give you freedom? Isn't that an oxymoron?"

Shep smirks, giving me a once over before taking a drink of his coffee and relaxing back into the plush chair. "What an interesting idea of marriage you have, Cecelia."

Do not pay attention to how he says your name.

This man is a snake charmer, that's all.

Stay strong.

"Just explain, please." I roll my eyes at him because if I'm even going to *consider* marrying him—for FIVE. MILLION. DOLLARS—I'm going to know every last detail.

"Well, if I'm married, my mother will be forced to stop her incessant search for the perfect Stepford wife for me to choose from, that's one reason," he begins, leaning forward and resting his forearms on his knees, his half-drunk cup of coffee between his palms—back to calm, cool, and collected. "The other and more important reason is, with this inheritance, I'll be able to fully commit myself to the business Maverick and I have created, leaving Dallas and my family behind for good." He pauses, a mischievous gleam taking over his blue eyes. "But, dear Cecelia." Scooting his body closer to mine, our knees brush as he leans in and places his full lips against my ear. "The cherry on top will be seeing you naked again."

Say what now?

Along with the expletive, I jump from my chair, like it's burning my ass, putting distance between me and Shep and his audacious words. The few customers in the shop stop what they're doing to turn and stare at me, causing my cheeks to flame red. Not wanting to cause more of a scene, I let out a fake laugh. "Sorry." Smiling, I try to brush off my behavior. "My friend here just told me a joke that was *very*...

funny and completely unbelievable." I narrow my eyes at him while returning to my seat.

"You expect this *fake* marriage to be *consummated*?" I ask incredulously, my eyes feeling as if they're going to fall out of their sockets. "You really do like having your cake and eating it, too!"

Shep struggles to keep from smiling that devilishly sexy smile that makes me weak in the knees, and it only pisses me off more.

"You *know* what I mean," I hiss. "Stop making my words dirty." I try to make my words sound affronted, like I'm taking offense to his suggestion of marital sex, but I'm anything but. No, in reality, his seductive tone and insinuation makes my skin burn with the memory of his touch.

"We'll be married for an entire year, CeCe. Why wouldn't we sleep together? You plan on staying celibate for that long?"

What he doesn't know is I've been celibate for much longer than that. When were we together? About two years ago? Yeah, that's how long it's been for me, but I'll be damned if I'm going to admit that to him.

"You don't think you can go without sex for a year?" I challenge him.

"Fuck, no," is his immediate reply.

"Oh, so then you'd cheat on me? Nice."

He lets out an exasperated breath. "Of course, I wouldn't cheat on you. No matter how you truly feel about me, you need to know I'm not a cheater. But," he pauses for effect and I find I'm dying for him to finish his speech. "If we get married, it must be convincing, especially when it comes to my parents. We have to be able to seem like we know each other…intimately, and that we're, you know, in love. Plus, I love sex and I'm really good at it, which you're well aware of, so why the fuck wouldn't we use our situation to fulfill our needs?"

There he goes, playing that pipe and charming me right out of my wicker basket. *Bastard.*

Wait, how did I become the snake in this scenario?

I sit and pretend I'm mulling his words over, but in reality, I'm trying to get the idea of sex with Shep out of my head. If I'm being truthful, I'm having a hard time thinking of reasons this would be a bad idea. Unlimited sex with Shep for a year without any real consequences, plus five million bucks when it's over? Okay, that line of thinking made me feel like a prostitute so let's not go there. But, really, what would the downside be, because there has to be one.

My mama always told me that if something seems too good to be true, it is.

"Let me think about it," I finally say, uncrossing and then recrossing my legs, trying to appear as unaffected by this proposition as he is.

"Excellent," he muses, a wide smile stretching across his perfect face.

The confidence radiating off of him screams victory.

"Don't start celebrating yet," I tell him, bringing him down a notch. "I said I'd *think* about it. It's a big decision and I'm afraid if we rush into it, we'll both miss something important to discuss beforehand. If we do this, how soon will we need to get married?"

"The sooner we marry, the sooner the clock starts ticking."

So, real soon. Right. That makes sense.

"Okay, give me a couple of days and then let's meet for dinner to discuss and make our final decision. Deal?" I ask, sticking my hand out to him to shake on it, but instead, he grabs it, kissing the top.

Fuck, he's good.

"I'll see you in two days, Ms. Calhoun."

As soon as he leaves, I pull my cell phone out of my pocket and open the group chat I have with Carys and Avery.

Me: Regulators, mount up.

Shep

Marriage.

Am I seriously considering getting married? And to CeCe Calhoun, of all people?

Don't get me wrong, she's the perfect candidate for this endeavor, but we have *history*, in addition to best friends who are a real couple. If this ends badly, it could cause a shit ton of drama and that's nothing either of us wants.

Instead of focusing on the excuses not to go through with this, I decide to think of the positive reasons for marrying CeCe.

For one, she's not from Dallas and knows nothing of my family. I wish I could say that wouldn't change, but I know for a fact the second my parents hear about my upcoming nuptials they'll be making plans so quick both of our heads will spin. Maybe we should elope…

Second, this plan we're toying with is mutually beneficial. We both, in time, would receive money that will greatly improve our lives. Being far from naive, I don't see a downside to this point.

Lastly, if ever there was a woman I could see myself tied to, it would be her. After she stops hating me, of course. She's beautiful, smart, hard-working, and sexy as fuck. Simply stated, she checks everything off my list—everything I know about, that is. But I have a feeling, if there were more qualifications, she'd check those, too. There's just something about her. It's a shame I'm not relationship material. I honestly hope our time together doesn't ruin her ideas or desires for a real relationship when this is all over, because I genuinely believe that CeCe deserves happiness.

Real happiness.

In short, I hope we're both able to enjoy our time together, followed by the spoils of our marriage, and then move on with minimal damage.

I'm such a romantic, I know.

Although, I'm strongly optimistic about doing this with CeCe, I feel like I need to share this turn of events with Maverick. I know without a doubt, he'll try to dissuade me but I'm hopeful he'll understand and lend his support once he hears me out.

When I walk into the lobby of the Blue Bayou, I can't help but be hit with memories of my weekend with CeCe two years ago. After hanging out with Carys and Maverick at their apartment out back, we kissed for the first time in the corner by the bookcase. Quickly after, we stumbled up the stairs, barely able to keep our hands off each other, and headed straight for my room. We didn't leave for two days.

Damn, that was a great weekend.

However, just like everything else in life, it had to end.

I know that sounds morbid, but it is what it is. We had fun and then it was time to go back to the real world. But, to not have that kind of time restraint with CeCe—an entire year with her, rather than just a weekend...the possibilities are endless.

"Good afternoon, Mr. Fancy Pants." Jules greets me in his usual style and I can't help but laugh. He's not wrong, my pants are fucking fancy, but I have a feeling he'd call me that even if I were wearing jeans. "Maverick is in the office. He said to send you right in." Jules motions to the room just behind him, reminding me of how Vanna White spins those letters on Wheel of Fortune.

"Thanks, Jules." I give him a nod of my head and step to the office door, knocking as I open it.

"Hey, man, come on in. Have a seat." Maverick gets up from the desk and greets me with a one-armed hug before guiding me to the sofa that's lined up with another large bookshelf.

They really love their books here.

"Want anything to drink?" he asks.

"No, thanks. I just had a coffee at CeCe's place."

Maverick pauses the sip of water he was about to take and eyes me hard. "Her apartment?"

Rolling my eyes, I clarify. "Neutral Grounds."

"Oh, right." His body relaxes and I almost feel guilty knowing he's just going to tense right up again when I tell him my plan.

"So, what's up? Have you thought about your grandfather's will?" Thank you, Maverick, for never being one to beat around the bush.

"I have and that's what I want to talk to you about."

"You know anything I can do to help, I will." Maverick's sincerity and always being willing to step in and lend a helping hand is one of the things I admire most about my best friend. Too bad he's about to lose his shit and regret his words.

"I know and I appreciate that, but before I tell you my plan, I need you to promise to listen first, react second. Can you do that?"

He slumps back in his seat. "Aww, fuck, man. What did you do?"

"Nothing… yet. It's what I'm going to do that you'll hate, but just hear me out, okay?"

His expression tells me he'll listen but he's already bracing himself for whatever I'm about to say.

"Keep an open mind," I warn.

"Okay, fine. Lay it on me."

"I'm going to marry CeCe." I allow my statement to fill the room and I'm a bit surprised I don't waiver in my delivery. My confidence in what we're planning is strong.

"Yeah, right," Mav guffaws, rolling his eyes. "Very funny. Now, tell me what you're really up to, man. I should've known you'd try to pull that shit over on me…Carys said CeCe had a lot to drink last night…"

He drifts off as his expression goes slack in realization.

"That's the real plan," I reiterate. "CeCe and I are going to be married and soon."

"Do we know another CeCe? Because there's no fucking way CeCe Calhoun—a *sober* CeCe Calhoun—agreed to marry you. Not in this lifetime, anyway."

"It was her idea."

Technically, if we're taking her drunk proposal off the table, it was my idea, but I know Maverick isn't going to be keen on this plan of mine, so I'm willing to stretch the truth a little. *Whatever closes the deal.*

"She was joking! And drunk! You can't hold her to something like that."

"I'm not *holding* her to anything. So stop acting like she's some innocent victim who can't take care of herself." *Whoa. Did I just come to her defense? Where did that come from?* Sighing, I continue, trying to be as calm and collected as possible. "We just talked. We're meeting up sometime tomorrow to hash out the details, but it's as good as done."

That's probably a little more confidence than I should possess at this point. She said she'd consider it. But I'm nothing if not confident, even when I shouldn't be.

"No." He stands up and starts pacing. "No fucking way. There's no way I'll allow this. Are you both stupid? What are you thinking exactly, because this makes no sense?"

I ignore his question regarding our intelligence for the time being. "It makes perfect sense, so sit down and let me explain. You promised you'd keep an open mind."

He mumbles something under his breath as he falls back into his chair, pinning me with that fucking Kensington glare. If I really wanted to piss him off, I'd tell him he looks like his father, but I don't have a death wish. So, I rationally explain the situation.

"First and foremost, CeCe and I are both business people and that's why this arrangement works so well. We'll get married and stay that way for a year. I'll receive my inheritance and I'll give her a small portion of it. Then, we'll be free to divorce and go our separate ways. *Amicably*. We'll both be able to use the money to improve our businesses or however the hell we want. It's as simple as that."

"Simple? You think marriage is simple?"

His humorless laugh makes my hackles raise.

"It is when love's not involved," I seethe, pissed that he can't just see things my way and fucking be in agreement with this. "There are no feelings between CeCe and I, which ensures this remains a business transaction."

"I see," he says after a few long seconds. "What about sex?"

His question catches me off guard. We've been best friends for years and have often participated in normal locker room-type banter regarding girls we've not been serious about but I've never mentioned my weekend with CeCe to him.

"Sex is good."

He's not amused. "Will you be having sex with her?"

"That's between me and my future wife, isn't it?" I goad him. "Come on, Mav. What do you want me to say? That I won't be sleeping with her or that I will? Which option would make you happy?"

"That you won't be sleeping with her and that this marriage idea is a joke you're not really planning on seeing through!" Shit, his jaw is twitching. He's really pissed.

"Why are you so against this?"

He gives me an exasperated look. "Because it's fucking ridiculous! CeCe is my friend. She's best friends with the love of my life. And you're my best friend, and even though you think marriage is just another business transaction, I think deep down you have a real heart in there, somewhere. Playing this game with her will only end badly. How do you not see that?"

"It's a year, for fuck's sake, and it's just a piece of paper I have to have to get the money left to me—a means to an end. Besides, I'm not CeCe's favorite person, so it's not like we'll be spending a lot of time together. We just have to convince my parents this is real and then go on with our lives. Trust me, Mav, the only way this can end badly is if feelings were involved, but they're not."

He doesn't look convinced but I think he realizes his complaints aren't changing my mind. After a few more seconds of seething and glaring, he breaks the silence. "If you hurt her in any way, I'll kick your ass."

"Duly noted."

"And then I'll let Carys kick your ass."

Okay, that scares me, I can't lie.

We both sit in silence, letting the dust from our disagreement settle, neither one of us knowing what to say next.

The thing is, I need Maverick on board with this. I need his support, even if he doesn't agree or understand. I don't have anyone else in my life rooting for me, which is why some of the decisions I make seem so fly-by-the-seat-of-my-pants. I go with my gut because it's all I have.

"Look, I know this situation isn't ideal for either CeCe or myself, but it's the best option I have. The *only* one I have. I can't marry someone my parents want me to and you know that. Wouldn't you rather I, at least, marry someone I know rather than taking an ad out in the local paper or doing one of those stupid dating shows on TV?" I wait for a second, not expecting a response but hoping for a change in demeanor, when I don't get one, I continue. "I promise, CeCe is on board with this and I'll do everything in my power to make sure she comes out ahead when this is all said and done. She still has plenty of time to marry for love."

"What about you? Don't you want to fall in love at some point?"

I don't even need a second to think of my answer to that. "That's never been in the cards for me. I've never wanted it and don't feel like I'd be missing out if I didn't get it. My heart of stone will survive, I promise." I smile at him, encouraging him to see things my way.

"I'm looking out for both of you, I hope you understand that. You and CeCe are probably more alike than you think but I've seen how charming you can be. Don't yank her chain or play with her emotions. Promise me, you'll be up front and honest with her the whole time."

"I will, I promise. We know what's at stake and what the reward will be. Our eyes are on the prize." I give him my most charming smile, knowing he hates it.

Maverick lets out a reluctant sigh. "Fine. You have my blessing but don't forget my warning. I care for you both and don't want this to blow up in your face."

"Thanks, Mav. I really appreciate it. Besides, if I fuck this up, you and Carys will have to wait to kick my ass once CeCe is done with it."

"We'll wait in line, don't worry."

We stand and hug before I take my leave but before I open the door, I turn and ask. "You'll be my best man, right?"

"You really are a charming son of a bitch, aren't you?" He laughs while shaking his head. "Yeah, I'll be your best man. Don't make me regret it."

"Oh, and you'll get Carys on board with this, right?"

He wads up a piece of paper and throws it at my head. Ducking, I hurry out, closing the door behind me and on Maverick's response.

"You're seriously fucking pushing your luck today!"

CeCe

Me: meet at Lagniappe @ 7?

I already asked Paige to stay late and fill in for me tonight and I have a feeling Shep will be compliant with my request. He seemed anxious to get this show on the road.

Shit show.

Huffing a laugh to myself, I glance down at my phone when it vibrates with a reply.

Shep: I'll be there.

I start to tell him Jules will be joining us but decide that's not necessary. The way I look at it, the ball is in my court. Shep needs me more than I need him right now and that power feels good. So, I'll keep my element of surprise to myself. Besides, it's not like Shep and Jules aren't already acquaintances. If Jules had his way about it, they'd be more than that.

And that thought makes me laugh again.

I need all the good humor I can get right now. It's the only thing keeping my nerves at bay.

What the hell am I doing?

It's the resounding question that's played over and over in my head for the past forty-eight hours.

WhatthehellamIdoing?

WhatthehellamIdoing?

WhatthehellamIdoing?

"Deep in thought, boss?" Paige asks as she walks past me with a tray of clean mugs. After almost five years of basically running this place by myself, never having a break, except when I was sleeping, it's nice having her around. I thought it'd be weird, relinquishing some of my duties, but it's been…nice.

"No," I lie. "Just trying to remember everything we need for the order I'm putting in." Pocketing my phone, I pick the order form back up and walk down the hallway to the stockroom. It's pretty well supplied. I like to keep it that way, just in case we were to have an off week. I'm always thinking worst-case scenario. Call it my upbringing and the fact that we never knew what the next day or week or month would hold. Or maybe it's the fact that I inherited this place from my uncle who lived through the Great Depression? Regardless, I never take my momentary success for granted, always preparing for disaster, which is one of the things that make my decision to go through with marrying Shep a no-brainer.

And the fact the said uncle I inherited Neutral Grounds from just so happens to have a long-lost son who wants to take it from me.

Jotting down the few things we need, buffering our supply of cups and lids, because those don't ever expire, I turn back around and make my way out to the main part of the store. After logging in the order online, I shut my computer down and untie my apron.

"If you don't need me, I'm going to head upstairs and shower away the day before I head out."

Paige waggles her eyebrows, reading more into this than she should. She reminds me of my little sister in so many ways. I'm sure not all twenty-year-olds are hopeless romantics. I know I wasn't when I was their age, but it seems to be a common theme. They're so whimsical and carefree. I wish I could have a little dose of that, but life has put a damper on my romantic side. It just doesn't go along with my need to safeguard myself…and my family and my business.

"Have fun," she sing-songs. "And don't worry, I'll lock everything down tight and leave the cash register print out and deposit in the safe."

She knows the drill.

"Oh, and I'll go ahead and break down the espresso machine and stock the shelves."

I pause at the door that leads to the stairs to my apartment. "Are you trying to get a raise?"

"No," she replies, rolling her eyes. "I'm just letting you know you can trust me…and you should take off more often…have some fun."

Now, it's my turn to roll my eyes. "Don't push it, kid."

"You're like what, five years older than me?" she asks with a laugh. "Act like it, CeCe. Live a little!"

Shaking my head, I smile. "Have you been hanging out with Carys?"

"Not too much," she says with a smile of her own.

She sounds like every other person in my life, so the culprit could be anyone—Carys, Avery, my sister, Rory…my mother—they're all the same. They think I work too hard and too much and take life too seriously, but they don't know what it feels like to be me. Well, Carys does, but she's inherently more carefree than I am. She loves the Blue Bayou, but the wherewithal to run it didn't come easy to her. She had to work at it and figure out a balance in her life to make it happen. Thanks to Maverick, she now has a vision for the hotel her family left her.

But for me, this business is my life. Sure, my family is important to me, but without this place, I wouldn't be able to support them. I was the breadwinner long before I was old enough. The need to take care of my mom and sister is my leading force, and this place gives me the ability to do that.

At least Shep understands that part of me. This fake marriage with him is probably the only one I'll ever be successful at. Anything more real and I'd fail miserably. There's just not time for two loves, something would have to give and I have a feeling it wouldn't be this place.

"Thanks again, Paige," I say before walking through the door. "And no ragers while I'm gone."

That gets me a good laugh.

See, I'm fun.

Half an hour later, I'm showered and dressed, staring at myself in the mirror. Is this the right outfit to wear to meet with Shep and announce I want to be his wife?

Who am I kidding?

How will I ever be able to pull this off?

No one will take me seriously. There's no way his family will believe he chose me over all his options back in Dallas.

Ripping the slip dress over my head, I toss it in the corner and then jump when someone knocks on my door. "Who is it?" My voice is high-pitched as I dig through my drawer and pull out a pair of my favorite jeans.

"It's Jules, honey. Did you forget we have a hot date?"

I smile, shaking my head as I reach for my favorite blue shirt and pull it over my head on my way to the door.

"Don't dress up on my account," Jules deadpans.

Blowing hair out of my face, I groan. "Stop. I've already changed three times and I decided that if Shep wants to marry me, he needs to know this is as good as it gets." Bending down, I grab my trusty sandals out of the bottom of my closet.

"Oh, it's good alright," he muses.

His comment makes me whip my head around so fast I almost hurt myself. "What's that supposed to mean?"

"Well, you've got the goods. You might not display them the way they should be displayed, but it's all there…and all in the right spots."

Pausing with one shoe on and the other dangling in my hand, I quirk my head. "Are you trying to tell me that if you were straight, you'd do me?"

"Oh, honey…I'd do you seven ways to Sunday."

Huh.

Okay.

As I slip the other shoe on and grab my bag by the door, I lean over and plant a big wet kiss on his cheek. "Thanks, I needed that little boost of confidence."

When Jules and I walk into Lagniappe, we're greeted by Micah, the restaurant owner, who must've already seated Shep, because he acts like he's expecting us.

"Your table is in the back," he says, leaning over for a hug from me and an air kiss from Jules. If Shep is Jules' number one and Mav, his number two, Micah is a close third…or maybe he'd prefer him in the middle of Shep and Maverick.

Okay, that's not what I want to be imagining for the rest of the night.

"How's Dani?" I ask, trying to clear my head of the ménage à trois vision I have playing in high def.

He hesitates for a minute and I want to ask, but then he recovers with a smile. "Great…she's great. I'll tell her you asked about her. She's supposed to be in town quite a bit in the next few weeks, leading up to Cami's new studio opening up. They have photoshoots and things lined up."

Excitement fills my chest. "I can't tell you how happy I am that Camille Benoit-Landry will once again be a permanent fixture in the Quarter. Is she planning on being at the studio on the daily?"

Cami and I have been friends since she was in New Orleans for college and have remained friends ever since. Now that her brother-in-law, Micah, owns a restaurant in the French Quarter, we've all become great friends, including Micah's wife, Dani, and Cami's brother and sister-in-law, Tucker and Piper. Even Micah and Deacon's parents, Sam and Annie Landry, make regular appearances. I love when my doorbell chimes at the shop and a Landry walks in.

"Uh, for the most part, at least in the beginning. She's hiring some bigwig from New York, a buyer from Sotheby's, to manage the gallery."

"Wow," I exclaim, in awe of my old friend and all that she's accomplished. "Well, tell them coffee is on me, so they need to stop by."

He gives me that classic Landry smile, like his dad and brother, minus the deep dimples. "Will do," he says with a deep nod. "Now, don't let me keep you. Appetizers are already on their way to your table."

I catch a whiff of something cheesy and delicious passing by as one of the waiters nods in our direction.

"CeCe…Jules, enjoy your evening."

Shep stands as we approach the table, pulling out the chair to his left, ever the gentleman.

"Jules," he greets, "didn't expect you to be joining us tonight."

He's not rattled or annoyed, just stating the obvious, getting it out in the open.

"I'm her legal counsel," Jules declares with a professional air as he straightens his tie. It's a vibrant purple floral that coordinates well with his pink shirt, complimenting his light grey suit perfectly.

To say I'm underdressed compared to the two impeccably dressed men at the table would be the understatement of the century, but I don't care. I feel comfortable and like myself, which is all I can be. There's no sense in putting on false pretenses.

This marriage will be fake enough for everyone.

"Legal counsel?" Shep asks, turning his attention to me. "Is that necessary?"

I shrug, letting out a sigh. "I'm just protecting myself." It's not a lie, but it's not the complete truth. Jules accompanying me to this… *meeting*…was Carys's idea. After my pow-wow with her and Avery, which did not go smoothly, they both insisted I look at this from every angle and make sure I know exactly what I'm getting myself into, which is how Jules ended up here.

"Fine," Shep says with a curt nod. "That's probably for the best."

There's an odd expression that passes over his face and I wonder, not for the first time, what's going through his mind.

What does he honestly think about this situation?

Is he really okay with his first attempt at marriage being a complete farce?

He did say a traditional marriage wasn't in the cards for him, but I'm not convinced. A good looking—no, *great looking*—guy like Shep, with all of his charm and wit and...assets. Any girl would be crazy not to jump at the chance to marry him. So, I find it hard to believe he never intends to do this for real.

Just not with me.

"Shall we get down to business?" I ask, needing something else to focus on besides Shep's future.

He smiles. It's a thousand watts and so genuine. "That's what I love about you, CeCe."

What?

He *loves* something about me?

How did I never know this?

I'm sure it's merely a figure of speech, but the fact that he put love and my name in the same sentence throws me for a loop.

"Always thinking about the bottom line."

I smile back at him and then glance over to Jules, who seems to be watching a ping-pong match as he looks at me and then back at Shep...and then back to me.

"Jules?" I prompt, drawing him into the conversation and hoping he'll be the buffer I need.

"Right," he says, pulling out a leather portfolio that has a list of the demands we came up with together last night over a bottle of wine. "CeCe has some of her own stipulations."

Shep leans forward, resting an elbow, so casual and confident. "Let's hear them."

I think Jules was right. I could've asked for the moon and Shep would probably give it to me. He obviously wants this inheritance pretty bad, so I'm not going to feel bad for asking for a few things I want.

But first, I need some sustenance.

Taking a piece of the flaky bread, I dip it in the ooey-gooey cheese and slowly consume a piece, settling my lingering nerves and my growling stomach. "Sorry, I forgot to eat today."

Coffee is a good filler, but it does not count as a meal.

"You should eat," Shep says, pushing the appetizer closer to me. "We have all night."

Jules motions to the waiter and asks for a bottle of wine.

After I've had a few bites and the wine has been poured, I start. "Okay, now I'm ready to get down to business."

Shep takes a slow sip of his wine and it's ridiculously erotic. I know he doesn't mean to be, but it's impossible to not notice. His face isn't perfect, per se. There are just enough flaws to give him character and make him unique, not like some photoshopped GQ model. His nose is a tiny bit crooked and his teeth are straight except for his front two that set a little forward, which is surprising. A rich kid like him has all the dental care at his disposal, unlike a kid like me, who had to just pray genetics went in my favor.

Then, there's his blond hair, which is actually a few different shades, natural highlights, I'm assuming. As much as Shep comes off as a pretty boy, he doesn't strike me as someone who'd dye his hair. Fork over thousands of dollars for a designer suit? Sure. Spend hundreds of dollars on skin care? Maybe. But I doubt he sits in a chair with foils on his hair.

The thought makes me hold back a laugh.

Clearing my throat, I decide it's time to lay it all on the table and stop obsessing over…my future husband.

"So, there are a few things I'd like to have decided before I agree to this…arrangement."

Shep nods. "Okay."

"First, I want to live in my apartment." This is the first and most important. "Actually, I *need* to keep living in my apartment. My mornings are early and my nights are late. It wouldn't make sense for me to live miles away and have to commute."

He thinks about this one for a moment, obviously having other ideas. I can see the wheels turning as he contemplates. "There will be times you'll have to make it appear as if you are living with me. I have a townhouse not far from here, so it wouldn't be a total inconvenience for you to stay with me…from time to time…" Drifting off, he thinks a little longer and I wait for his verdict. "Yeah, okay. I'll agree to it, but only if you agree to be available when and if I need you."

What?

Like a booty call?

The question must be loud in my expression because he quickly continues to elaborate. "Not like that," he says with a sly smile. "I mean, if my parents were to show up or a business colleague. We'll need to put up a good front if we're going to pull this off for a year. I have a feeling if my parents feel like this is a ploy to gain the inheritance, they'll contest it somehow. Neither of them was pleased they were left out of the will. I wouldn't put it past them to keep me from what's mine."

I nod. And then I swallow, thinking about exactly what I'm considering agreeing to. It's a lot. And I know there will be times I'll have to play the part of the happy wife. I've thought a lot about what he said, including the part about sex. "I also don't want you to sleep with other people."

His eyebrows shoot up. "Well, there is an alternative offer on the table where that's concerned," he counters.

Clearing my throat, I glance around and remember that Micah set us at a table that's secluded in the back of the restaurant. No doubt Shep requested this spot for privacy. God bless him. Thankfully, Jules already knows this little tidbit of information, so I'm free to discuss.

"About that," I start, picking up my wineglass and downing its continents. "Well, I'll…uh…"

"You can't expect me to be celibate for a year," he adds, cutting off my rambling, obviously thinking I'm going to turn down his offer. But what he does is piss me off and I don't even know why.

My face heats as I let his statement sink in. *Celibate for a year.* Try two fucking years.

"Are you telling me you'll be able to not have sex for an entire year?" he asks incredulously.

Now my cheeks are on fire.

Jules nudges me with his foot under the table and I shoot daggers in his direction.

"Is there something I should know?" Shep asks, looking at me and then at Jules.

"CeCe?" Jules prompts, folding his hands in front of him.

"Well," I start and then stop, swallowing. "I'm…I mean, I could—"

"Ha." Shep barks out a laugh, tilting his head back and drawing my attention to his chiseled jaw.

Fuck.

Fuck him.

Damn it.

"Are you some kind of nun?" Shep asks in disbelief. "Listen, I'm more than willing to be monogamous, if that's what you want, but there is no way in hell I'll be celibate. It's one or the other. Unless, there's something I don't know about…*someone*."

His expression shifts and I see the moment his thoughts turn. He's considering that there's someone else in my life, a man…another relationship.

"No, no one else…just me and the shop… andIhaven'thadsexintwoyears," I mutter, getting it out in the open, even if it does come out as rambling gibberish.

Shep's eyes squint, focusing in on me and I direct my gaze at the white linen tablecloth. When he clears his throat, I look back up at him, briefly, in time for understanding to hit and his eyes go wide. "What?" he asks, shifting in his seat and moving his gaze to Jules. I suddenly get the feeling he wishes it was just the two of us as he leans toward me for his next statement, lowering his voice. "You haven't had sex since…*us*?"

"Yeah," I confirm, wishing I could crawl into a hole under the table and disappear. "So, monogamy it is."

It's a rash, spur-of-the-moment decision, but damn it, if I'm going to be married to Shep Rhys-Jones, I'm going to get every benefit I have coming.

Pun fucking intended.

He smiles and it's so fucking smug, I want to smack it off his face, but it's the hint of something else—Nostalgia? Desire? —that makes me press on with my final demands.

"Also, I'll only accept one million dollars." I almost choke, because *only*? What the fuck and how is this my life? But after much contemplation last night, I decided that five million dollars was too much. With great reward comes great responsibility and I don't want that kind of burden. It gives me hives to think about that amount of money.

"And," for my final request, I pause, taking a drink of my wine before continuing, "I want to elope."

Shep

"YOU SURE ABOUT THIS?" MAVERICK MUTTERS UNDER his breath as we wait in front of the courthouse.

CeCe and I were just here a few days ago to get our marriage license.

Marriage license.

I had to let that sink in over a few glasses of whiskey last night. The thought crossed my mind to call Maverick over for one last night of bachelorhood, but thought better of it. I didn't want to spend the night with him trying to talk me out of what I'm one hundred percent sure of. This is what I want. There's no going back.

Besides, in a year, I'll be a bachelor again, so there's no sense mourning that part of my life.

This is temporary.

"I'm sure," I finally say, adjusting my tie. I went with a black Tom Ford suit. It's my good luck suit that I've worn for several big business deals and they've all gone according to plan, so I put it on this morning in hopes it would bring me the same good luck in this endeavor.

I wonder what CeCe will wear?

Not that it matters. She could show up in her faded blue jeans for all I care…I do love the way her ass looks in those. And for the hundredth time since our talk the other night over dinner, about being monogamous, I'm imagining getting her out of *whatever* she's wearing.

Having CeCe to myself for an entire year might be more of a reward than a hundred million dollars…and the knowledge that my father got nothing. I have to admit, that's almost as good as the money, but CeCe is better.

CeCe, who hasn't been with anyone since our weekend together.

"What's that smug ass grin for?" Maverick asks, eyeing me with the same calculated stare he's used since I told him about my plan… *our plan*. I'm not alone in this. After the dinner at Lagniappe, it's clear that CeCe has thought through this entire process and she's also one hundred percent onboard.

"What?" I turn to him and give him my biggest, most genuine smile. "A guy can't be happy on his wedding day?"

"You can drop the act with me," Maverick says, still leveling me with his stare. "No feelings, remember? *Happiness* is a feeling."

Chuckling, I slap him on the shoulder and squeeze. "Loosen up, Mav. This is all going to work out, just you wait and see."

About that time, a car rolls up to the curb in front of us and out steps Carys…and then CeCe. Her dress is a pale-yellow lace—simple and understated—with a lower cut neckline. And she's wearing these shoes that wrap up her ankle, accentuating her toned legs.

Legs for days.

Even though she's shorter in stature, her legs seem to take up more than their fair share of real estate, which is not a bad thing. Quite the opposite, actually.

"Ahem." Maverick clears his throat and nudges me with his elbow. "I think you've got a little drool," he mutters.

"Shut up."

CeCe gives me a tight smile as she walks up the steps. "Ready?"

"As I'll ever be," I tell her, making eye contact and hoping, somehow, I can convey how much I appreciate what she's agreed to and also that she can relax. Just like I told Maverick the other day, this is all going to work out. I can feel it, and besides, I'm wearing my lucky suit and it hasn't failed me yet. "You look beautiful," I tell her.

Her eyes travel to mine and for a moment, I think she's going to bolt or tell me she's changed her mind, which makes my stomach do a weird tightening maneuver. But I watch as the slight hesitation is erased and is replaced with a breathtaking smile. I'm not sure if it's pure moxy or genuine confidence, but she looks completely calm… and downright gorgeous.

"Thank you," she finally says, exhaling.

As soon as we walk into the waiting area, someone calls our names. Fortunately, the day we got our license, there had been a cancelation, so we were able to get an appointment with the judge on short notice.

We stand in front of the judge and when he instructs me to, I hold CeCe's hands. Her fingers feel small against my palm and I have an odd sensation come over me—something foreign that says I need to protect her. I don't know where it's from or what to do with it. Of course, I don't want CeCe to get hurt, not physically or emotionally, but it's uncharacteristic of me to feel so protective over someone, especially a woman.

"Shepard Rhys-Jones and Cecilia Louise Calhoun," the judge begins. "Today you celebrate one of life's greatest moments and give recognition to the worth and beauty of love as you join together in the vows of marriage."

At the mention of love, I feel my neck heat and the button on my collar is suddenly tight. I want to pull at it and get a little more air flowing into my lungs, but I'm holding CeCe's hands, so I can't.

When I glance over at Maverick, I expect to be met with a look of disapproval, but his focus is on Carys. It's like the two of them are in a world of their own. If I'm being honest, the two of them almost make me believe in true love and soulmates and all that bullshit.

Almost.

"Shepard, do you take Cecilia to be your wife?"

Oh, shit.

My eyes flash back to CeCe's and I'm met with something resembling challenge.

Do I take her to be my wife?

This is real.

We're really doing this.

"I do."

"Do you promise to love, honor, and protect her, forsaking all others and holding only unto her?"

CeCe continues to hold my gaze, trapping me with those deep brown eyes.

"I do."

She swallows and I swear I can see her shoulders visibly relax.

"Cecilia," the judge says, turning his attention to her. "Do you take Shepard to be your husband?"

"I do," she replies quickly.

After she repeats her vows, we spend the next five minutes listening to him talk about our wedding bands—some simple gold bands I picked up yesterday—being symbolic of our marriage…no beginning and no end.

*Oh, but there is…*three hundred sixty-five days, to be exact.

Finally, he congratulates us, announcing, "You may kiss the bride."

I think about opting for a chaste kiss to the side of her mouth, keeping it PG and without *feelings*. But that's not me. Besides, I've thought about kissing CeCe again for the past two years. Her lips have haunted me as I've tried to erase her from my memory, replacing it with random women who never compared.

So, I'm cashing in two years' worth of denial.

Wrapping one hand around her waist, I pull her flush against me, enjoying the way she inhales sharply in surprise, and then I cup her cheek with the other. For a split-second, I just enjoy the feel of CeCe against me, drinking in her sweet smell and quick breaths of anticipation, and then I go in for what I want, brushing my lips against hers. When she doesn't pull back or slap me—which is totally plausible considering what a little spit-fire she can be—I take that as permission to commence with our first kiss as *Mr. and Mrs. Rhys-Jones.*

Cecilia Louise Rhys-Jones.

That's quite a mouthful.

CeCe Rhys-Jones.

That's better. I like the sound of that.

Maverick interrupts the small bubble we're wrapped in with a loud *ahem*. When I reluctantly pull away, I notice CeCe's eyes are still closed and I can't help the smug smirk. She was totally into it, into me, and it makes me want more.

"Congratulations," the judge says. "We'll just need to step over here and sign the certificate."

Right, we're on a schedule.

Business.

"Of course," I tell him, placing my hand at the small of CeCe's back and leading her over to the wooden podium. Maverick and Carys are our witnesses. The judge lets us know when to expect the certified copy in the mail, which is important. It's why we're doing this. I'll need to send it to my grandfather's lawyer as soon as possible…and then the clock starts ticking.

"Come to Blue Bayou," Carys says as we walk back out into the heat of New Orleans. "Avery and I put a little something together."

"Carys," Mavericks says, her name sounding like an admonishment.

"What kind of *little something*?" CeCe asks hesitantly.

Carys turns to Maverick, giving him the smile she always reserves just for him. It's one of the first things I noticed about her—the way she looked at my best friend. I knew from day one that whatever Carys felt for Maverick was forever, even though they aren't even engaged yet, I know they're both in it for the long haul, without a deadline or an end date.

"Very little," she assures CeCe while still looking at Maverick. "Promise."

We all start to walk out to the curb when Carys adds, "I mean, you only get married for the first time once."

Finally, the thin layer of tension that's been hovering cracks and we all chuckle at her honest comment. It's true. This will be the only first wedding CeCe and I will ever have, and the only one for me, so I might as well live it up.

"To Blue Bayou," I say, placing my hand on the small of CeCe's back once more, loving the way it feels and the fact that she's allowing me to touch her like this. It feels intimate…familiar…which is what everyone should feel after pledging their life to another.

My wife.

When we all walk into the courtyard at the Blue Bayou, Carys was telling the truth about very little when it comes to the amount of people—there's only the four of us, plus Avery and Shaw and Mary and George—but when it comes to everything else, she was a damn liar. There are even more hanging lights than normal and a table full of food and booze, courtesy of Shaw and his sister, Sarah, if I had to guess. Instead of a cake, there's a platter of Carys's famous macarons, and in the background, the sound of light jazz permeates the space.

It's perfect.

For a couple of hours, I almost forget that this is all fake… pretend…a marriage with a deadline. I let myself smile and enjoy CeCe, stealing glances and a brush of my hand against hers. I don't go in for a kiss again, even though I have been known to push my luck, I play nice, just enjoying the evening.

When everyone starts saying their goodbyes is when I'm brought back to reality.

"Uh, I guess I should go too," CeCe says, brushing her hands down her dress…a dress I'll remember for the rest of my life, even if we do go our separate ways. When I think back to this day and marrying CeCe, I'll think about how she looked when she stepped out of the car at the courthouse.

If I'm being honest, she took my breath away.

"Yeah," I reply, running a hand through my hair. "I should too."

"Five o'clock comes early and I can't expect Paige to fill in for me two days in a row." CeCe laughs and it comes out nervous, like she's unsure of herself…us…where we go from here.

"Yeah, I've got an early conference call in the morning," I tell her, wanting to reach out and brush a strand of her dark hair out of her face, but I stuff my hands in my pockets instead.

"Right," she adds, filling the awkward silence we suddenly find ourselves in. "So…"

What do I say here?

There's no judge having me repeat after him, no manuscript or *how to be fake married* manual. "Well, uh…thanks for…"

Smooth, Shep.

Real fucking smooth.

Thanks for marrying me.

"I guess you can call me…if you…" CeCe says.

"Yeah, I'll call you."

What now? Are we going to fucking shake on it?

What I want to do is carry her back to my apartment and hide her away for a few days. I want a repeat of our weekend together, but I have a feeling that's not going to happen. At least, not yet. But if I give her some space and show her I'm not going to push…maybe soon?

"Want me to walk you—"

"No," she says, cutting me off. "I…I need a few minutes to… process."

Right.

"Be safe," I tell her, that nudging to protect her coming back.

"Of course."

I stand in the center of the courtyard and watch her until she turns the corner, headed toward Neutral Grounds. This morning, she was just CeCe Calhoun, coffee shop owner and a one-weekend stand. This evening, she walks away my wife.

My wife.

CeCe

I'M WORKING BY MYSELF THIS MORNING, WHICH IS starting to feel weird. Which is weird. When I hired Paige, I honestly thought I'd hate it—having someone who constantly needed my instruction. I'm horrible at delegating and much more comfortable at doing everything myself.

It was actually Avery who helped me realize how nice it could be to have the help. She lived with me for a short time and instead of rent, paid me in hours working the shop.

Even a stubborn, independent, self-reliant person like myself can change.

But change is hard. Over the course of my life, I've been trained, through disappointment and letdowns, to believe that I'm the only person who can guarantee my happiness and security. I can't depend on anyone else to do it for me, even my mama. Like everyone else, she's only human. And even though she means well, she's not the best at caring for others. It's why I stepped in at such a young age. After my dad left, she was a mess and Rory was just a baby. Someone had to be the adult and that someone was me.

As I go through the course of the morning, serving my regulars and greeting newcomers to the shop and the city, my thoughts occasionally turn toward Shep and the fact that I am married.

To Shep.

Typically, when people get married, part of the appeal is having someone else to depend on.

But even with my newly hired help…and my new husband… I'm still flying solo.

Part of me thinks I always will.

It's just who I am.

Which is why I agreed to this sham of a marriage.

"Have a good day," I call out to a couple as they leave. Ironically, they came to New Orleans to elope. What a coincidence. I didn't tell them that I'm also a newlywed. Actually, I haven't mentioned it to anyone besides Avery and Carys. Since it's temporary, I don't see any reason to involve anyone I don't have to, including my mother. Or Rory. They're both busy living their own lives. Rory is home for the summer, and even though she will be back soon, she'll be living on campus and going to class. She has a part-time job and a social life that keeps her busy.

Surely, I can keep this to myself for three hundred and sixty more days.

It's been a week since we said *I do*, followed by the most awkward goodbye ever. I swear, I almost told him "thanks" or something equally embarrassing, which is why I had to get the heck out of Dodge before I made a complete idiot of myself in front of my new fake husband.

Well, I guess he's really my husband.

My husband.

Yeah, I've been bouncing that one around in my head like an intense game of pinball.

After *the kiss*—yes, it will forever and ever be known as *the kiss*, because…*damn*. He literally swept me off my feet with that one kiss. I wasn't expecting it. Internally, I braced myself for a quick peck and then he just leveled me with those delicious lips and his tight grip on my waist. I lost myself in that kiss…and later, I lost myself in the impromptu reception Avery and Carys threw for us. It wasn't until Avery asked me what we planned to do for the next twelve months that I remembered…we're just pretending.

So, I quickly shut those errant feelings down and got back to business. It was time for everyone to leave anyway, and I quickly made my departure, turning Shep's chivalrous offer down and walking myself home, using the few blocks to clear my head.

And stare at the new gold band on my left hand.

Married.

Wow.

My cell phone ringing draws me out of my inner thoughts and back to the real world.

Well, speak of the devil.

"Hello?" I answer, batting down the flock of birds taking flight in my stomach with the sight of Shep's name on my caller ID. He did say he'd call. I just wasn't sure how long he'd wait…

"CeCe," he says, sounding all business and making my spine straighten.

I don't know what I was expecting, but that wasn't it. Who the heck really knows anymore?

"Listen, I need you to go to Dallas with me." He continues talking without any pleasantries. "My mother is planning a reception for us this weekend. We'll need to leave Saturday night. Will that work for you?"

What?

No, no, no.

I'm not ready for this. I'm not ready to pretend in front of people who don't know our arrangement. We've only been married five days.

I'm not ready.

"This…Saturday?" I ask, buying myself a few seconds to process his request.

"Yes, I have a flight booked for Saturday night, nine fifteen. It's the latest flight out of New Orleans to Dallas. We'll return on Monday morning. You can handle that, right?"

What?

"I'll have a car pick you up at eight. No need to check luggage, just bring a carry-on. You can even shop for a dress on Sunday afternoon if you'd like. The reception will start at seven."

When I still don't say anything, he asks, "Did I lose you?"

"Uh, no…I'm here," I reply, my mind reeling. "I'm here…I just… I've never left the shop for an entire day." We do have fewer hours on Sunday and I guess Paige can handle the place for a day…maybe. "I'll figure it out."

"Great," he says quickly. "Call if you have any issues with the plans."

"Okay."

"See you Saturday."

I almost stop him and tell him I think we need a crash course in Shep and CeCe so we can effectively sell our romance, but before I can say another word, he's gone. Hung up. On to the next item of business for the day.

Okay.

When the black sedan pulls up at the curb, right at eight o'clock, just like Shep said it would, my heart is in my throat. It's basically been lodged there for the past few days, ever since his phone call. Not only do I have to meet the parents and sell a fake marriage, but I'm also being thrust into Shep's world without a safety net.

I always have a safety net, but right now, I feel like I'm free falling.

On top of all of that, I'm leaving Neutral Grounds in the hands of Paige and seven-month-pregnant Avery, who is supposed to only be on back-up and used for emergencies. Shaw is adamant she not be on her feet right now, which I completely agree with. I don't like it any more than he does, but she's the only other person who knows my business.

My business.

That's why I'm doing this. For the money. I have to keep telling myself that when I start feeling that fight or flight sensation take over. I can do this…I can fly to Dallas and meet Shep's parents and play the part of the happy newlywed.

Stepping toward the car, I take a deep, fortifying breath and then immediately lose it when Shep slides out of the back. He's wearing a navy-blue suit that's tailored perfectly for his long, lean body. When he stands to his full height and adjusts his cuffs, I have to swallow down a moan that tries to escape.

Holy Jesus.

You know what's real torture?

I know what's under that suit.

From the moment he walked out of the hotel room we shared and didn't give even a backward glance, let alone his phone number, I knew I'd regret that fact.

Knowing what he's hiding under those clothes and not being able to do a damn thing about it…well, that's enough to make any woman go insane.

My eyes are stuck on his blond hair as he rakes his fingers through it. It's grown a little longer since he moved to New Orleans. I'm not sure if it's the laid-back atmosphere or if he's just due for a haircut. Regardless, I love it. And I want to run my hands through it.

That will be enough, Cecelia Louise.

This is business.

Get your shit together.

"Here," he says, reaching for the strap of my bag. "Is this all you have?"

I look up at him just before I slip into the backseat of the car. "You said to pack light."

Shep chuckles, shaking his head as he places my bag in the popped trunk.

"What's so funny?" I ask when he slides in beside me.

The driver pulls away from the curb and for a second I think Shep's going to ignore me when he pulls his phone out of his suit pocket and begins typing away. "Most women think packing lightly means an overpacked suitcase."

"I'm not most women," I declare, watching as the city passes us by.

"Don't I know," Shep mutters under his breath while his fingers are still flying across the screen.

I think about asking him who he's talking to, but it's none of my business.

Right?

That wasn't part of the agreement. We didn't negotiate personal details of each other's life. Actually, now that we're married, I've thought of several things we probably should've discussed before we made it official.

Protocol.

Family history.

What we tell people about us and our *relationship*.

"What do I need to know about your family?" I ask, tackling my biggest concern first. I know we have a two-hour flight, but I have a lot of things weighing on my mind.

Shep puts the phone back in the inner pocket of his suit jacket and lets out a deep sigh before he begins. "My father is Phillip. My mother is Jane. They're your typical high-society people who have more money than they'll ever be able to spend but still want more. Pretentious. Self-absorbed. They're both only children and are a product of marrying for money…I come from a long line of modern day arranged marriages. So, technically, we fit right in."

"Except, I don't have money." That's where the comparison ends. I'm not like his mother and father who joined their mass fortunes. I've done a little research of my own and I know his mother is an heiress of a small hotel chain. When her father passed, she inherited an estimated three hundred million dollars. I can't even wrap my head around the hundred million Shep is going to inherit, let alone three hundred million.

What do people do with that kind of money?

Shep's throaty laugh pulls me out of my thoughts. God, that's a sexy laugh.

"What's so funny?" I ask, trying to distract myself from the onslaught of everything else that's sexy about Shep.

"Nothing," he says quietly, shaking his head as he turns to look out his window.

"Are they going to hate me?"

The car is quiet for a moment and my stomach drops a little. I know I'm nothing like Shep or his family. There's no use for me to try to pretend. After a quick emergency help session with Avery and Carys, we decided that I should just be myself. Shep knew who he was marrying. He knows I'm not high-society. And one thing he's never asked me to do is be anyone different.

"Probably." His words are honest and I appreciate it, even if they do make me feel nauseous. "But they wouldn't like anyone who's not on their shortlist of people I should marry."

"So, why not marry one of them?" It's been on my mind since the morning I woke up and recalled my offer to him at Come Again the night before. Why doesn't he just pick one of his many suitors? Why me?

"Because that's what they expect of me and I'm tired of falling in line," he mutters, his words coming out so low I'm not sure if they were even meant for me to hear. "I'm ready to start living my life on my own terms. If I would've married one of the women my mother throws at me, it would've been a life sentence. That's not what I want. I just want to do what I need to do to get my inheritance and cut ties."

For some reason, this time, his honesty doesn't make me feel better. It just makes me feel…cold. And a little empty.

It's not the first time I've been slapped with the truth of our arrangement, but it cuts a little this time. But I'm grateful for the sting. It's a sobering reminder of what we're doing here and I need that going into the lion's den.

Get in.

Get out.

And don't get eaten alive.

Fifteen minutes later, I get an answer to one of my earlier mental questions. *What do people do with that kind of money?* They charter private jets.

As the driver pulls up, I swallow the nervous lump in my throat. "I've never flown before."

Shep's hand pauses on the door handle and he turns to me. "Never?"

"Nope." My eyes flit from the sleek plane back to Shep.

I would never admit this to him but I spent the better part of last night worrying about every possible thing that could go wrong and thinking of ways out of it. That's me. That's what I do. I think about all the worst-case scenarios and then I think of how to fix them.

When I walk into a new place, I always look for the closest exit.

The couple of times I've stayed at a hotel, I've always located the nearest set of stairs.

In case of an emergency.

So, last night, I laid in bed on my phone googling all of the things that can go wrong on an airplane and how to survive a plane crash.

Take a non-stop flight.

Check.

Watch the skies.

Check. No bad weather in sight.

Wear long-sleeved shirts and long pants made of natural fibers.

Check. Check. Even though it's hot as shit, I made the sacrifice and wore a thin, linen button-up shirt with a pair of wide-leg pants and some flats. The look I was going for was casual, yet put together, and safety first, of course.

Select a seat on the aisle, somewhere near the end half of the cabin.

Now, see, how am I going to do that when this plane looks like it only seats about twenty people?

"Well, allow me to pop your cherry," Shep says, seduction rolling off his tongue.

I want to glare at him—burn holes through his meticulous suit for making me think about sex at a time like this—but instead, I take his proffered hand and step out of the car. "And relax," he whispers, slipping my hand through the crook of his elbow and leading me to the steps of the plane. "It's going to be the best ride of your life."

Are we still talking about the plane ride?

Damn him.

Damn him for being so sweet and making me lose my resolve.

Because even though I should be fortifying my walls, I'm not. Instead, I'm latching onto him and absorbing his air of confidence and surety, clinging to it like a damn lifeline.

"Mr. Rhys-Jones," the flight attendant greets as Shep enters the cabin of the plane. "So nice to see you again."

"Rachel," Shep greets, still holding onto my hand, which is now tucked safely behind his back. The heavens shine on me and I get a front-row seat to Shep's ass, and it is a glorious sight. "Will anyone be accompanying us today?"

"No, sir," she replies in a mellow, soothing tone. "The plane will be all yours."

When I take the last step, my mouth gapes at the interior. If I thought the outside of the plane was sleek, I don't even know what to classify this.

Rich.

Filthy stinking rich.

It's the things movies are made of.

Like, I'm Julia Fucking Roberts and this is the set of *Pretty Woman*.

"This is my…wife," Shep says and I practically swallow my tongue when my heart leaps into my throat at the mention. "CeCe."

That's the first time I've heard him call me that…*his wife*. He should win an Oscar. The way his tongue caresses the word is so believable. It's accompanied by adoration, something you only hear in people's voices when they speak about something—or someone—they truly love.

Bravo.

The Oscar for Best Performance in a Fake Marriage goes to Shepard Rhys-Jones.

Thankfully, I'm able to rally and give her a smile. "Hello."

"This is her first time flying," Shep informs, garnering me an astonished look from Rachel—the tall, blonde flight attendant. She's more Shep's style and as I really look at her, I see the familiarity in her gaze when she looks at him and the genuine surprise when she hears his announcement. But it's not just because I've never flown before, no it's more than that. She's shocked Shep is married. And she's probably shocked Shep would marry someone who's never been on a plane before.

She's shocked because she knows him.

Like, *knows him* knows him.

In the biblical sense.

After we're seated in the plush leather seats that are more comfortable than any chair I own or have ever sat in, I buckle my seatbelt and swallow down the nerves that have come back full force and are competing with the realization Shep has more than likely fucked the flight attendant. Which means she knows what he looks like under that suit and I don't like it. In my small bubble that is the French Quarter, I'm the only one who's ever seen that, at least to my knowledge. But the realization that I'm possibly getting ready to face a slew of women who know Shep—*my husband*—in an intimate manner is unsettling.

In real life, it's none of my business.

However, in this fake reality I'm living in, I feel like it is.

I've never been the jealous type. Truth be told, I've never had a reason to be jealous. Sure, I've had a few boyfriends—one fairly long-term relationship in high school—but I never got attached.

I never practiced writing my name with a boy's last name.

I never planned out my wedding.

I never daydreamed about my future children…or given them names.

I don't have a hope chest.

I don't have a five-year plan that includes two and a half kids and a white picket fence.

So, why am I sitting here stewing over the stewardess?

"Nervous?" Shep asks, stretching his long legs out in front of him, drawing my attention back to the here and now. "Need a drink?"

"Yes, a little…and no, I'll be fine."

To distract myself, I go back to my pre-flight checklist.

Listen to your safety briefings.

Hopefully, we get one of those.

Locate your nearest exit.

Check.

Count the seats between you and the nearest exits in case the cabin should fill with smoke.

That's easy. Two. Check.

Practice opening your seatbelt a few times.

Reaching to my waist, I unlatch my seatbelt and then slide it back into place…and repeat.

"What are you doing?" Shep asks with his head leaned back and his eyes closed.

"Practicing opening my seatbelt."

"Why?"

"It's part of the How to Survive A Plane Crash article I read on CBSNews last night."

There's a brief stretch of silence before Shep pulls his long legs up and leans forward, practically cornering me in and using up my personal space. "Do you always do that?"

"What?" I ask, tucking hair behind my ear.

That's my nervous tick.

Anytime I feel unsure of myself or anxious, I tuck my hair.

Shep rakes his fingers through his.

We all have something.

"Prepare for the worst?"

Well, shit.

"What? I don't," I lie.

"Yes, you do," he insists. "I've watched you. You might think you fly under the radar, and you might fly under most people's, but not mine. I see you, Cecelia."

"Don't call me that."

He chuckles, that low, throaty sound that does things to my body, things I don't approve of and didn't ask for. Things I thought I'd never feel again. At least, not after our weekend together.

"Why?" he asks, nailing me with his icy blue eyes. "I like it."

Clearing my throat, I brush my hair back again, tucking strands behind my ear. "Well, it's CeCe to you…and everyone else."

Cecelia was my grandmother's name and the only people who have the right to something so sentimental are my mother and sister, but even they don't use that name. Well, my mama does when she's mad at me or when she's really trying to get me to listen to her. It has to be important.

It's too familiar.

Speaking of familiar…"So, you and the flight attendant?" I ask in an effort to redirect the conversation and get this attention off me and onto him.

I don't miss the smirk before Shep asks, "What about us?"

My cheeks heat. I expected him to lie or divert. I didn't expect him to be so forward, but I should have. Shep loves to get under my skin, so of course, he's going to take this opportunity to make me squirm.

"You fucked her."

One of his well-groomed eyebrows lifts and he shrugs—so aloof and cool. "And?"

I'm trying to stay one step ahead of him, but it's hard. I never know what's going to come out of his mouth. How am I ever going to keep up with him when we're with his family? They're going to smell my lies from a mile away.

"Did you ghost her too?"

Oh, there it is. I did *not* mean for that to come out. *Shit.*

"Mr. Rhys-Jones," a male voice says, coming over a hidden speaker and saving us from that awkward conversation. "We've been cleared for takeoff."

Shep leans over and his lips are brushing my ear when he whispers in a low, guttural tone, "Fasten that buckle and hold on tight."

Shep

Did you ghost her too?

CeCe's question is playing on repeat in my mind as the plane begins its ascent, but I quickly forget it when I feel her hand clutch the sleeve of my suit. Glancing over at her, I notice the set of her jaw and how her nostrils are flared and her eyes are closed.

"You good?" I ask, reaching for her hand.

When she takes mine willingly, I can't help but think how perfect it feels. And how good it feels…and right.

Breathing deeply, she mutters, "I'm fine."

She's obviously not, but she's working hard to convince herself as much. But that's CeCe. She's self-reliant and self-contained. She's not needy and she doesn't want anyone taking care of her. Those are a few of her characteristics that make me attracted to her. As much as I'd like to lie to myself and say she's just another fuck from my past, I can't. Because she's not. She's Cecilia Calhoun and she's different from anyone I've ever been with or known. There's a goodness that's soul-deep and it shows. She has this magnetic quality about her that makes you feel better about yourself by just being near her.

It freaked me out two years ago.

When we spent the weekend together, I went into it thinking it'd just be a quick one-night stand. But the next morning, I woke up and saw her lying beside me and I couldn't stop staring at her. My hands itched to touch her, but the thought of waking her was enough to keep me from it. I just wanted to watch her sleep. Eventually, I tried to put some distance between us by jumping in the shower, but when I came out and she was slipping on her shoes, I couldn't let her go.

So, instead, I kissed her.

And pushed her against the hotel room door, taking her once more.

And then on the desk.

And again, in the shower.

We christened every surface of that hotel room, until we were spent and the only thing either of us could do was crawl in bed and fall asleep. Later, we'd ordered food and had it delivered, and all I wanted was her presence and her conversation. When we fell asleep again and I woke up with her sleepy, warm body wrapped around mine, the only thing I could think about was spending another day with her…and another…and another. And I knew.

I had to get the fuck out of there or I was never going to leave.

So, I packed my shit and slipped out of the room and caught a flight back to Dallas.

That saying about catching flights instead of feelings could be my life motto.

In a matter of forty-eight hours, she'd gotten under my skin. I couldn't stick around and make a mess of things. Because, let's face it, that's all that would've happened. I'm no good at relationships.

On my way back to Dallas, I thought about her—played our weekend together over and over in my head—and tried to picture plausible outcomes, but all of them ended with CeCe hating me and in turn, Maverick being pissed off at me.

I couldn't risk it.

The only true relationship that exists in my life, outside of my fucked-up family, is Maverick.

So, why now? How did I let this happen—married to CeCe?

Good fucking question.

All I know is when she offered, I jumped. After the night at Come Again, I went back to my apartment and mulled over all my possible options and marrying CeCe was the only one that felt right.

Just like her hand in mine.

When her grip begins to loosen, I glance over and watch as her eyes stay glued to the open window. It's dark, so there's not much to see, especially now that we're thirty thousand feet in the air. But still, she seems to be mesmerized and a lot less nervous.

"Not so bad, right?"

She huffs a laugh, dropping my hand and rubbing her palms down the front of her pants. "Yeah, it's not so bad." Turning she meets my eyes and I wish I knew exactly what she was thinking, but CeCe always keeps her true feelings close to her chest. "Pretty awesome, actually."

"I can't believe you've never been on a plane before."

CeCe's back stiffens and she sits a little straighter in her seat. Glancing down at her lap, she tightens her seatbelt again as she mutters, "Well, we didn't really take vacations when I was growing up and I've worked at the coffee shop since I was eighteen…so."

She's defending herself, but I didn't mean it as a dig. I only meant I'm surprised she's never been anywhere because she seems like someone who's seen the world, but maybe she just has that air about her because she's seen the world come through her doors.

New Orleans is one of those cities that attracts people from all over and it's comprised of all walks of life. CeCe reflects that.

"I didn't mean anything by it," I offer, not wanting to get off on a bad foot, especially since we're getting ready to have to be a united front. "I also didn't realize you'd worked at Neutral Grounds since you were eighteen."

Relaxing a little, she settles back into the seat. "I have," she confirms and for a second I think she's going to stop at that short answer, but then I notice the way she worries her bottom lip with her teeth and I know there's something else she wants to say. "It was my uncle's shop. He left it to my mom who passed it on to me."

I think I knew that bit of information. It's something Maverick has mentioned in passing, maybe when I bought the building next door to her.

"It's actually why I agreed to this..." she says, drifting off as her eyes go back to the dark window. "Someone is threatening to take it away from me."

"What?" Why haven't I heard about this before now? Not that I'm privy to every detail of CeCe's life, but bits and pieces usually make their way to me, especially important stuff, like someone trying to take the shop.

"It's a new development. Jules is helping me look into it, but I'll probably have to hire a lawyer and fight it in court. It's going to cost me. But I have no choice, the shop is all I have."

My blood is pumping faster. I'm angry, on CeCe's behalf. That protectiveness I've been feeling since the judge pronounced us husband and wife is in overdrive. How dare someone try to take what's hers.

"Why didn't you tell me?" I ask, my voice rising even though I don't mean for it to.

CeCe shifts in her seat and turns toward me, her eyes widening at my tone. "It's not something I'm just going around telling everyone."

I want to tell her I'm not *everyone*.

I'm her husband.

But I shut that shit down and try to play off my reaction. "Well, I could help you."

"You already are."

"What's that supposed to mean?"

She lets out a deep breath and turns back to the window, avoiding my stare. "You're giving me a million dollars."

"Not for a year."

Shrugging, she glances over her shoulder. "At least I know now if I have to take a loan out to fight this, I'll be able to pay it off. It feels like I have a safety net again."

And that's what it all boils down to with her.

The pre-flight checklist.

The knowledge she'll be able to pay legal fees.

She always has to know what her Plan B is…and Plans C and D.

I wonder what her strategy is when it comes to meeting my parents.

"So why are we doing this?" CeCe asks, pulling me out of my thoughts.

"What? Flying?"

She shakes her head, leaning deeper into the seat and exhaling. "No, this…going to a reception…meeting your parents," she clarifies. "I thought you'd just need a piece of paper and we'd need to…I don't know, not kill each other for three hundred and sixty-five days. It seems like a little too much to go to this length for a temporary… *arrangement*."

Her air quotes make me laugh while contemplating an answer to her question.

"Pretense," I reply. It's the one word that explains my family. "The one thing you should know about the Rhys-Joneses is that we are *always* keeping up a pretense."

Her eyes bore into mine, like they can see my soul and she's stripping my reply down to bare bones, examining it like a cadaver. "Do your parents know we only married for your inheritance?"

"Yes," I say, simply. "Not by my admission, but due to my sudden change of marital status…yes. They might be a lot of things, but they're not stupid. Plus, they'd do the same if they were in my shoes." Bringing one leg up, I cross my ankle over my knee, shifting in my seat to face CeCe. Shit's about to get real. "I've told you before, my parents got married for money. There's nothing surprising about what we're doing. But don't be shocked if my mother still brings suitors around. She'll probably invite women she thinks I should've married instead of you to the reception tomorrow night. There's no sanctity to the institution in their circle. Whatever gets you higher on the ladder is all that matters. But they're all the same—plastic, trust fund babies with fake degrees and titles that don't mean shit. Be on guard and don't tell anyone anything. If they ask about your family, divert to the weather…or how you're just dying to get the newest Hermès bag."

"The what?" she asks, confusion thick in her tone.

Waving it off, I continue. "Just don't give them shit. They don't deserve to know anything about you."

"Right," she agrees, nodding, but obviously worried now that I've thrown all of that on her.

Reaching over on instinct, I place my hand over hers, grasping her fingers. "Look, just be yourself…it'll be fine."

She exhales, turning her gaze out the window. "At least I have a night to sleep on it and get my shit together," she mutters.

Oh, fuck.

I might've left out one small detail. "Actually, we'll be staying with my parents."

CeCe

My interest in looking out my window at the dark unknown evaporates.

Turning to look at Shep—my *husband*, who just dropped a bomb the size of Hiroshima—dead in the eyes. “What do you mean we’re staying at your parents’ house? What happened to your fancy house?”

“Shit,” Shep mutters, wiping a hand down his gorgeous face. “Settle down.” Exhaling harshly, he rearranges himself in the seat before running a hand through his hair, mussing it up even more. Have I mentioned I like this version of Shep even more than the kempt, tidy version? The more he grows his hair out and lets his true colors shine, the better.

“My house is being painted,” he explains. “The furniture is all covered and it isn’t suitable to spend the night in. Besides, it’s only for two nights and my mother insists we stay there. I’m sorry…I should’ve warned you, but you’re you.” He waves a hand in my direction. “You’ll be fine.”

He obviously gives me way more credit than I deserve. If he only knew exactly how much this is freaking me out and exactly how much I've been stressing over meeting his parents and actually having to play the part of his wife, he would've warned me. Shit, he might've even sedated me.

"Sure, I'll be fine." I huff out an exasperated breath, trying to convince us both of the statement. When a semi-sardonic laugh escapes, I lean forward and think briefly about taking my seatbelt off. I'm starting to feel a bit claustrophobic. The air is too still. And this careening tin can is starting to feel too small.

Pressing my palms into my eyes, I will myself to calm down. "Yeah, no worries," I mutter, more to myself than the man sitting beside me. "I just have to talk about things I know nothing about, while being paraded in front of people I know nothing about, who coincidentally hate me because I'm married to their prize pony. All while pretending to be in love with you. Piece of cake."

Shep shifts, drawing my attention back to him and reminding me I'm having a meltdown with a captive audience of one. I swear, I see a hint of a smirk and it makes me seethe. As he composes himself and takes my outburst in stride—being his typical calm, cool, and collected self again—I want to smack that smile right off his face.

Whoa, where did that come from?

Get yourself together, Cecelia.

"Our agreement was that we get married. We never negotiated on falling in love," he teases. "I understand, it may happen regardless, but I won't hold it against you." His joking tone makes my shoulders ease a bit, even though I'm still considering bodily harm.

However, when he pulls my hand away from my face and brings it to his mouth, kissing the top, I melt. Whatever tension that had crept in with the knowledge I'll be facing his parents tonight fades. The feel of his lips on my skin, the way his breath warms the area as it escapes his nose, it becomes all I can think about. But I'll never let him know what he does to me. There's too much power in knowledge like that and Shep already has enough of that. Instead, I jerk my hand from his and cross my arms, making him snicker in response.

Does nothing get to this guy?

"Relax," he soothes. "It's less than two days. And yes, they're horrible, but I assure you, you'll make it out alive. In fact, I'll guarantee it. I'll even offer hazard pay."

That damn cocky smile is back in place and the air in the cabin finally goes back to normal.

I should probably spend the rest of the flight grilling him about his parents and the people I'll meet at the reception tomorrow night, but I decide instead to soak up as much serenity as I can, while I can.

Shep leans back in his seat, crisis averted, and somehow, I manage to doze off for a few minutes. When the captain announces our descent, I put my seat back in its upright position and tighten my seatbelt.

I've read the ascent and descent are the most dangerous parts of flying.

As soon as we're safely back on land and cleared to deboard, we're ushered down the steps and out to a waiting car. I feel like I cheated on my first flight. I didn't have to wait in long security lines or deal with a swarm of strangers. There was no one elbowing me the entire flight. Well, I did have to put up with Shep's charm and sex appeal, so that makes up for some of what I missed out on.

However, this plane-side service is something anyone could get used to, even me.

"I still can't believe you've never been to Dallas," Shep says as we settle into the back seat of the sleek sedan. "It's not even that far from New Orleans. Traveling was how my fucked-up family survived. I mean, we didn't spend our vacation time together but it was still an escape from our everyday lives. How do normal people manage?"

I don't take offense to his question because I can tell he's genuinely curious. He has absolutely no idea what it's like to be *not*-rich. And, although I hate the word *normal*, because who has the right to decide what it means, I answer him.

"Vacations were a luxury we couldn't afford," I admit. Being vulnerable in front of Shep is starting to feel easier and I'm not sure if I should be worried by that, but I just go with it. "We felt lucky just being able to drive to the beach in Alabama for a couple of days during the summer. *Managing*, as you put it, is what we simply consider living. If you don't know what you don't have, you don't miss it." I sigh, leaning back into the seat and feeling the exhaustion of a long-ass day settle over me. "I've always wanted to travel, though. I'd love to see the world but that's pretty much impossible at this point."

"Why do you say that?" Again, I can tell he's truly interested. I don't usually like being the focal point of a conversation, but with Shep, I oddly don't mind it as much.

"Because, I run my own business and have only one other employee to help out. Also, there are these things called bills and responsibilities I have to take care of. It'd be incredibly selfish for me to travel—"

"I'll take you anywhere you want to go."

"No, that's not what I mean."

"We need a honeymoon anyway, right?" he asks. "You pick the place and I'll take care of the arrangements."

"You're not listening to me. I can't abandon my life to go traipsing across the globe with you. Gah, you really are clueless sometimes."

When I feel Shep stiffen beside me, I turn to look at him. I've obviously hit a nerve because his body language just made a one-hundred-and-eighty-degree turn. His face that was casual and inquisitive is now devoid of emotion and his relaxed posture has been exchanged for rigid and cold.

I instantly miss the way he was before and I feel terrible for causing this kind of change in him. I want the happy, teasing Shep back. The guy with the megawatt smile and eager conversation. The man I married.

Before I can apologize, though, the car stops. When I look out the window to see where we are, I know immediately we've arrived at Casa de Rhys-Jones. It's not a house. No, that's far too menial of a description for what I'm seeing. *It's a freaking mansion.* Seriously, there's no other way to describe it. If it wasn't so late at night, I'd expect a line of people waiting outside to pay admittance for a tour.

Shep steps out of the car and offers me his hand, which I accept, not just because I need help out of the car, but also because I need something to ground me.

What has my life become?

I feel like I'm in some weird movie or alternate universe.

"The house is dark so, hopefully, my parents are in bed," he says, sighing in relief as he shoulders both of our bags and we walk up to the massive doors. "Let's keep it quiet. We might be able to avoid the Spanish Inquisition until morning. My mother and father are scary enough during the daytime but if they're awakened in the middle of the night…" He shivers rather than filling in the blank and I feel like I'm going to throw up.

"Spoken like someone who's been caught sneaking in a time or two," I whisper, trying to keep the mood light.

A half-smile appears and I'm grateful. "You could say that."

Once Shep uses a keypad to unlock the front door and quickly disarms the security system, he leads me inside and places our bags at the bottom of a massive stairwell. I mean, I assume it's massive. I can't see the entire thing because of the darkness but a staircase in a house like that would have to be huge.

"Shit."

The curse coming from Shep surprises me but when I see what he sees, I want to repeat his sentiment.

"They're awake, aren't they?" I ask, timidly, already knowing the answer when I see the dim light coming from a room to our right.

"And they're waiting for us." He grabs my hand and starts walking down the hallway. "Let's get this over with." When he pauses and grabs both of my hands, there's a desperation in his eyes and tone as he whispers in the darkness. "I just want to say thanks for doing this and I apologize in advance for anything my parents do or say this entire weekend. Promise you won't hold it against me…or divorce me before we even get started."

There's a laugh that tries to bubble up inside me. I don't know if it's hysteria from the stress of this whole ridiculous situation or pity for the man in front of me, but I nod my head and squeeze his hands. "Okay," I assure him and watch as his shoulders visibly relax.

He turns, obviously giving himself a mental pep talk, before reclaiming my hand and striding into the room with confidence.

The massive space we step into could only be labeled as a sitting room because every piece of furniture in here, with the exception of a few small tables, is a chair or sofa. There's literally nothing else to do in here but sit. In the corner of the room is an unlit fireplace and standing in front of it is a man who I can only assume is Shep's father. To his right, a woman sits on a chaise lounge, staring icily at us. Both of them are drinking martinis, as if it's the most natural thing to do at this time of night and I feel like I just stepped into a horror movie.

Again, that inappropriate laughter is back, and I have to tamp it down.

"For fuck's sake, what are you, The Addams Family, now?" Shep spits out before flipping the light switch on and saying exactly what I was thinking. If I wasn't scared shitless, I'd let the laughter spill out. "Enough of the theatrics, please. You're being ridiculous."

I appreciate Shep's candor with his parents, but my mama would tan my hide if I spoke to her like that, even to this day.

"We can't enjoy an evening cocktail while we wait to meet our new *daughter-in-law*?" his mother asks, batting her eyelashes. I really try not to judge people before getting to know them, but a fool could see this woman is a snake. And a manipulative one, at that.

Shep rolls his eyes before turning to me and grabbing my hand. "Mother, Father, this is CeCe, my wife. CeCe, these are my parents, Phillip and Jane."

"Hello," is all I manage to get out, but it sounds clear and confident. To my ears, at least.

Score one for CeCe.

Shep's mother walks over to me, ignoring her son, and gives me air kisses on both of my cheeks. I should've expected that, I guess, but it still catches me off guard and I end up standing there, frozen like a statue, side-eyeing Shep.

She then takes a step back and makes no attempt to hide the fact she's assessing me. With a fingertip on her chin, she looks me over—up and down, from head to toe—before giving me a tight smile. "So lovely to meet you, dear," she says before turning to Shep. "Since the reception is formal, I assume she'll need to go shopping tomorrow."

Heat floods my face in embarrassment but Shep is quick to come to my defense. "You don't have to worry, Mother. I'm looking forward to spoiling my wife in many ways this weekend." I'm shocked at the suggestive tone he takes with his mom but it's not enough to stop the warm feeling in my belly. I know how it feels to be spoiled by him in the bedroom and I'd be lying if I wasn't looking forward to experiencing that again.

"Of course, you are," she mutters before returning to her drink and chaise lounge.

When his father looks me over, it's in the same manner as his wife but instead of feeling like I'm a disappointment, I get the impression of quite the opposite. *Ew*. Before he can get much closer, Shep puts a possessive arm around my waist, pulling me into his side, as if to say *mine*, like he's staking his claim.

Yeah, I'm definitely freaked out now.

Shep turns me toward the room's exit. "We're going to bed. We'll see you sometime tomorrow." His parents say nothing in response. No "goodnight", "sleep well", nothing. They just go back to their weird sitting and standing.

This is truly some Twilight Zone-shit.

I don't think I start breathing again until we're up the staircase, which was massive, and in Shep's room with the door closed. I'm using the word *room* loosely, of course. It's more like his own wing of the mansion. It's a huge space with a couple of different sitting areas that ultimately surround what I'm guessing is a California king bed. I would've killed for this kind of space while I was still living at home but I also imagine it must've been terribly lonely for anyone to grow up here. There's nothing cozy or personal. Distant parents and no siblings—no wonder Shep has little concept of what commitment or family means. I'm thankful he found Maverick and had him as a positive influence.

"Are you okay?" His voice is quiet, like he's bracing himself, expecting me to freak out or have another meltdown.

"I am, but I have a question."

"I'd be worried if you didn't," he says with a small laugh.

"What was that thing…with your dad…"

He immediately shakes his head. "A warning. He's never touched anyone I've been with, at least not to my knowledge. Unfortunately, he's known to struggle with keeping his hands to himself around beautiful women, so just wanted to give him a reminder." It's so matter-of-fact that it makes me cock my head in disbelief. "If he makes you feel uncomfortable in any way, at any time, you tell me. Understood?"

His tone brooks no argument and the look on his face tells me he's dead serious, so I immediately nod my consent.

"The bathroom is down the hall that way," he says, pointing. "Go ahead and get ready for bed. We're going to need a good night's sleep. I can only imagine what is waiting for us tomorrow."

I grab my bag and quietly walk to the bathroom. Part of me hates leaving Shep alone right now, he's obviously bothered by all of this more than he would ever admit. But the other, more urgent part of me, really needs a shower to wash away this crazy day. While bathing, I try to wrap my brain around this insane situation I'm in. I don't regret the initial agreement between Shep and me, but I'm starting to doubt my ability to pull this off.

There's always been this part of me that feels like I don't fit in. I wasn't popular in high school and never went to college. My three closest friends, Cami, Carys and Avery, I met once I was living on my own and finally feeling like the person I was meant to be. Now, though, being thrown into a world I thought only existed on Bravo TV, all my old insecurities are resurfacing. At least I'll have Shep's help to navigate my new, temporary surroundings and he really does seem to want to make this as easy as possible. I just hope it's enough to survive the weekend.

Things will be back to normal once we're back in New Orleans, I tell myself. But even I can hear the doubt in that statement. Who knows what the next year will hold?

Once I'm clean and dressed for the night, I make my way back to the room, coming to an abrupt stop when I see Shep stretched out on the bed.

He's shirtless, only wearing plaid pajama bottoms, and he's reading a freaking book.

A mother trucking book.

And he's wearing glasses!

This must be a cruel joke.

How did I not know he wears glasses? I thought I remembered every detail from our weekend together, but I guess the shock of how perfect he looks like this rotted a part of my brain. It's probably a good thing, now that I think about it. If I would've remembered this version of Shep, I never would have gotten over him because I am now. Over him. Totally and completely.

I just have to be married to him for a year. And sleep in the same bed tonight and tomorrow night.

Nope, I can't do it.

I'll have to pick one of the millions of couches in this house and sleep there because there is no way I can sleep next to this man and not want what we had two years ago.

Not possible.

"Are you going to join me or do you plan on sleeping standing up?" His voice startles me and I try to ignore the look of amusement spreading across his stupid, gorgeous face.

"I don't know if I can do this," I admit.

His amusement quickly shifts to something more serious.

"Why not? We're just getting started. You haven't even given it a—"

"I don't mean the marriage," I say, ending his momentary panic. "I mean this sleeping arrangement. I can't sleep next to you. You know, in a bed." I'm talking with my hands now and I know I look ridiculous, but I can't help myself.

Shep carefully places a bookmark in his book and places it and his glasses on the nightstand before gracefully climbing off the bed. I swear he's moving in slow motion as he walks over to me and I try really hard to swallow the lump in my throat. When he reaches me, he simply grips my hand and leads me to the opposite side of the bed.

"Are you nervous about consummating our marriage?"

Umm, what? Is that what's happening?

"Shep, I'm not having sex with you here. Are you crazy? In your parents' house where they can hear or maybe even watch! A place like this probably has cameras in every corner. No, not happening."

Laughter fills the room and I'm mesmerized by the movement of his Adam's apple as he tips his head back. I'm also confused as to why he's laughing.

"There she is. There's the woman I married." His large hands cradle my face. "Relax, CeCe. I have no expectations of sex this weekend. I only said that to get a reaction from you because you're thinking too much."

"You don't know that." My jaw juts out to emphasize my stubbornness.

"I do know that. When you get quiet, it means you're overthinking things. You need to loosen up and I hear getting laid is great for that, but if you're not ready, I can wait."

"I'm sorry I said you were clueless earlier in the car." I've been wanting to apologize since the words first left my mouth but haven't been able to find the right time. Not that this is the right time, necessarily, but I know I won't be able to sleep until I get this off my chest. "Just because we come from different backgrounds, doesn't mean you're any more clueless than I am. It just means we've had different experiences and that's okay. It was wrong of me to lash out like that."

Shep watches me closely. Maybe he's trying to decide if I'm sincere or not, I'm not sure, but I hope he sees I am. It wasn't a nice thing for me to say and, honestly, I didn't mean it. Shep's actually a very capable person, probably one of the least clueless people I know.

Finally, he leans toward me and places his lips on my forehead. He kisses me twice there before resting his forehead against mine. "Thank you for apologizing, but it's not necessary."

"I hurt your feelings."

"My feelings recovered. I'm more resilient than my upbringing may suggest, but I do really appreciate your apology."

He moves to the side and motions for me to get into the bed, so I do. When we're both settled under the covers, I try to force myself to relax but it's too damn hard. You know how it feels, the first time you share a bed with someone that's not a family member, like a friend at a slumber party and you're so aware of every movement you make because you don't want to accidentally kick your bed partner or push them out of bed? Multiply that by, like, a million and you might be where I am right now.

I'm sharing a bed with Shepard Rhys-Jones. The man who is hotter than sin and who I also married for money. And even worse, I've seen him naked and allowed him to do very dirty, albeit amazing, things to my body and I can't have a repeat performance. Not right now. So, yeah, relaxing is not in my wheelhouse at the moment.

Oh, god, what if I snore?

"Come here."

"What?" I look over and find Shep watching me with his arm stretched out toward me.

"Move your body over here." He points to where his shoulder and chest meet, like that's where he wants me to be and that can't happen.

Can it?

"You're thinking again and it's keeping me from falling asleep, so get your ass over here so we can snuggle. Surely, then, we'll both be able to settle down enough to sleep."

I'm not sure what comes over me but I actually do what he says and snuggle into his chest. In an instant, I feel as though I've been transported back two years and Shep and I are in his room at Blue

Bayou. I'll never forget the way his skin tastes, the sounds he makes, or how it feels when he moves inside of me.

Damn him for making me remember.

Damn him for giving me something worth remembering.

And, damn him for making me want it again.

Shep

When I wake from the best sleep I've had in ages, I immediately feel like something's amiss.

Squinting against the early morning light, I recall what it is: CeCe's no longer tucked into my side, where she slept all night.

Just a few hours ago, sometime around three-thirty, I woke up and needed to go to the bathroom, but there she was, sleeping so peacefully. I couldn't bring myself to wake her, so I ignored the urge and went back to sleep.

And now, I need to pee like a fucking racehorse.

As I pull myself out of bed, I look around for a sign that would lead me to CeCe's whereabouts. Surely, she didn't go downstairs and face my parents alone.

She's way smarter than that.

"CeCe?" I call out on my way to the bathroom. When I don't hear a response, I pop the toilet seat up and relieve myself. Mid-stream, I'm startled when the bathroom door flies open and CeCe's surprised shriek fills the room.

"What the hell?" she asks.

Turning around, I see one of her earbuds dangling in her hand, the other still lodged in her ear. "I could ask you the same thing? Where were you hiding?"

"Closet," she mutters, throwing a thumb over her shoulder. "Have you seen how huge that thing is? My entire apartment could fit in there." Her eyes are no longer on my face. They've traveled down… below my waist.

Smirking, I finish peeing.

She's the one that walked in on me. It's not my fault she didn't hear me when I called out and that she's now getting a front-row seat to the show.

"Enjoying the view?" I ask, when I sense her still standing frozen in the doorway.

She huffs, turning around. "Ew, no!" I don't believe her. You want to know why? When CeCe lies, her voice goes up an octave. The bigger the lie, the higher the pitch. And she's at choir boy level right now.

When I return to the bedroom, she's walking around mumbling to herself. I think I catch a *men are so gross* and *hasn't he ever heard of locking the door when you're peeing.*

"You know, I did hear about that one time at prep school. I think it was in my Marriage 101 class, but of course, since I never intended to be married, I kinda fucked off the entire class."

She laughs, shaking her head. "You probably failed."

"Big time."

"You're so stupid."

Now I'm the one laughing. When I outwit her, she always shoots back with grade school comebacks.

"Really?" I taunt. "Pretty sure you didn't think I was so stupid the last time we were together."

CeCe's back straightens and her beautiful smile drops.

"No, you're right," she says, leaning over to pick up her toiletry bag. "I was the stupid one then."

Brushing past me, she makes her way to the bathroom but before

I can go after her, the door shuts and I hear the lock slide into place.

Apparently, she didn't miss the lesson about locking the bathroom door when it's occupied.

Also, we're going to need to air this shit out before it explodes. Between her off-handed comment about me ghosting her last night on the flight here and now this, there's obviously some underlying issues.

Call me ignorant. Actually, call me stunted, because I am, especially when it comes to relationships, but I assumed our one weekend together was just that…a weekend. And, yes, she's the one woman I've never been able to totally forget about, but I didn't think the feeling was mutual. The few times I've been around her over the last two years, she's always acted so aloof, like my presence meant nothing to her…like she barely remembered my name.

She even got it wrong once and called me Seth or something like that.

I'm not going to lie. It stung.

But I needed that. It was a nice wake-up call that she wasn't pining away for me, so I should forget about her.

Now, I'm wondering if it was all a coping mechanism. Maybe she was struggling to forget me as much as I was her? Maybe the private details from our time together still haunt her dreams like they do mine?

Fuck.

Gripping the ends of my hair, I walk down the hallway and listen closely at the door. I expect to hear the shower running, or at least water from the sink, but it's quiet.

When I tap lightly, something falls to the floor.

"CeCe?"

There's some shuffling around and it sounds as though she's down on the floor, maybe picking up whatever fell. "Uh, just a second…I'll be out in a minute."

"Okay."

I should suggest we talk, but I'm hoping we'll get an opportunity later today. Maverick asked me to check in on a piece of property we're in the process of flipping. Most of our properties are in the New Orleans, southern Louisiana area, but we still have a few investments in Dallas.

"We're going to go for a drive," I tell the closed door. "Dress casually."

"Okay," she calls back after a few seconds.

"Also," I hesitate for a second, not wanting her to take this the wrong way. She's been a little touchy this morning. Maybe she didn't sleep as well as I did. "About tonight...do you need something to wear?"

"No," she says, but thankfully, it doesn't sound like she's mad. "I brought something with me...borrowed it from Carys. I'm good."

"Great," I say, shoving down the slight disappointment I feel at her answer. There was part of me that wanted to take CeCe shopping. I want to give her all kinds of things, but that also scares the shit out of me. I'm glad she is who she is, and who she is, is someone who takes care of herself. I can't fault her for that. Of course, she brought something.

That's CeCe.

She's not a woman who can be bought. It'll serve me well to remember that.

Thankfully, my mother and father are both nowhere to be found when we make our way downstairs. Stopping by the kitchen, we find Maggie putting the finishing touches on a delicious looking cake.

"Mr. Shepard," she greets with a wide smile.

"Maggie, this is CeCe," I say, placing my hand on CeCe's lower back. "CeCe, this is Maggie."

"So nice to meet you," CeCe says, leaning forward to shake her hand. Maggie wipes hers off on her apron and accepts the greeting, patting CeCe's hand vigorously.

"So lovely to meet you." When she glances over at me, there's an unspoken conversation—*I like her*—followed by a wink. "I hear congratulations are in order."

CeCe glances over her shoulder at me and there's a faint blush on her cheeks, but she handles it beautifully. "Thank you so much. It's been such a…whirlwind." Her laugh sounds more like a newlywed who still can't wrap her mind around her windfall of happiness and less like someone who thinks she might have lost her damn mind.

She's good.

Of course, I already knew that.

"We're headed out for a drive," I tell Maggie, pulling CeCe back to me. Sure, I'm playing the part, but I also feel better when she's close.

Maggie walks quickly around the island and begins pouring coffee in to-go cups. "At least take some breakfast with you."

With our still-warm croissants and coffees in hand, we make our way down the long hall that leads to the garage. When I open the door, I swear CeCe's mouth drops to her toes. She turns to me, eyes wide in wonder. "What the hell?"

I shrug, punching a few numbers into the keypad on the wall, raising the garage door behind the Porsche 911. "What?"

"Please tell me this is some kind of car museum that just so happens to be attached to your parents' house."

"Or the garage," I say, hitting the auto start on the cherry red dream. I will admit, she's a beauty. When I open the passenger door, I turn to see CeCe still standing in shock—wide-eyed and adorable.

"Careful or you're going to spill your coffee."

That jolts her out of her car-induced stupor. She laughs, shaking her head and then taking a sip of her coffee. "Uh, are you sure I can take this in there?"

I glance back to the car and the smooth black leather. "You can do whatever you want in this car." There's a shit-ton of sexual innuendo laced in those words and I mean every bit of it.

Huffing another laugh, she averts her eyes, looking around at the twenty or so cars that are parked, just waiting on their turn to hit the road. Some rarely see the light of day. Others, like the Porsche, are treated to drives on the regular. "I bet your father might—"

"It's mine," I assure her, cutting off her train of thought and leaving my father out of it. I meant what I said last night, I don't want any part of him touching any part of her. "And what's mine is yours, remember?"

She swallows and hesitates for a few more seconds, but thankfully, finally acquiesces and climbs in the car, albeit gingerly, careful to not spill a drop of coffee or a crumb of croissant.

When I stuff my face with the last two bites of my own croissant and brush the crumbs into the floorboard of the car, CeCe's eyes widen. "What are you doing?"

"It's a fucking car, CeCe, not a museum exhibit," I admonish.

"And it probably costs more than my life," she says, exasperated with my lack of care.

Pushing the pedal down, I accelerate, whipping the car out of the garage and into the drive with ease and precision, but stop on a dime to look her in the eyes. "Nothing is worth that."

That shuts her up for a few minutes, until her curiosity gets the best of her. "Where are we going?"

"Mav and I have a piece of property we're flipping. He wanted me to stop by and check on the progress. It's good to make your presence known from time to time. Keeps people on their toes."

She nods and takes a dainty bite of her croissant. "For fuck's sake, just eat the damn thing."

"Shut up," she mutters, shoving a bigger piece in her mouth.

"What?" I ask in mock astonishment. "You're not going to call me stupid?"

When she laughs, I gun the engine and enjoy the way my body molds into the seat and CeCe's hand grips my arm. I miss this car. Maybe it needs to move to New Orleans with me.

"Wow." CeCe's eyes are glued to the window. "You and Maverick own this?"

I put the car in park and turn off the engine. "Yep, one of the few houses like this we've purchased. Typically, we opt to invest in things that are more multi-purpose, like dilapidated buildings on the verge of being demolished. We really love making something out of nothing and breathing new life into it. Mav is definitely the visionary where that's concerned, but he's teaching me how to have a good eye, seeing things for what they can be, rather than what they are."

"That's amazing." Her gaze shifts to me and I suddenly feel uncomfortable under her scrutiny.

Opening the door, I blow off her compliment. "It's business," I tell her, hoping she'll drop it. Normally, I eat that shit up, but coming from CeCe, someone I admire, it makes me want to bolt.

I'm glad there's no one in my head to psychoanalyze that shit.

"Can we go inside?" she asks.

Walking up the drive, I look around to see if the progress they've documented is actually happening. "Sure," I tell her, sliding my shades up to check out the roof, which looks like it's been replaced. The beams of the old front porch have also been replaced and have a fresh coat of paint.

"How old is this place?" she asks, running a hand along the banister. "Reminds me of a ranch you'd see on television…like Dallas…you can't tell me you're not asking yourself who shot JR every time you come here."

"What?" I ask, humored by her rambling.

"Big white ranch…80's television show…JR Ewing?" Her eyes go wide as her hands stretch out in question and then she slaps them down to her sides when I don't respond. "For fuck's sake, Shep. You grew up in Dallas and you don't know who JR is?"

Finally, I crack a smile and laugh. I love fucking with her.

"You're so stupid," she says, stomping around me and trying the door, which is locked…which makes her cross her arms over her chest and let out a frustrated huff.

"Excuse me," I say cockily, using the key in my pocket to unlock the door. "After you."

No *thank you*, she just walks around me and into the house, like she owns the place.

God, I love her.

Whoa.

Yeah, that…well, I just meant I love the things she does…not *her*. I mean, sure, I like her. I mean, I did marry her for God's sake…for an inheritance. But let's not get carried away.

"I'm going to have a house one of these days," CeCe muses, her head tilted back as she takes in the grandiose foyer.

I'll give you one. It's right on the tip of my tongue, but I swallow it back down.

"Wanna see the bedroom?" I ask, waggling my eyes.

She rolls hers in response and balance is restored once again.

After I do a thorough investigation—of the house, not CeCe—and she takes inventory of every room and characteristic of the house, continuing to compare it to Southfork, we make our way back out to the Porsche.

"Ready for another ride?"

She twists her lips to the side, squinting up at me. "Can I drive?"

I'm not prepared for the way my heart leaps into my chest. Sure, I said what's mine is hers, but I didn't intend for her to cash in on the Porsche. "Uh…well, I—"

"Kidding," she says, punching my shoulder lightly and laughing her ass off as she leaves me behind on the sidewalk. "But it sure was fun to see you swallow your tongue."

"I didn't swallow my tongue."

CeCe nods, reaching for the handle, but I beat her to it, opening the door for her. Her teasing smile turns soft as she gazes up at me. "That's really nice of you."

"What?"

"This," she says, sliding into her seat. "Opening my door for me. You did it earlier too. I didn't take you for someone who's so chivalrous."

Funny thing is I hadn't even thought about it, and it's definitely not something I learned from my father. He and my mother barely ride in the same vehicle together and when they do, someone is usually driving them.

So, don't ask me where I picked it up.

After I climb into the driver's seat and start the car, I look over at her. "Maybe you don't know me as well as you think you do."

Maybe I don't know myself as well as I thought I did?

CeCe brings out things in me I didn't even know existed.

Which is probably why I make the split-second decision to take her one more place before we head back to my parents' house and face the reception from hell.

"I've got one more place I want to take you," I tell her, backing out of the drive. "Feel like grabbing a cup of coffee?"

She turns, her eyes going wide with delight. "Are you kidding me? I love going to other coffee shops. It's my absolute favorite thing to do, on the rare chance I get to." The pure joy at the thought is so evident on her face, making her even more beautiful.

It really is the simple things with this woman.

The drive is quiet, only the faint hum of the radio in the background, but it's comfortable and the most relaxed I've been in a while. Without overthinking it, I reach over and place my hand over CeCe's and when she doesn't pull away, I relax even more.

Ten minutes later, we pull into a park in the Bishop Arts District of downtown Dallas.

"Where are we going?" CeCe asks, her eyes roaming the busy street.

"The best coffee shop ever," I tease, knowing it'll get under her skin. And it does.

When she cocks her head and juts her chin out in challenge, like she does every time she disagrees with me, I smile. "Fine. At least, the best coffee shop in Dallas."

She narrows her eyes and I think it's meant to scare me, so I try really hard not to laugh.

"You're a shithead."

"Oh, so I've graduated from stupid to shithead?" I goad. "You have a way with words, don't you? What a way to talk to your husband. Didn't they teach you anything at…where did you go to school?"

CeCe steps out of the car and her expression grows serious. "I went to a small high school about an hour from New Orleans. K through twelfth grades. They didn't really teach much past the basics. And don't even get me started about my parents—"

"I was kidding," I say, cutting her off. We seem to be good at stepping on each other's toes. But I guess that's what happens when you don't know everything about someone but you're thrust into a situation where you're supposed to. It's all trial and error...with a lot of errors. But I don't hate it when things get a little tense, not like I normally would, because I learn things about CeCe each time. "I'm sorry. I didn't mean to—"

"No," she says, stopping on the sidewalk and facing me. "I'm sorry. I was being too sensitive. I don't know what's wrong with me. Maybe I'm hangry. That croissant didn't last long."

I go to brush a strand of her hair behind her ear, but so does she, and our hands bump together, making us laugh. "Let's get you some food."

"Okay," she agrees, letting me brush her hair back and then take her hand, leading her down a flight of steps into the underground coffee shop. As soon as the door opens, the familiar sound of jazz fills the air.

This is probably the only thing I miss about Dallas, other than the Porsche.

"Coffee and Jazz?" CeCe asks, gripping my arm and leaving a wake of heat. "Okay, this might be better than my place."

Glancing over to the stage, I see Finley right away. His wide grin and head nod let me know he sees me too. Giving him a wave, I guide CeCe to the counter so we can place our order.

"This is great," CeCe gushes as we find a table and wait for our coffee and food.

Pulling a chair out for her, I wait for her to have a seat. "I thought you'd like it."

"How did you find this place?" she asks. "It doesn't seem very... Shep."

I smirk, sitting across from her and resting my elbows on the table. "What did I tell you about not knowing everything there is to know about me?"

"Who knew you were such a mystery?" she teases.

The ease of our conversation and the comfort of having her in my presence is something I've only experienced with a couple of people—Maverick being one and never with a woman.

I think about telling her I know Finley and he's how I found this place…actually, I found this place for Finley. But I decide to leave a little more mystery hanging in the air and let her experience it without pretense.

How very un-Rhys-Jones of me.

Smirking, I lose myself in watching CeCe soak up her surroundings. After a few minutes, our coffee is delivered, followed by the best sandwich in Dallas.

Eventually, the band finishes their set and Finley makes his way over to the table.

"Shep!" His usual, wide grin is on full display. "Hey, man!"

Standing, I pull him into a hug. "Dude, you sound great!"

"Thanks." When he steps back, his eyes immediately go to CeCe who is staring up at us, confusion on her face. "This must be—"

"CeCe," I finish for him. "My wife."

That phrase is getting easier and easier to say and every time I do it, I start to believe it more than the last.

"Hi," CeCe says, standing and reaching across to shake his hand. "You were amazing."

"Thank you," Finley says, ducking his head, never the one to take praise as well as he should. Especially from a pretty girl like CeCe Calhoun.

"Finley is Maggie's grandson," I tell her and see the amazement in her eyes.

"Oh, my gosh." She looks from me back to Finley. "I should've guessed. You have her eyes."

"The Lawson genes are strong."

Motioning to the extra chair, we all sit. "Finley Lawson is a name you need to remember," I tell CeCe, knowing this will get a rise out of him. "He's going to be the biggest name in Jazz music one of these days…better than Miles Davis and Duke Ellington combined."

"Stop," Finely says, rolling his eyes.

"Better than John Coltrane," CeCe chimes in, giving me a wink.

Finley's eyes go wide. "Wow, y'all have been married for what… two weeks? And you're already in cahoots?"

We all laugh, but I can't help but notice the way CeCe's eyes sparkle when she looks across the table at me. I like it.

I'd give her the next fifty years to stop.

CeCe

It's so surreal.

Still, even after two weeks, it's like I'm living in an alternate universe.

The man sitting beside me, calmly maneuvering his way through Dallas traffic is feeling more and more like an enigma, yet also more and more real.

I thought I knew exactly who he is.

Born with a silver spoon in his mouth.

Always gets what he wants.

Sleeps with someone, ruining her for everyone else.

All of that is true. But what I'm learning is those things are just surface deep. Underneath it all, he's…more—chivalrous, thoughtful, and desperately trying to break away from his family and forge his own path.

On top of all that, he's now introduced me to Finley, the housekeeper's grandson, and it's opened up so many more questions and feelings. I can't keep track of them all.

What's a guy like Shep doing hanging around with a kid like Finley? Well, I use the term kid loosely. He's probably in his early twenties, but sometimes, I feel like I'm a fifty-year-old in a twenty-eight-year-old's body. Everyone younger than twenty-five seems like a kid to me.

"So, how did you become friends with Finley?" I finally ask, breaking the comfortable silence we've been in since we left the coffee shop. "I mean, besides the obvious."

When Shep doesn't answer right away, I lift my head from the plush leather and turn to look at him. He shrugs, eyes on the road. "Maggie got custody of him about ten years ago. I was in college and I'd come home to work for my father on breaks. He would be around the house a lot…no one around to interact with except Maggie. Don't get me wrong, she's great…the best, really. But he didn't have any friends, you know?"

"So you became his friend?" I prompt, wanting to hear more.

He shrugs again, checking his mirrors before switching lanes and making an exit. "I guess you could say that. That first summer he was with Maggie, we played basketball and I took him to the movies. He told me about wanting to play the saxophone, so I bought him one."

Turning my head, I smile out the window. "You bought him his first saxophone."

"Yeah, best three hundred bucks I ever spent."

There's that deeper level I was talking about.

"I also paid for lessons," he says with a chuckle. "I taught him a lot of things, but I can't take credit for him being a musical genius."

Oh, but you can, Shep. You made it possible for him to discover his talent. That's what I want to say, but I've noticed he doesn't respond well to praise, which is weird for a guy as cocky as Shep. I want to keep the ease of the conversation for as long as I can, milking these last few stress-free minutes. "I bet you taught him a lot of things."

"Someone had to." He smirks and my stomach flips, just like it does every time he turns on the charm. "I couldn't let the kid go through junior high thinking he could get a girl pregnant from kissing her."

Laughing, I tilt my head back. "Oh, my God, was that what Maggie told him?"

"I never figured that one out, but any kid under my wing was going to have game."

Familiar houses start coming into view and I know we're close to being back to his parents' house and my heart starts to pound. I'd love nothing more than to stay in this bubble with Shep. Today's been… great—unexpected, but great.

I can't help staring at Shep's profile. The smile on my face making my cheeks hurt.

"Ready for this?" Shep asks as he pulls the car back into the garage.

Staring straight ahead, I let out a deep sigh, resolve seeping to the surface. "Let's get this over with."

"That's my girl."

My girl?

His girl?

Yeah, that's a dangerous road for my mind to travel down, because after a day like today…actually, after the past two weeks, I could see myself *truly* being Shep's girl. But that's not what this is about, is it? No. No, it's not.

It's about putting up a good pretense, playing the part, and getting paid.

"Let's go be the best fake husband and wife these rich people have ever seen."

Shep's eyes bore into mine and he winks. "So fake it's real."

The air inside the car feels heavy…as heavy as his gaze. "Right," I say, swallowing as I blindly reach for the handle to open the door and free myself. I need some space.

Somehow, we manage to make it into the house and up the stairs without having to stop and talk to anyone, not even Maggie. I'm assuming she's either off for the evening or helping get things set up for the reception.

"I'll take my suit and get dressed in another room so you can have some space."

Did he just read my freaking mind?

"Thanks," I say, not arguing. Maybe if I can put my earbuds in and turn on some music, I can drown out the nagging voices in my head telling me this is all starting to feel too real and perhaps I'm feeling too much for someone who's temporary.

I wait for Shep to gather his things and leave before I walk to the closet and grab the dress I hung in there this morning…right before I walked in on Shep peeing.

Yeah, that's an image I won't be getting out of my head any time soon.

Sure, I told him he's disgusting, but really, I could hardly pull myself away from him. Once I saw…*it*, I was lured in. It's like my body took that visual as a cue.

I remember that.

I remember how it felt…and how it made me feel.

I want that.

Shaking my head to clear it, I take the dress to the bathroom and remove the plastic. As I hold the shimmery fabric out, I pray Carys was right and this dress won't make me stick out like a sore thumb. I'm not a fashion disaster, but I don't have the need for high fashion, like ever.

My entire closet is made up of jeans and t-shirts with a couple of skirts and dresses thrown in for good measure. When Shep threw this on me last minute, I didn't have time to get everything at the shop ready for me to be gone for two days *and* shop.

So, of course, Carys came to my rescue.

If it had been up to me, I would've just worn the dress I got married in.

Gah, that still sounds so weird.

What am I doing?

Groaning out my frustration, I strip and hop in the shower to wash off the day and freshen up. I'm going to need it. And all the deodorant known to man, because I can already promise I'll be a sweaty mess. There's no getting around it.

Once I'm out and dried off, I pull on the deep-cut, pale pink bra and matching panties, which are all mine. I draw the line at dresses and jewelry. But they do match perfectly with the dress. It's also a pale pink with a plunging neckline. The soft satin has a sheer mesh overlay, adorned with rhinestones and pearl-embellished floral accents.

Carys said it gives me a flowy silhouette and I must admit, it does make me feel pretty.

Giving myself a once-over in the long mirror, I like how the pale pink makes my olive skin tone seem a little more tanned than I really am. I'll take that.

After I put a few curls in my hair and swipe some mascara on my eyes and brush some blush on my cheeks, I'm good to go. Any more and I'll feel as fake as this marriage.

Before I leave the bedroom, I spritz some perfume and slide into the creamy white pumps.

The second I open the door, Shep is waiting, looking like he just walked out of a men's fashion magazine. Swallowing, I bite down on the corner of my lip to keep from smiling like a loon.

"Wow," he says with a quirked eyebrow. "You look gorgeous."

Smoothing out the front of my dress, I feel the blush creeping up on my cheeks. "Thank you. You don't look so bad yourself," I say, barely above a whisper as I draw my eyes back up to his.

There's a drawn-out pause and when I see Shep's hand reach out for me, I awkwardly begin to fidget and look around the empty hallway, using the distraction to keep him from doing whatever was on his mind. Touching me? Kissing me? That's not an option right now. I would crumble.

"We should…" I tilt my head to the side, motioning down the stairs.

Shep clears his throat and adjusts his bow tie…a fucking bow tie.

I'm dead.

My ghost will be attending this reception.

"We should," he agrees, holding an arm out for me to walk ahead of him. "After you, Mrs. Rhys-Jones."

Oh, God.

Thankfully, I don't have much time to over-analyze that statement or how it made me feel, because the second we enter the foyer, we're whisked away to the backyard…lawn? I don't even know what to call it. Basically, they have a park behind their house and it's decked out in white lights. Tall tables with white tablecloths are scattered around. Candles and flowers and lots of people in tuxes and evening wear round out the scene that's laid out before me.

When Shep said his parents are all about pretense, he wasn't lying. I mean, I knew he wasn't. But this is a reception fit for royalty. Everything looks expensive, even the waiters walking around with trays of finger-sized foods and flutes of champagne. Is this even real life?

Maybe I slipped in the bathroom and hit my head?

This could all be a result of a massive concussion.

"There they are," Shep's mother says, a wide smile on her face and her arms opened wide. She looks like the epitome of proud mother-of-the-groom, a polar opposite from her chilly introduction last night. "Shep…CeCe." First, she leans in and kisses both of Shep's cheeks… and he lets her. Then, it's my turn, and even though I go through the motions, I feel like I'm floating outside my body, hovering about as this alternate reality plays out.

We move between clusters of strangers, all of them smiling and congratulating after Shep introduces me as his new wife. The protective stance he took last night with his father is in full effect, with his hand on the small of my back and my body tucked in close to his. Every once in a while, he places a tender kiss on my forehead or cheek, occasionally letting his lips linger, painting the perfect picture.

At first, I feel stiff, and it's all I can do to remember to smile and use my manners. But after about a dozen introductions, I start to loosen up and relax into my role.

When I glance up and notice a smudge of lipstick from some old lady who tried to molest him, I gently reach up and swipe it away with the pad of my thumb. The tender smile he gives me in return doesn't feel fake…not in the slightest.

"Hey," a familiar voice says, drawing me away from Shep's gaze and back to reality.

Finley and Maggie walk up to us, like beacons of light in a dark angry sea.

My first genuine smile since we walked down the steps splits my face. "Hey, so glad y'all could make it." Maggie approaches with open arms and I step right into them, needing a soft place to land, if only for a moment. For some reason, since the first second we were introduced earlier today, I felt like she was good people.

After I met Finley, and saw how he and Shep interacted—the carefree, yet tight bond they have with each other—I knew my instincts were right.

"You look beautiful," Finley says as I'm passed from Maggie's arms to his. He's tall, like Shep, so I have to stand on my tiptoes to give him a proper hug.

"Thank you," I tell him.

Shep leans in to give Maggie a kiss on her cheek and then grips Finley's shoulder. "So glad you came."

"We wouldn't have missed it," Maggie says, her eyes dancing around the crowd. "Not sure what your father will say about it though."

"But do we really care what he says?" Shep asks, mischief in his eyes.

That same gleam is reflected back in Maggie's as she scrunches her nose and gives her head a shake. "Nah."

"Didn't think so." Shep steps back and glances around. "Would the two of you mind to keep CeCe company for a second? There's someone I need to talk to."

The three of us follow Shep's departure and I can't help but watch as he confidently steps into a group of older, very business-like men. They look like they could be his father's age, but the way Shep inserts himself into their conversation is impressive. Within seconds, he's dominating their attention and it's seriously sexy.

Clearing my throat, I turn back to Maggie and Finley. "So—"

"You're good for him," Maggie interrupts, her eyes moving past me to where Shep is commanding the stage. "He's different around you—more relaxed and himself."

It's on the tip of my tongue to ask her if she knows this is all a ruse. If Shep were to be completely honest with anyone, I imagine it would be Maggie. But I don't want to say anything out of line or anything that could be used against Shep. So, I simply smile.

"We watched Finley play today," I say, my eyes going to him in an effort to redirect the conversation. "He was fantastic."

Maggie's face lights up with pride. "He's wonderful," she says, patting his arm. "Did Shepard tell you he bought Finley his first saxophone?"

"He did," I say with a nod, feeling a little pride myself. Where did that come from? I don't know, but it's definitely there. Knowing Shep took interest in someone like Finley changes so much of how I see him. He goes from the heir to a multi-million-dollar trust fund, who was born with a silver spoon in his mouth, to someone who is considerate and caring. There's no reason why Shepard Rhys-Jones should be anything other than what he was groomed to be—an entitled, rich asshole. Just like his father. But he's not. He's different. He's good.

And it makes me want him even more.

"You should come to New Orleans," I tell Finley. "Talk about jazz clubs…they're a dime a dozen down on Frenchman. And there's this great new place in the French Quarter. Sometimes, I just sit outside at night behind the shop and listen to the music carrying over the breeze. Well, when there is a breeze." I laugh, brushing my hair behind my ear as I feel someone staring at me from across the yard.

Shep

"I SHOULD BE IN TOUCH," HE SAYS, SLIPPING A business card from the pocket behind his lapel and handing it to me. "But if you don't hear from me in a week or so, give me a call."

Mr. Archer and I shake hands on our verbal deal. He owns a piece of property Maverick and I have had our eyes on for quite a while, and it seems as if the timing is right for him to sell. I hadn't intended on doing business during my wedding reception, but when opportunity knocks, you answer.

"Will do, sir," I tell him, taking the card and slipping it into my pocket, anxious to get back to CeCe. When I turn around, she's not where I left her and Maggie and Finley are nowhere to be seen. I didn't expect them to stay long, but I thought they'd at least wait until I came back.

Excusing myself around and between groups of people, I make my way across the lawn. She's not by the tower of cake or the rows of champagne, although I wouldn't blame her if she was.

Cake and champagne would be a worthy distraction from this

madness.

When my mother walks up to me, I ask. "Have you seen CeCe?"

"No," she says bluntly, rolling her eyes as she brings her martini glass to her lips. Always a fucking martini. Gin and vermouth are my mother's signature scent. "But I did want to introduce you to Dominic and Frangelica's daughter. She recently graduated from Yale and has moved to Dallas to step into a vice-president position at their company. Your father—"

"Stop," I warn, adjusting the cuffs on my suit to keep from strangling her. "I'm. Married."

Her shrill laugh makes my stomach sour. "Oh, God, Shepard, like anyone believes this farce." She waves her free hand around at the people. "I can't believe you'd bring someone like her…here. You must really hate her."

"She's my wife," I clip.

"Yes, and you brought her here and threw her to the wolves." It's when she steps back that I see CeCe flocked by the Crawfords. "Bravo."

The smile my mother gives me makes my blood run cold. "What did you do?"

"The strongest steel is forged in the fire of a dumpster," she says with a shrug before taking a sip of her cocktail. "If she's *truly* going to be a Rhys-Jones, I want to see what she's made of."

I know, it's wrong for any child to hate their mother, but mine has zero redeeming qualities. I've always known that, but seeing her disregard for someone I hold in such high regard just put the nail in her coffin.

She's dead to me.

"Excuse me, Mother." Brushing past her, I quickly make my way toward CeCe, only to be stopped again by one of my mother's country club floozies.

Her long red fingernails scrape down my chest. "Oh, Shepard…I was so *sad* to hear you're officially off the market." Her words are drawn-out and overly dramatic. "Although," she says, dropping her voice to a whisper as she leans in close to my ear. "I always did enjoy a challenge."

Removing her hand from my arm, I don't even give her a reply as I brush her off and walk away.

Fucking cougars, man.

In a few long strides, I'm standing behind CeCe, glaring at her company. "Felicity…Foster," I greet, startling CeCe. When she whips around, there's relief in her eyes. For someone who always seems to have a handle on the situation, she seems rattled. "Hey, baby. You good?"

"Uh," CeCe starts, cocking her head, obviously taken aback by me calling her *baby*. With my eyes, I try to tell her to go with it and thankfully she does. "Yeah," she finally says, reaching up to adjust my tie. "Fine."

Pulling her into my chest, I rest my chin on her head and let out a sigh when I feel her relax against me. Call it instinct. Call it possessiveness. Call it whatever the fuck you want. All I know is I don't want Felicity or Foster to even breathe the same air as CeCe, nevermind carry on a conversation with her.

She's too good for them.

"Shepard," Felicity says with a nod and a raise of her eyebrows. "I thought we were going to have dinner together. And here you are… married."

"What can I say?" I ask, looking down at CeCe. "When you know, you know. I couldn't live one more day without her being my wife."

CeCe's eyes go wide at my proclamation and I hear a muffled *bullshit* covered by a cough come from Foster.

"Haven't seen you in a while, man," I tell him.

He smirks, his eyes darting down to CeCe and giving her a once-over, and I want to punch him in the face. Typically, I'm more of a lover than a fighter, but having him within a foot of her has my blood boiling. *Don't even look at her, motherfucker.*

"Felicity and I were just talking to your *wife* about where the two of you met," he says with a pointed nod. "New Orleans…Sin City of the South…*impressive*."

"Tell us, CeCe," Felicity begins. "Are you a stripper?"

"Enough," I growl, putting myself between CeCe and Felicity. But the next thing I know, CeCe has snaked her way back around and is confronting her.

"What if I am?" CeCe challenges. "How would it make you feel to know you were pushed aside and ignored all because of someone you've deemed beneath you? To know *you*, with your perfectly fake hair, tits, and ass, still aren't good enough to get a man like Shep? I don't know about you but, it makes me feel fucking fantastic."

Turning, she stomps off in the direction of the house and I don't waste any time following her.

"I'm sorry," I say, once the glass doors close behind me. "I should've prepared you better…warned you…shit, I don't know. Maybe I shouldn't have agreed to this."

CeCe's back is to me, but she slowly turns to face me and I'm afraid there are going to be tears, but thankfully, she just looks pissed. Pissed, I can handle. "It's probably better you didn't try to prepare me or warn me, I might've chickened out." She laughs lightly, rubbing her temples. "Those people are horrible."

"Try growing up with them."

She pauses, slowly bringing her head back up to look at me. "How did you turn out so…normal?"

"You think I'm normal?" I ask with a chuckle. "Not even close."

"Well, you're certainly not them," she says, her voice lowering as she looks out the window.

Walking closer, I reach out and take one of her hands. "You okay?"

She lets out a deep sigh. "I'm fine."

"I'm especially sorry you had to deal with those two…I fucking hate them."

CeCe shivers and scrunches her nose, looking entirely too adorable for her own good. "Foster gives me the creeps. He's like one of those slimeballs you see on those reality television shows. You know the ones where you're yelling at the girl. NOT HIM. RUN THE OTHER WAY."

"That's exactly who he is," I tell her, leaning forward and placing a kiss on her forehead and then resting mine against hers. "You want to call it a night or do you think you can manage a couple more hours?"

"Don't leave me," she demands, pulling on my lapels.

"Wouldn't dream of it," I insist.

We walk back out into the fray, hand-in-hand.

We smile.

We touch.

We kiss.

We sell this marriage so hard that even I forget it's not real.

"My cheeks hurt from smiling," CeCe whispers as she brings her champagne glass up for a drink.

Pressing my lips to her hair, I inhale, unable to stop myself. "Well, if it helps, you look beautiful doing it."

"Sweet talker," CeCe muses.

My father just gave a riveting speech intended to be in honor of mine and CeCe's nuptials, but instead, turned out sounding more like he was receiving an Oscar on behalf of the Rhys-Jones family.

We're so proud of where we are as a family.

After a tough year, and the loss of a patriarch, we're coming out on top.

The Rhys-Jones name and brand is just as valuable and steadfast as it's ever been.

When the music begins to play, people slowly make their way onto the makeshift dance floor in the middle of the lawn. Typically, there would be a first dance and all that mother-son, father-daughter bullshit but I didn't want any of that and I knew CeCe wouldn't either.

I slipped the DJ a substantial amount of cash to bypass my mother's instructions and just play some fucking music.

The soulful melody of Ella Fitzgerald and Louis Armstrong's *Cheek to Cheek* begins to play. "Dance with me," I tell CeCe, pulling her arm behind my back so her body is pressed against mine. The wide look I get makes me chuckle. "Don't look at me like that. You're my wife…we're supposed to be this close, remember?"

Her lips curve up in a smile. "Yes."

"Yes, you remember? Or yes, you'll dance with me?"

"Both."

As I spin her around the dance floor, the last bits of fake facade seem to crumble at our feet.

She's looking at me like I hung the moon.

And I'm holding her like I never want to let her go.

I forget I'm surrounded by assholes.

I forget I'm trying to escape my own identity.

Because I'm with her and that's all that seems to matter and there's no other place I'd rather be.

"Mind if I cut in?" My father's question disrupts the perfect sense of peace I've managed to maintain for the last three songs. I clench my teeth to keep from growling my displeasure for his interruption.

"Actually—" I begin, but he cuts me off.

"Come on, Shepard…surely you don't want to make a scene. Everyone expects me to have a dance with my new daughter-in-law." The way he's looking at CeCe followed by the smirk he gives me is enough to make me want to punch him. "Besides, you can't be that insecure. What do you think? I'm going to fuck her right here in front of God and everyone?"

My back goes stiff and I drop my hold on CeCe, ready to put my father in his place—forcefully. But she's there, putting herself between me and the man who *should* want the best for me. That's not him, though. We're not the happy, perfect family he and my mother would like everyone to believe. He'd love nothing more than to sabotage what's supposed to be one of the happiest moments of my life, regardless of its validity.

"CeCe, step back," I warn, not wanting her to get in the middle of my life-long beef with my father. I shouldn't have brought her here. It was a bad idea.

And I don't give a fuck that this is a temporary marriage. As far as my father and everyone else is concerned, CeCe is my wife and she deserves respect.

She pushes on my chest, standing on her tiptoes to get my attention. "Hey, look at me."

I do, because she asked me and I'd do anything for her.

"It's a dance. One dance," she says with a shrug.

Brushing a strand of her hair back, I tuck it behind her ear, letting my thumb linger on her jaw. She's amazing. I want to tell her that right here in front of everyone, but she'd hate me for it, so I won't. I also want to grab her and run away with her, keeping her for myself and protecting her from the nastiness of this world. But I can't do that either.

"I'm fine," she whispers with a strength in her eyes that I love. This time, she's the one who leans in and kisses me, gripping my hand in assurance before she steps away and faces my father.

CeCe

I TRY NOT TO LOOK AT PHILLIP OR REGISTER THE WAY his hands feel like they're burning through my skin—and not in a good way—but I also can't look at Shep. If I did, I know I'd see fury and possessiveness all over his face. But Phillip is looking for a reaction from his son and I refuse to be the catalyst for that.

We've made it this far and the night is almost over. I can make it through five minutes on a crowded dance floor with Phillip Rhys-Jones.

"You know this isn't going to last."

It's not a question, it's a statement. And one that I refuse to acknowledge. It feels like a trap. If I start defending Shep, it'll sound like I'm trying to convince him this is real. Which it's not, but if it was, I still wouldn't acknowledge a comment like that. It doesn't deserve my time and energy, so I don't give in to him.

"So, how much is he paying you?"

Okay, that's a question and I honestly didn't see it coming.

Stupid me.

He must feel the way I tense beneath his touch. I tried to quell it but couldn't.

"Ahh, that's it, huh," he continues. I don't even have to look up to know there's a smug grin on his face. My heart starts to beat a little faster. What does it matter if he knows about our agreement? Shep seems to think it's common, unspoken knowledge, so maybe I should be brutally honest and rub it in his face.

Yeah, I agreed to marry your son for a year so he can claim his inheritance and save himself from the depths of hell.

That's what this place is, and Phillip Rhys-Jones is the devil himself.

"That money is supposed to be mine." This time, when he speaks, his tone holds brittle anger I haven't heard from him before and his hold on me tightens. "You're fucking up my plan and I don't appreciate it."

His plan?

What plan?

The money is Shep's, providing he stays married for a year. End of story.

"Shepard is stupid and reckless," he mutters, almost to himself. "He's too much like his grandfather and he doesn't even know it."

There's a long pause and for a split second I think the song will finally end and save me from my misery, so I take the opportunity to say my piece. "This is Shep's life, not yours. He gets to choose who he marries, and now, he'll also have the freedom to choose what he does with the rest of it."

Phillip's evil laugh makes me regret even responding. I should've kept my mouth shut, but like Shep, I'm beginning to feel protective. I can't stand here and let Phillip spew his nasty words. Along with everyone else at this shindig, he needs a good dose of reality.

"Oh, Cecelia." The use of my real name makes my back stiffen and Phillip pulls back to look me in the eye. "Don't seem so shocked. I know everything there is to know about you. I know about your poor upbringing and your uncle's shop, deadbeat father, and younger sister you're putting through college. I imagine I know more than Shepard does."

My stomach drops.

"You're a noble, young woman, but I have news for you...Shepard's life isn't his own. He thinks it is, but he's wrong. This is a family effort. We don't stay on top by marrying down. Everyone is responsible for doing their part. Shepard marrying you contributes nothing."

When the music stops, I drop my arms from Phillip's hold and turn toward the edge of the dance floor where Shep is standing. His hands are in his pockets, but if I had to guess, they're balled into fists, and his face is nothing but hard lines.

I think about reaching for him, but decide against it, just wanting to get out of here—away from all these people. And far, far away from Phillip Rhys-Jones.

"CeCe," Shep calls out, but I keep walking. I know he'll follow me and what I have to say isn't meant for anyone here but him. My mind starts going into overdrive on my walk to the house and I make a spontaneous decision to not say anything until we're away from here. I wouldn't put it past Phillip to have our room bugged, like some Bourne Identity shit.

"Wait." Shep's hand gently comes up and grabs mine, making me halt before I can open the glass doors and escape the madness. "Are you okay? What did he say?"

Blowing out a deep breath, I look past Shep to the party going on behind him. Everyone is talking and dancing. A few are still partaking in champagne and mixed drinks. All of them are completely oblivious to the two people this party is supposed to be in honor of.

Except Phillip.

He's now standing where Shep was a few moments ago, and he's assumed the same stance—hands in pockets, hard stare. It's scary how similar the two are, but in appearance only. Thankfully, Shep is nothing like his father. And somehow, I'm going to help him accomplish what he's set out to do.

Not because he's paying me.

But because I care about him, like really and truly care about him.

Glancing up, I give him the best smile I can muster and squeeze his hand. "I'm fine. Just tired. Can we go upstairs?"

He examines me, eyes starting on my face and trailing down my body, like he's looking for physical damage. Of course, he won't find any, but I can't hide the way my hands are shaking from the adrenaline coursing through my body. I can still feel Phillip watching us and I won't be able to relax until he's not.

"Let's go," Shep says, pulling me into the house and up the stairs. At first, when he flings the bedroom door open, I think he's going to explode and start ranting about his father, but instead, the calm and collected Shep is back in full force. "Pack your bag."

"Where are we going?" I ask, standing in the middle of the room and trying to keep my head from spinning. What a fucking day, man. I feel like I've been on a giant roller coaster. My time with Shep earlier when we were driving around was great. I felt like he let me see a part of him that not many people know. Since then, I've been turned on, pissed off, and thrown to the vultures. And after I felt like I'd been picked to pieces, Phillip swooped in to finish me off.

He doesn't look at me as he walks around, collecting his things. "Anywhere but here."

"I just want to go home." It hits me so hard. All I can think of is getting back to New Orleans. I need to be in my own element so I can process the past day and a half. It's hard to get your head on straight in the middle of a whirlwind.

Everything will go back to normal once we're back in New Orleans.

"Whatever you want." Shep's words are simple, but they hold weight, like there's a deeper meaning, something below the surface. When I meet his eyes, the blue is so dark I almost can't see it.

I swallow down the surge of feelings.

Somehow in the breadth of a second, there's a silent conversation, an understanding.

Whatever I want.

I want Shep.

That's the root of every emotion vying for control inside my body. I want Shep on the most basic level. I want him in my life. I want to be a part of his. I want what's best for him. I want him to be happy.

Without another word, he pulls his phone out of his pocket and begins talking, his tone demanding. Fifteen minutes later, we're changed out of our party attire, packed and hopping in a car outside of his parents' mansion, heading to the airport for the last flight to New Orleans.

I have a feeling we won't be on a private jet, but I don't care.

Whatever gets me home is all I care about.

"I'm sorry," Shep whispers, his gaze focused on the side window as the driver makes his way out of the fancy neighborhood and onto the highway. "I should've known this would be a mistake."

For a moment, I hold my breath, thinking he's regretting not just bringing me to Dallas, but all of this…marrying me. I want to say something, but I'm scared. If I open my mouth, I might admit something I can't take back, or wouldn't want to. Even though I trust Shep, I don't know how deep that trust goes. Sure, he's nice to me and chivalrous and sweet. He seems to have my best interests at heart, but to what extent? It's obvious to me now, he comes from wicked, money-hungry people and my mama always says the apple doesn't fall far from the tree.

As much as I've tried to be my own person and forge my own path, I know I'm like my mother. I come off as someone who isn't interested in the frivolity of love. I can't afford it. But it doesn't mean I don't love the idea of it. I love seeing my friends in love. I love watching couples come in and out of my shop and seeing their love in living color. It's beautiful.

But for myself, I know I'm too much like my mama. I didn't fall far from the tree. If I let myself love someone, it would be deep and life-altering.

And as much as Shep might try to break away from his family, he's still a Rhys-Jones. Deep down, I'm sure there's a part of him that's fighting to be like Phillip. When and if that part of him rears its ugly head, where would that leave me?

Where is the safety net in that?

"You're too quiet," Shep says, turning toward me and reaching for my hand. "Get out of that pretty little head of yours and come over here." He shoots for our typical, friendly banter, but there's an intensity I can't ignore. It's kind of desperate, which is something I've never seen from Shep and it makes my body respond. Heat begins to simmer in my belly and I give in to his gentle pull, sliding across the seat until my body is next to his.

At first, he just slips an arm around my shoulder and leans in to kiss the top of my head. It's innocent, a gesture that could be shared between good friends, but we're not good friends. Are we? No, we're Shep and CeCe and our relationship has been complicated from the get-go. We've never been anything as simple and straightforward as *good friends.* So, when his hand begins to stroke my arm in a sensual, much more than a good-friends way, I'm not surprised when my eyes roll into the back of my head.

Thank goodness it's dark and he can't see what a touch from him does to me.

"There you go…just relax," he soothes and my entire body responds. That tone, the way he says those words, takes me back to our weekend together so long ago. I remember what it was like to have his seductive words whispered in my ear. The way he coaxed me into submission is something I knew I'd never experience with anyone else ever again, which might explain why I never tried.

Well, that and the fact that no other man ever understands my level of commitment to my business. But Shep does. He's never questioned it.

Needing to touch him too, I slide my palm across his stomach, appreciating the contrast between the softness of his shirt and the hardness beneath. When my pinkly dips lower to the waistband of his jeans, he groans and I smile, leaning my cheek against his chest.

"Don't start something you don't plan on finishing," Shep warns.

Maybe I do…plan on finishing, that is.

I've thought about his proposition during our negotiations about monogamy and I've decided he's right. We're married and have vowed not to be with anyone else for the next year. Plus, we've already had sex, so we know we're good together. At least, he's never told me any different. And I know he's the best I've ever had.

Two consenting adults who are obviously attracted to each other should enjoy the act of sex.

That's all it would be—a carnal display of our inner desires. It's simple…science, really.

I mean, have you seen Discovery? Every time I flip the channel there are two animals going at it. Why should we fight that?

"CeCe." Shep's words are strained and I realize, during my inner debate, I let my fingers slip below, stroking the light trail of hair that leads to glory.

Shep

Holy fucking shit.

I can't believe I survived the last thirty-something hours. Come to think of it, I also can't believe it's only been that long since CeCe and I left for our trip. At times it felt like we were in Dallas for days and other times it felt as though time was moving too fast. Those were the fun moments, of course, when it was only me and CeCe, living in our bubble, getting to know each other better and, I think, coming out better for it.

Showing CeCe around Dallas— introducing her to the people and places that mean something to me—went better than I ever could've imagined. I thought I was being optimistic hoping for us to be civil to each other for the duration of the weekend. Instead, I think we came to an unexpected, unspoken agreement that we'd both let our guard down and enjoy our time together as much as we could. And, we really did enjoy ourselves.

Well, I certainly did, especially on the drive to the airport a few hours ago.

The way CeCe's fingers traveled over my skin, slipping in and out of the hair that trails down my stomach…it wasn't just sexy, it was familiar. It was as comforting as it was exciting and although I would've loved for her to work her way down further, I was thrilled simply by the fact she was touching me.

Too soon, though, and we were at the airport, rushing to make our flight and with it being a commercial one, there was no way to continue what she'd started. Mark my words, one of these days I will have my way with CeCe while in the air. But the Mile High Club is much more fun when you're traveling in a private jet.

Which reminds me, I should start planning our honeymoon.

CeCe slept for most of the hour and a half flight back to New Orleans and she's asleep again in the car that's driving us to my townhouse. She's obviously worn out but not in the way I'd prefer.

For now, I just want her in my bed any way I can have her.

The car pulls up to the front of my place and I get out, trying my best not to disturb CeCe. Thankfully, she stays asleep against the window as the driver and I place our bags inside my front door. I don't want anything getting in the way of me carrying CeCe—my wife—to my room. I guess this would be like me carrying her over the threshold in the traditional sense but maybe, she needs to be awake for that?

Hell, if I know.

CeCe stirs as I lift her out of the car and take her inside.

"Where are we?" she whispers, making me smile with her sleepy voice.

"We're home." At that, her brows furrow, so I amend. "Well, it's my place but I've already told you what's mine is yours, so feel free to move in whenever you'd like."

She sighs, laying her head against my shoulder. "It makes more sense to stay at my place because of my work hours, you know that."

"Is that your invitation for me to move in with you?"

"My apartment is tiny, there's no way you and your big head would fit."

"Big head?" It's obvious she's fully awake now so I don't hold back my laughter. "I'll show you my big head." I toss CeCe onto my bed and immediately cover her body with mine. She gasps and I feel it everywhere. I honestly meant for my actions to be playful but now the air between us is so charged and alive, I don't think I can move.

CeCe's deep brown eyes are open and clear, holding me captive to her gaze. She must see the question on my face because she quickly glances at my mouth and nods her head. I don't wait for her to change her mind or chicken out; I take full advantage of this moment and kiss her. She greedily accepts my tongue into her mouth and I know there's no coming back from this—from her.

I'm done.

We devour each other for what feels like ages, my jaw aching in the best of ways, when we finally break free to catch our breaths.

"Wow," CeCe says, sighing. "And I thought our wedding kiss was good."

I don't try to hide my smirk. "I've wanted to kiss you like that all weekend, among other things."

"Other things, hmm? I wouldn't mind doing *other things*." She bites down on her bottom lip, eyeing me carefully.

I don't know why her words surprise me, but they do. I was afraid she'd want nothing to do with me after the disaster we just left in Dallas. I feel like the luckiest man alive simply by her allowing me to kiss her but to hear she wants to take things further and she wants it now, I'm speechless.

Well, almost. "O-okay," I manage to sputter out.

She laughs and soon I follow, and it's exactly what we need to relax and collect ourselves. I lean forward and kiss her gently this time. There's no pressure, no anxiety, no worries. There's only the two of us wanting to connect in the most basic, yet intimate way possible, sharing a part of ourselves that's secret and special to only each other.

And, god, do I want her.

CeCe runs her fingers through my hair before cradling my jaw in her hand. It's moments like this that separate her from other women I've been with. That was just sex, a release, a fleeting moment. But my time spent with her is different. This is more.

I knew it when we were together two years ago, and I know it now.

We kiss again and it's just as passionate as before but it's also intense and controlled, setting the stage for what's to come. Reluctant to leave her mouth but desperate to taste more of her, I kiss, bite, and lick my way along her jaw, down the column of her neck to her collarbone. I remain there for a bit, the taste of her skin igniting something feral inside me.

The breath she releases is shaky but her voice is strong when she commands me to remove her shirt and bra. I waste no time undressing her completely but I do take a few seconds to simply look at her. She's the most beautiful woman I've ever seen and where some women may feel shy or insecure lying naked under a man's watchful eyes like CeCe is right now, that's not her. She's thriving under my gaze, coming alive.

And, now I get to make her come undone.

I quickly remove my clothes and settle back down between her legs, my mouth immediately finding her nipple. CeCe's reaction to my mouth on her sensitive skin is fascinating and I love watching her face morph as I bite and suck her. Although I'd love to stay here forever, I find I'm no longer able to resist the temptation waiting lower.

CeCe spreads her legs as I travel down her body, opening herself up for me, and fuck, I want to devour her. I *will* devour her. All it takes is one lick, one taste, and I'm barely able to control myself.

She's just as sweet as I remembered.

It doesn't take long before CeCe grips my hair, grinding her pussy against my mouth while begging for more. She always comes fast when I eat her out, but I don't mind because it means I'm closer to being inside her. Maybe one day I'll be strong enough to prolong her pleasure but today is not that day.

Slipping two fingers inside her, I pump them as I suck on her clit. "Fuck, yeah, Shep. Just like that. Don't stop!"

When she begins to climax, I can feel her clench around my fingers, so I suck harder, causing her orgasm to rip through her as she screams my name.

I do love the sound of that.

Once she's calmed down a bit, I sit back on my knees and CeCe follows me, grabbing my face, and kissing me hard. I love that she doesn't care about tasting herself on my lips. It shows me she's desperate to have her mouth on mine and that's fucking hot.

"You. Inside me. Now," she demands in between kisses, pulling me on top of her as she lays back on the bed.

"Let's consummate this bitch," I say, reaching over to grab a condom out of my bedside table drawer. Realization dawns and I look back at CeCe. "I don't mean you're the bitch I'm consummating…but I guess, you kinda are but I didn't mean it disrespectfully. Shit, I don't know why I said it at all."

"Shep," she says loudly, getting my attention and putting an end to my rambling. "Shut up and consummate this bitch." She's laughing which means I haven't offended her and I'm so relieved this is really happening and she didn't kick me out of bed. Except, I forgot I haven't bought any condoms since I moved in.

"I, uh…"

"I'm on birth control and it's been a while, if you remember."

"I swear, I'm clean. I would never put you at any kind of risk." I mean those words for all aspects of our lives, not just here in my bed. Hoping with every cell in my body she believes me, I kiss her softly. "I trust you," is her reply and the weight of those words coming from her nearly leaves me breathless.

We kiss again and I enter her slowly, feeling every inch of our connection as her body stretches to fit me, molding around me. It's not just a physical bond, it's emotional and the way it feels as I push in as far as I can go, is… otherworldly.

"Fuck," I gasp out, trying to keep a hold on what little control I have left. "Never, it's never been this good." She tightens around me and I'm torn between making this slow and sensual and just fucking her brains out.

CeCe runs her hands down my back, stops at my ass, and grabs it, pushing me further into her. Yeah, we can take it slower next time.

Pushing her knees up toward her chest, I'm able to drive into her even deeper. CeCe grabs onto the headboard behind her, her pelvis meeting mine thrust for thrust and it's not long before I feel the familiar tingle move down my spine, causing my balls to tighten. Thank fuck, CeCe starts making her delicious sounds again, signaling she's close, so I push harder and faster until we're both screaming our release.

Eventually, I pull out and roll onto my back, taking CeCe with me, so she can lay against my chest. We're both sweaty and need a shower but I'm too exhausted to move.

It's the best feeling in the world.

Too soon, though, sunlight peaks through my blinds and I feel CeCe escape my hold on her.

"No, come back. It's too early," I groan and reach for her, my eyes barely able to stay open.

Laughing, she says, "You said that three hours ago. It's now almost eight in the morning and I need to get to work."

"But I want you, CeCe. Can't we do it just one more time before you leave?" I'm obviously not above begging. *What has this woman done to me?*

"You also said that three hours ago."

"And it worked, so get back in this bed."

She puts her hands on her hips but I don't miss the smile trying to show itself. "Shep, we fucked three times already. How are you still this insatiable?"

I throw the blanket and sheet off my body, showing her my hard-on. "It's you. You do this to me. Now, get over here, you sexy wench."

CeCe bites down on her lip, which means she's seriously thinking about my offer, so I go in for the kill. I grab my shaft and pump it a couple of times, my eyes never leaving hers. Her cheeks flush and her eyes darken. When she licks her lips, I know I've won.

She huffs out a breath before pulling her top over her head. "One more time and then I have to leave. And don't forget your meeting with Maverick later."

"Please don't mention Maverick when I'm about to make love to my wife," I murmur as I pull her body under mine. She tenses briefly but relaxes as I kiss her, sliding into her warmth once again.

After walking CeCe to the corner closest to Neutral Grounds and watching her until she disappeared inside—which, by the way, felt like the most natural thing in the world, like I was meant to wake up next to her, make love to her, and walk her to work—I made the short trek to Blue Bayou.

Walking up to the main doors, I smile when I see one is already propped open. Carys loves to welcome in the New Orleans breeze, as she puts it. There's no fucking breeze, but I think I get what she means. After being here for a while now, there's just something about the morning air. Sure, it's a bit heavy in these summer months, but it also smells sweet and there's a newness I can't get enough of.

"Welcome—" Carys starts, then stops when she looks up and sees it's me. "Oh, hey, Shep. Welcome back. Mav's in the office." Pointing over her shoulder, she goes back to whatever work is in front of her.

They really do make a great team.

"Thanks," I tell her, stopping for a cold glass of water and a macaron. Taking one bite, I moan my appreciation. "Oh, man," I mumble around the flaky cookie. "So good."

She laughs, shaking her head. "You should really eat something more nutritious for breakfast."

I want to be crude and tell her I had CeCe for breakfast, but I opt for a safer route.

"Wait, macaron isn't a food group?" I ask, teasing as I walk behind her and pull her blonde braid.

Her foot makes contact with my shin and I wince. Should have seen that coming. "Shit, Carys," I groan, leaning over to rub at the sore spot as I open the door to the office. "You know I'm old now. You have to take it easy on me."

"Are you bothering my woman?" Maverick mutters from behind the desk.

"She kicked me."

"You deserved it."

As I make myself at home in the leather chair across from him, I toss my arm across the back. "Fuck, it's good to be home."

"Home, huh?" Maverick asks, looking up from the computer with a sly smirk.

I remember when I came here for the first time. If I'm being honest, I was a little worried. Things at Kensington Properties were a bit volatile and I knew Mav was on the verge of losing his shit. So, imagine my concern when I called him up for lunch one day, only to be told he was gone and his receptionist wasn't sure when he was coming back.

But this place was the best thing that ever happened to him.

Shit, it was the best thing that ever happened to us. If it hadn't been for him finding the Blue Bayou and Carys Matthews, he would've never taken the leap to leave Kensington and we both would still be stuck back in Dallas working for our fathers and hating our lives.

As much as I enjoy the finer things in life and I do miss some of the amenities of my house in Dallas, New Orleans is growing on me…immensely. The more time I spend here, the more I feel relaxed. Things are different down here.

And I spoke the truth. It feels more like home here than anywhere else. Deep down, I know that has a lot to do with CeCe, but I'm not ready to go there just yet.

"Yeah, home," I tell him with all seriousness. "Stop looking at me like that."

He chuckles, holding his hands up in surrender. "Hey, no one is happier to hear you say that than me…just a little surprised is all. I thought it'd take you a little longer to adapt."

"Well, being back in Dallas this past weekend helped speed up the process."

"How was it?"

I raise an eyebrow in question, like he even has to ask. "It was Phillip and Jane. How do you think it was?"

"That bad, huh?"

Groaning, I lean my head back and stare at the ceiling. "Worse, man. I knew it would be…tense," I tell him, raising my head back up to look at him. "But I never dreamed they could be so…"

"Cruel?"

I let out a sigh and rest my elbows on my knees. "Cruel, pretentious assholes. I swear my mother still thinks I'm going to marry Felicity Crawford." Just the mention of her name sends chills down my spine. "I thought I knew how bad they were, but it was different this time…I don't know, taking CeCe there." I pause, searching for the right way to explain it, but I come up short. "It was bad. We left early and flew back late last night."

"Fuck," Maverick says, running a hand down his face. "How's CeCe?"

The smirk on my face is unavoidable and Maverick cocks his head.

"She's good."

"Really?" he asks, skeptical yet interested.

He has no idea just how good she is. But that's my golden nugget of truth. Only mine.

"Yeah, she handled those assholes like a champ," I tell him, shaking my head at the memory of her putting Felicity and Foster in their place, cutting them down a notch. And taking on my father, which I still want to know what he said to her. At every turn, she showed me what she's made of—grit and determination and so much tenacity. An average person would've crumbled, but she didn't, because she's extraordinary.

When I look back up, Maverick is watching me with a knowing glint in his eyes, but he remains silent, fingers steepled at his chin.

"Okay, fucking Godfather, speak," I demand when he starts creeping me out.

Standing from his chair, he walks over to the door and peeks out of it briefly before silently closing it and turning to me. For a second, I think I'm getting ready to get the third degree about something… maybe CeCe talked to Carys already about Dallas…or maybe even about us.

"I'm proposing to Carys," he says in a conspiratorial whisper and when I go to congratulate him, he shushes me. "I want it to be a surprise and I thought it'd be fun to turn it into a celebration. She'll want CeCe and Avery there, and you and Shaw, of course. I've already told Mary and George…they've known for a few days actually…and I'll tell Jules. Well, right before it's happening because that fucker can't keep a secret to save his damn life."

"About fucking time," I tell him with a smile, standing to slap him on the shoulder and pull him in for a hug. Fuck that side hug shit, Mav and I go all in. "Happy for you, man."

He pulls away and runs a hand through his hair. "I kinda owe it to you," he says and I frown.

"Me?"

"Yeah, all this going to the courthouse and making shit happen. It got me thinking. I love this woman, more than life itself, so what the fuck am I waiting on?"

I nod, feeling him for the first time on this subject. In the past, he's talked about Carys and how much he loves her and I've always thought good for him…at least one of us needs to find true love. But I never thought it would be me. I don't do love. I don't do fucking relationships. Well, I do the fucking part, just not the relationships.

Until now.

"I'm doing it tonight. Think you can get CeCe here?"

I simply nod again, afraid to open my mouth and have all my inner thoughts flying out before I can stop them. I think for the first time in my life, I actually know what love feels like.

CeCe

"I THOUGHT YOU'D BE A LOT LESS...I DON'T KNOW, chipper?" Paige has been digging for information about the weekend ever since I walked into the shop three hours ahead of schedule. Mine and Shep's original flight wasn't supposed to arrive until noon, which would've put me back here no earlier than twelve-thirty, so I'd told Paige not to expect me before one.

"Why's that?" I ask, restocking the pastries after a particularly busy morning rush. Amazingly enough, the place didn't burn down while I was away...actually, everything looked exactly as if I was still here. Paige did well. "Isn't everyone chipper after a couple of days away from work?"

"Everyone but you," Paige says with a snorted laugh. "I figured you'd come in hot this morning, guns blazing. I mean, you were away for two days, which is the longest you've been away from this place in five years. I know we talked, but you sounded stressed when you called to check in, which I'm sure had something to do with being away, but it had to have been stressful meeting Shep's parents for the first time. Are they rich? Like, really rich? I know how it was stressful when I finally met my boyfriend's parents for the first time and they're middle class all the way."

When Paige gets on a roll like this, I just let her talk. Sometimes, by the time she gets to the end of her monologue, she doesn't remember her original question and I get to avoid talking about things I'd rather not.

Besides, the stressfulness of the weekend seems light-years away this morning.

"Super rich," I deadpan, not wanting to get into any of that. Although, her bringing up Shep's parents does make me remember my conversation with Phillip during our dance last night. Was that really just last night? Wow. I think Shep's dick made me lose track of time.

If Shep and his dick hadn't kept me in bed so long this morning, I would've been here even earlier. But since I couldn't resist him, I strolled in about ten, like I own the place. Oh, wait, I do. Seems I'm not only chipper, I'm also full of jokes.

It's amazing what quenching a two-year dry spell will do for your psyche.

"So, it was good?" Paige asks, leaning her hip against the counter and pinning me with her stare. She's obviously not going to give this up until I give her something.

Sighing, I stand and wipe my hands on my apron. "Yeah, I mean, as good as can be expected. Shep didn't really give them time to adjust to the idea of him being married…so it was a little…tense. But nothing I couldn't handle." And that's putting it mildly, but for some reason, I don't want everyone to know Shep's business.

And I'm definitely not telling her how amazing the sex was last night…and this morning. I've barely allowed myself time to process that tidbit of information. There were moments I felt like I was hallucinating or having an out-of-body experience—no way can that much pleasure be real. Then, there were other moments of complete clarity. It's like the whole world was in high-def and I could see every detail and hear every sound and feel every sensation—Shep's eyes, the planes of his body, his moans and whispers, and the way he felt…the way *we* felt. It was real and raw and somehow better than I remembered it.

Maybe it's because he kept calling me his wife and the permanence that word brings. There's this promise in his touches, like he's silently telling me we have time. But how much? What happens at the end of our year?

There's been a small voice telling me to look for the nearest exit. This is starting to feel too normal, too real. It got louder when we were leaving Dallas but spending the night in Shep's bed drowned it out to a faint whisper.

Now, in the light of day, it's back.

If it feels too good to be true, it usually is.

"CeCe!" Paige's voice cuts through my thoughts and my head pops up as my eyes find hers.

"What?"

She smiles and shakes her head in bewilderment. "Where'd you go?"

"When?" I ask, blinking as I glance around to make sure there aren't any customers waiting.

"Did something happen in Dallas that you'd like to share?"

Paige knows about my agreement with Shep, but not many of the details. I've put her in the same category as my mom and Rory—they're all on a need to know basis. She doesn't need to know that the Hurricane Shep wreaking havoc in my brain right now—is a category 5.

I shrug my shoulders. "I'm just in this weird limbo between being tired and wired…you know, early morning flights and too much coffee."

"Okay," she drawls. "Whatever you say, boss."

As a few more customers filter in through the doors, we both go back to work and she drops the twenty questions. Maybe I need to think about working another employee into the budget. I think Paige suffers from lack of companionship when I'm not here.

Not that I plan on being gone anymore.

And then there's that lingering problem with Theo…

About that time, the bell above the door chimes and in walks Jules. "Hey, hunties!"

Everyone in the shop turns to watch him sashay in, or according to Jules, he shantays. Of course, he looks as polished as always, sporting a suit that fits him like a glove and a loud ass tie. His complexion and brows are much more on point than mine. Come to think of it, I could use a Jules night in. We haven't had one in a while and he makes the best homemade face masks.

"Hey, Jules," Paige calls out with a wave as she delivers a drink to a customer.

He throws her a wink and a wave.

When he makes his way to the side of the bar, I meet him there and give him two air kisses, drinking in his decadent smell. I swear, he's just good for my soul. As he pulls back, he grips my biceps, giving me a good, long look. "My, my. The Big D was good to my girl."

I try to keep the blush at bay, but am betrayed.

"Spill. The. Tea." Guiding me toward the stairs that lead up to my apartment, he calls out over his shoulder. "Paige, honey, cover the front." When we're out of earshot, he mutters, "We've got the back."

Laughing, I turn to him and roll my eyes. "There's no tea to spill."

"And you're a goddamn liar."

Groaning, I pinch my eyes and turn away from him. "I hate you."

"You love me, now spill."

"Fine," I say with a huff and then mumble, "the Big D was good to your girl."

The slow, wide smile that takes over his face is bright enough to light up the dimly lit staircase. "I knew it…a couple of days away, locked up with a piece of meat like Shepard Rhys-Jones. Mmm." When he bites his knuckle, I laugh again. "Tell me this double-dip was as good as the first time around."

"Better," I admit.

When he places his hand on his forehead and begins to plead, "Good Lord, give me strength," I lose it.

"Is it weird I missed you?" I ask, adjusting his tie and then remembering the real reason he's probably here. "Do you have any good news for me?"

His face drops and so does my stomach. "I wish I did," he says with a sigh, stepping back to reach into his messenger bag for a sheet of paper. "One of my professors, who's a lawyer, was able to dig a little deeper than I could on my own. He found that Theo has filed a will contest, stating he's the heir-at-law. You'll be receiving a notice from the court in the next few days and, CeCe," he says, growing even more serious, especially for Jules, "you're going to need to have as much documentation as possible. According to one of the lawyers at the office where he's seeking legal counsel, he's claiming he wasn't properly notified after his father's death and that according to the hand-written will on file with the state, he's the next-of-kin."

My heart stops.

"But…but he was," I stammer. "My mama said some sort of letter was sent out and he didn't respond. It's why the judge gave everything to her."

Jules takes a deep breath and hands me the paper. "Gather any of this documentation you can find. My professor said he'll help you as much as he can, and so will I, but you'll need to have representation if this goes to court."

Rubbing my temple with one hand, I begin to pace the small space as I hold the paper with the other, reading over the list. "Okay," I mutter. "It's okay…I'll find this stuff…I think."

"You've got a good filing system, right?"

Looking back up at him, I'm almost offended. "Of course, I do."

He raises his hands in surrender. "Don't shoot the messenger." We stand there for a moment, staring at each other, both in our own heads as we think through this. "I just don't want to see anyone take this place from you. You work your ass off. This is your shop. Fucking Theo Duval doesn't win. You do."

His little pep talk lights a fire under my ass.

He's right. This is my shop. And my filing system is meticulous. I can provide any and all evidence they need that my Uncle Teddy intended on leaving this place to my mother, knowing she'd pass it on to me. If he had wanted his son—who I'd never even heard of before now, to have this shop—he would've told me. We spent five years together, working day in and day out. He told me everything…about everything…or at least I thought he did, but apparently, there are a few things he didn't share.

One thing I know for sure, before I go in front of a judge and plead my case, I'll know it all.

"If it's not here," I tell Jules, thinking out loud, "my mama will have it. She never throws shit away."

When my pocket vibrates, I retrieve my phone and see a text from Shep.

Shep: We're going to the Blue Bayou tonight.

Shep: Mav's proposing.

Shep: Don't tell Jules.

Shep: Pick you up at 8.

I clear my throat to hide my shock and awe.

Maverick is finally going to ask Carys to marry him.

When Jules tries to take a peek, I quickly tuck the phone back into the pocket of my jeans and cross my arms. "Shep," I offer up, hoping me telling a smidge of truth will help cover the fact I can't tell it all. But I know why Shep said not to tell Jules.

He'd take it straight back to Carys, even if he didn't mean to.

I'm not sure how that's going to work out for him once he becomes a lawyer. Who the heck ever heard of a lawyer who can't keep a secret?

"Sexting already?" Jules asks with a waggle of his brows. "Did he send a dick pic?"

"God, you're deplorable."

At promptly eight o'clock on the dot, I'm locking the front door of the shop. When I turn around, ready to text Shep, he's there, waiting on the bench out front, looking every bit the part of a GQ model—one arm thrown over the back of the bench, an ankle crossed over a knee, the sexiest grin I've ever seen, and a suit that makes him look like a million bucks. But I know he doesn't need the suit. It's just an added bonus.

The strain from my day, all of the digging I did in the hours after Jules left and before Paige left for the day, turned up pretty fruitless. Sure, I have backlog after backlog of store business. I have tax returns, payments, and correspondence between me and my Uncle Teddy, detailing the daily business. What I didn't find is a copy of the handwritten will my uncle left and any other documentation that would indicate his intentions after he died.

"Mrs. Rhys-Jones," Shep greets as he gracefully stands from the bench and strides toward me, making me swallow, not just at the sight in front of me, but his greeting. I almost want to tell him to stop, because I know he's just playing the part. But I don't say anything, because I like it. Pretend or not. I like it when he calls me his wife.

I smile and fall into step beside him, loving the way his arm brushes mine.

I might've missed him a little today.

Maybe.

Just a little.

"How was your day?" he asks when I stay silent.

The sigh that escapes is unavoidable. Today was another roller-coaster day. It felt better being back in my element, but I still have Phillip's words messing with my mind and all the crap with Theo and the will. "It was fine…definitely a Monday."

Shep's hand reaches for mine and he pulls me to a stop in the middle of Jackson Square.

"Doesn't sound fine," he says, brushing a strand of hair behind my ear.

The gesture is so familiar and comforting. So real and normal. I can't help but lean into it. I also can't remember the last time someone asked me how my day was or comforted me. Sure, I hang with my girls, but we're all busy women—one of us is pregnant, one of us runs a busy hotel, one of us is in law school…and I was a one-woman show until Paige came along. It doesn't leave a lot of time to ask about the mundane.

"Better now," I tell him.

"Want to talk about it?"

Glancing around to the people milling about around us, I think for a second about blowing it off, but I don't want to. I want him to know. He's one of the smartest business people I know and I'd like his input. "Remember that stuff I told you about someone trying to take the shop from me?"

Shep's jaw tenses and he squints his eyes before saying, "yes."

"Well, it's my Uncle Teddy's son, who I knew nothing about. A few weeks ago, I got a letter from a Theodore Duval, which was my uncle's name, so imagine my surprise when I realized there was another one and he wants to stake a claim on Neutral Grounds." I bite my lip to keep my frustration at bay. "Anyway, Jules stopped by today to let me know his friend, a law professor, did some digging and found out Theo, my uncle's son, has filed a will contest. Now, I have to find as much proof as I can that Uncle Teddy intended on the shop going to my mama…and me. It's not going as smoothly as I hoped."

I can tell he's thinking hard about the information I just gave him before speaking. "I want his name, everything you know about him," he begins, wheels turning. "I'll—"

"No," I tell him, bringing him to a halt. "This is my problem. I'll fix it…and if I don't, then that'll be on me."

"You're so stubborn."

I shrug, unapologetic. "I like to think of it as self-reliant."

He smirks. "That too."

"We should go," I say, rolling my eyes and turning to continue our walk, but Shep stops me, his hand slipping down my arm until his hand is holding mine.

"If you need help…anything…I'm here for you and I want to help. Let me help."

Internally, I cringe, because it would be so easy to let him step in and *help*, but this is my shop. I've kept it afloat all these years. I've brought it into the twenty-first century. *Me.* If I let Shep step in, then it'll be like it's partly his and no longer mine. It would change things.

"Thank you," I tell him. "I mean it." And I do. It's nice of him to offer. "I might need—"

I was getting ready to say advice…but he kisses me—lips firmly taking mine, tongue sweeping across, wetting my skin until I open, allowing him to deepen it. I let him steal my breath for a few moments, until someone whistles bringing us out of the haze.

"We should…" I trail off.

"Head to my place," Shep suggests…suggestively, and I laugh. "Maverick and Carys won't even notice we're missing. They'll be all *I love you…no, I love you…*blah, blah, blah."

Now, we're both laughing, me at Shepard's impersonation of Maverick and Carys.

He brushes my lips with the pad of his thumb and the laughter gets swallowed down.

"Let's go, Mrs. Rhys-Jones."

Hand-in-hand, we walk the short distance to the Blue Bayou, slipping in the side entrance to the courtyard. Of course, it's lit up in the typical white twinkle lights and cafe lighting. Since Maverick came to stay for good, he's made great improvements. This place is straight out of a fairytale and it draws business. They've hosted a slew of weddings and parties. Now, it seems as though it'll be the backdrop for my best friend getting her happily ever after.

Everyone is here—Shaw, Avery, Mary, George, Jules…everyone except Carys. We say our hellos, getting our hugs in just before Maverick gets everyone's attention.

"Thanks for coming," he says with a wide, sure smile. No nerves in sight. "Carys is up checking on a false alarm in room 304." The slight blush on his cheeks makes me fight back a giggle. I know what happened in 304. That was his room when he stayed at the Blue Bayou. Carys spilled the tea. Jules made her give us all the details over wine one night.

Just before the back door opens, Maverick cuts the lights, leaving nothing but the walking path lit by candles. When Carys walks into the courtyard, she doesn't even know we're all standing in the shadows. All she sees is Maverick, on bended knee.

Even if the place was lit up like Fort Knox, I still don't think she'd see us, because she only has eyes for him. The love the two of them share is so vivid…I've never doubted how Maverick feels for my best friend. Well, maybe the first time he came into the shop and asked about her, but he proved himself quickly.

"Carys Matthews," Maverick begins as Carys's hands go to cover her mouth. "I knew I wanted to marry you shortly after I met you. I remember thinking back then that I knew I'd love you in three weeks, three months, or three years…or thirty…for the rest of my life. When I moved here to be a part of yours, I didn't see any reason to rush things. We might've fallen in love fast, but we have the rest of our lives to cultivate it. But recently, I've been thinking…what the hell are we waiting for? I know I love you and you're it for me…forever and always. I want you in every way."

He pauses, pulling a small box from his back pocket and opening it, showing Carys what's inside. A choked sob leaves her as she drops down on her knees in front of him. "Marry me," he pleads. "Be mine in every way possible. And let me spend the rest of our lives proving how much I love you."

She throws her arms around him and cries. "Yes, yes…three weeks…three months…three hundred years," she chuckles. "Yes."

"How about two weeks?" Maverick asks as he leans back to slide the ring on her finger.

"Two weeks for what?"

"To marry me," he says, standing and helping her to her feet. "Right here, in our favorite place, surrounded by our family and friends." When he flips a switch and the courtyard is once again bathed in light, Carys looks around, realizing we all had a front-row seat to the best proposal I've ever witnessed.

It's only then I realize I'm crying. Wiping the tears from my cheeks, I look beside me to see Shep watching me. He doesn't say anything, just gives me a soft smile, brushing a strand of hair behind my ear.

"Oh, my God," Carys exclaims, turning back to Maverick. "Yes!"

We all swarm them, doling out the congratulations and examining the perfect ring. "I'm so happy for you," I tell her, when I finally get my chance with the soon-to-be bride.

Who would've thought I'd be the first one to get married out of me, Carys, and Avery?

Sure as hell wasn't me.

"Will you be my matron of honor?"

"Absolutely."

Shep

I'VE SPENT THE BETTER PART OF MY DAY THINKING about CeCe, which is crazy, because I have plenty of work sitting in front of me to keep me busy—contractors to touch base with, property owners to send proposals to, profit and loss reports to look over. This little venture Maverick and I started over two years ago has turned out better than either of us could have dreamed.

Who knew doing work we actually cared about—and still made money on—could be so rewarding?

And now that I'm permanently here in New Orleans, it's full steam ahead.

Yeah, I said it. *Permanently*. I haven't made it public knowledge, but I've already put my house in Dallas on the market and have had a few serious inquiries. I have no doubt it will sell fast. If I can swing it long distance, I won't even go back. I'll hire a company to move the rest of my belongings here and I'll put them in storage until I decide what to do with them.

For now, I'm happy in this townhouse.

I'd be even happier if CeCe would agree to move in with me. But I know how stubborn she is and if I push her on this, she'll definitely push back.

And that thought has my dick growing hard.

What is this woman doing to me?

She's making me think about love and making things permanent, all while effectively ruining me for any other woman…ever. A year with her will never be enough. I'm not sure a lifetime will be, but it's a good place to start.

Looking at my watch, I realize it's after three o'clock and if I'm going to tackle some of this shit, I better get on it. Picking up the phone, I dial Mav's number.

"Hey, man," he says.

"Hey," I reply, clicking around on my laptop until I find the information I'm looking for. "I just wanted to run some specs by you for that new property."

He's passed on a lot of his knowledge, but the actual remodeling and refurbishing part of our business is still his domain.

"Hit me with it."

We spend about half an hour talking floor plans and square footage and how much we'll need to put into this particular place before it'd be ready for resale. Once we come to a unified decision to make the purchase, I write down Maverick's negotiations and send an email to Mr. Archer.

"One more thing," I tell Maverick. "What do you know about this fucker who's trying to contest CeCe's uncle's will?"

Maverick is quiet for a few seconds. "She told you about that?"

"Yeah, of course," I tell him. "We are married."

He chuckles and I want to punch him through the phone for his sarcastic tone.

"What?" I bark.

"Nothing," he says. "Just didn't expect you to take this so seriously."

I stand from my chair and begin to pace my office. Maybe I need to just go over there and have this out with him…clear the fucking air.

"What the fuck is that supposed to mean?"

He exhales loudly. "Fuck, Shep, I don't know...you're you and this isn't...you."

"And exactly what am I?" I ask, getting more pissed off by the second.

"Oh, I don't know," Maverick says, sounding as exasperated as I feel. "You're a fuck 'em and leave 'em kind of guy. You never bang the same chick twice because repeat performances lead to feelings and you don't do fucking feelings. You're words, not mine." His volume rises until he's practically yelling into the phone. "And now, you're married," he says, drawing it out and following it up with an incredulous laugh. "And I have to admit, you're doing a pretty good job of playing the part...it's very believable, but don't you think that's going to, I don't know, confuse things down the road?"

Standing facing the window that looks out on the street below, I huff, "Confuse who, Mav? Because I'm definitely not confused...I know exactly what I'm doing."

"Don't hurt her," he warns, but it's completely unnecessary.

"I would never hurt CeCe. That's the last thing in the world I'd ever want to do."

"Good," Maverick says after a few seconds of dead air. "Back to your question regarding the will contest. I only know what Jules has told us and it sounds like this long-lost cousin might have a leg to stand on. Jules is working with one of his law professors to find out anything and everything they can, but from what he says, it'll more than likely go to court."

"Who is this fucker?" I ask, my wheels turning. "Does he even know what he's trying to claim? Running a business in the French Quarter isn't for the faint of heart. It takes someone who knows the clientele. So, what does he want? The business or the building?"

Maverick sighs heavily. "Fuck if I know."

"Might be a good thing to find out. Think you could get his contact information from Jules?"

"Shep," he says hesitantly. "Don't overstep."

Plopping back down in my chair, I lean back. "You know CeCe isn't going to ask for help, but I want to help her anyway…help *me* help *her*," I plead, knowing he'll cave.

"Fine. I'll see what I can find out and I'll give it to you tomorrow when we meet up at the St. Ann property."

Any day I win a negotiation with Maverick is a good day. "Thanks, man. See you tomorrow."

I spend the remainder of the day and evening making phone calls and sending emails. When I finally lift my head long enough to read the clock, I realize it's nearly nine o'clock and my only thought is that I didn't talk to CeCe once today. I thought about sending her a text message earlier, but I didn't know what to say.

Maverick was right about one thing. I've never done relationships, so the fact that my first one is marriage means I skipped a few steps, like dating…or courting. Do people even do that anymore? Unlike most men my age, no one has ever told me or showed me how to treat a woman, except for Maverick. Watching him with Carys is the only real-life example I have of what a relationship should look like.

Picking up my phone, I think about calling him and asking for some advice, but then the screen lights up with a text from CeCe and my heart squeezes in my chest.

Like, literally stops and starts at the mere sight of her name.

How is that possible?

CeCe: I made enough spaghetti to feed an army. Did you eat?

Smirking at my phone, I quickly type my response.

Shep: I could eat.

Way to play it cool.

CeCe: Text me when you're here and I'll come down and let you in.

She doesn't have to tell me twice. Rolling my chair back, I stand and shut my laptop. As I head to the front door, I grab my keys and flip off the lights. It's nice living in a place where I don't need my car. I enjoy walking the streets of New Orleans, especially at night. Plus, as an added bonus, my next-door neighbors happen to be Shaw and Avery.

The longer I'm here, the more I start feeling the sense of community Maverick raved about for so long. I didn't get it until I moved here, but now, I understand what all the fuss was about.

A few lights are on next door, but I don't see Shaw's Jeep out front, so I assume he's still at the bar. It's crazy to think in a couple more months, they'll have a baby.

Now, there's something I've never even considered.

In the past, my only thought about the subject of children was I didn't want any. Why would I? My parents made me feel like a possession, something resembling a status symbol—a pawn to advance them in the game of life.

I wonder how CeCe feels about kids.

It's crazy, but thinking about having kids with her doesn't sound so bad…or scary.

What's also crazy is that I went into this thinking it would be temporary and now I'm thinking about making it more permanent than anything in my life has ever been.

Maverick's reaction today on the phone got my hackles up, but I get it. All he has to go off is my track record and it's not great. I've never been a *good guy* and definitely not marriage material. If anyone considered it, I can guarantee it was only for my money…or my family's money. The Felicity Crawfords of the world are the only women interested in marrying someone like me.

Except for CeCe.

She's different.

She volunteered before she even knew what I had to offer.

Sure, she was intoxicated, but I could tell her offer was genuine. That's the kind of person she is—one willing to step in and help someone with no expectations of getting anything for themselves in return.

Which is why I want to help her, even though she thinks she doesn't need my help.

When I get to the dark, locked storefront, I pull out my phone and shoot her a message.

Shep: I'm here.

A few seconds later, the stairway light flips on and then CeCe is there, walking toward the door. Her dark hair is in a messy bun on top of her head and she's wearing a pair of baggy sweats and a t-shirt that hangs off her shoulder.

When she opens the door, with a smile on her face, I wonder how I got so lucky…and how she got so beautiful. No one should be this appealing in sweats but fuck me if she's not the most gorgeous woman I've ever seen.

"You gonna come in or should I just grab you a plate to go?" she asks, leaning on the door frame with a peculiar expression.

Running a hand through my hair, I chuckle, shaking my head and then take a step toward her. When I lean in, using the door to trap her, she inhales deeply. "I'm definitely coming…in, that is. You look beautiful."

A breathy laugh escapes her as she maneuvers around me. Once we're both inside, she shuts the door and locks it—two deadbolts. On our way up the stairs, she pauses to set the alarm and then glances at me over her shoulder. "Don't judge my apartment, fancy pants."

"What?" I ask. "I'd never."

"Okay." Her tone says she doesn't believe me, but I'm telling the honest truth. I'd never judge CeCe, about anything. She could live in a cardboard box out back and I wouldn't look at her any differently.

I might insist she lives with me, but I wouldn't judge her.

Her sweet ass is swaying in my face, so I'm unable to form a coherent sentence in response.

When we top the stairs, CeCe stands back with an anxious look on her face. "This is it."

It's definitely small, but I can't help the smile that works its way onto my face, because more than that…it's her. It smells like her, mixed with the delicious aroma of spaghetti. It looks like her—simple and eclectic. Everything here feels like it holds significance, as if it earned its place, it means something.

Which makes me feel like I might mean something.

"I love it," I tell her, reaching out for the hem of her t-shirt and pulling her to me. As my lips hover above hers, close enough to touch, but not quite, I take some calming breaths, willing myself to slow down and not show all my cards…not yet.

CeCe's eyes flick from my lips up to meet mine and then her tongue darts out to swipe across the plump, pink skin. So kissable. So fuckable. "Was this…a booty call?" I ask, wanting to ease the tension that's settled.

She smirks and I lean the rest of the way in, capturing her mouth with mine. Tonight, there's a faint taste of wine mixed with the sweet taste of CeCe and it's intoxicating. What I intended to be a sweet, soft kiss of appreciation for her inviting me over, turns into a demanding, needy plea for something more…more of her.

When she moans and slips her hands up my shoulders and into my hair, I push her back against the wall, using my body to show her how much I missed her today. Holding her face in my hands, I devour her—delving my tongue into her mouth.

Her soft skin beneath my palms, mixed with her delectable taste and seductive sounds, I'm engulfed by CeCe and I want to drown in her…never coming up for breath.

Reluctantly, I pull away, nipping at her bottom lip for one last taste.

"Hungry?" she asks, her voice sounding somewhere between drunk and sleepy.

I love both versions of CeCe.

I love all versions of CeCe.

Leaning back on my heels, I look down at her, still holding that sweet face in my hands and I'm overcome with the feelings and truths overtaking my thoughts. In this moment, they hit me so hard I want to shout them from the rooftops of New Orleans, but I refrain because that feels like too much too fast. "Famished."

We both know we're not completely talking about dinner, but we pretend anyway. For now.

"Follow me," she says, slipping around me and making her way to the small kitchen. There's a table by the window that looks out on Jackson Square. It's set for two, and once again, I'm hit with the overwhelming sensation there's no place else in the world I'd rather be than right here, with her.

She instructs me to sit as she walks to the stove and makes two plates of spaghetti, placing one in front of me. "Cheese?"

"Of course," I reply, leaning back to take her in.

My chest is doing this weird thing…tightening and warming all at the same time. I rub at the area over my heart and try to shake it. But I can't. It's her. It's every fucking time I've been in her presence lately, especially since we came back from Dallas.

"Is that good?" she asks. When I look down at my plate, there's a healthy amount of shaved parmesan on my pasta. Probably a little more than I'd typically prefer, but I got preoccupied, which is becoming a real problem when I'm with her.

"Looks great."

She pours two glasses from an opened bottle of wine and sits down across from me. The soft smile on her face makes me smile in return.

"Thanks for coming over," she says, placing a napkin on her lap before digging in.

"Thanks for inviting me."

When my stomach growls, I glance over at her and she laughs. "So, you really are hungry?"

"Starving," I say with a chuckle. "Actually, I can't remember what I ate today."

She takes a bite and then frowns. "Not good," she mumbles, covering her mouth while she chews.

On my first bite, I close my eyes and let the flavors assault my tongue. This is the best fucking spaghetti I've ever had. "Fuck," I moan when my mouth is finally clear. "This is good."

She shrugs noncommittally. "I'm pretty good at a few things, spaghetti happens to be one of them." Taking a drink of her wine, she smiles around the glass and arches an eyebrow.

Oh, she's good alright…

"How was your day?" I ask, before taking another bite.

"Fine, I guess," she says, then corrects herself, "Well, business was good, but I'm still having trouble finding all of the documentation Jules asked me to locate."

"Can I help?" I ask, wondering if I should tell her I'm thinking about contacting Theodore Duval myself and see exactly what he's after, but when she gives me an abrupt no, I decide against it.

"I'll find everything," she sighs. "It's just going to take a little longer than I thought."

We both eat in companionable silence for a moment and I glance out the window.

"Nice view," I comment.

"Best view in the city," she says, following my gaze. "I love sitting here at night with all the lights off, just watching the square and the people."

"Kind of stalkery of you," I tease.

She rolls her eyes and laughs, bringing her wine glass up for another drink. "Well, when you live alone, you get inventive."

"You don't have to live alone," I tell her, without thinking.

When she quirks an eyebrow, I laugh. "I'm just saying. But I won't push. If you want late-night booty calls, then late-night booty calls are what you'll get."

She laughs again and I join her, loving the sound and the feel of this moment. If I could fold it up neatly and stick it in my pocket, I would. I'd keep it forever.

After we clear our plates, I wash while CeCe dries…and relentlessly teases me about how she assumed I didn't know how to scrub a dish. *Isn't that what maids are for?* She's such a little shit, and I tell her so. Washing dishes turns into me chasing her around the small kitchen with the dish towel I stole from her and her squealing.

Good thing she doesn't have any downstairs neighbors because they might think she has an intruder.

And when we start making out like horny teenagers on her couch and then end up fucking in her oversized chair, they really would be concerned...probably even call the cops...because I have her screaming my name while she comes on my dick.

Yeah, I could get used to this. All of it. The dinner, the banter, the teasing, the fucking ...and especially this. Right now, CeCe is curled into my side, sound asleep, and it's the most peaceful I've felt in my entire life.

Later, when I wake up, after the best sleep I've ever had, I immediately realize something is missing.

CeCe is no longer pressed against my body, but a warm blanket is thrown over me, maybe even *tucked in* around my chin.

Did she tuck me in?

Has *anyone* ever tucked me in?

Tossing it off, I sit on the edge of the bed and rub my eyes. Her bedroom is also small, but it's tidy, everything in its place, just like the rest of her apartment. She's definitely a woman who doesn't need a lot of things. It's obvious she's perfectly happy in this tiny apartment and it suits her.

There's coffee wafting in the air. Standing, I pull on the button-down shirt and jeans I wore over here last night and then slip into my shoes. As I walk out of the bedroom, I can see that CeCe is nowhere to be found. Glancing down at my watch, I see it's only five forty. In the fucking morning. I mean, I'm an early riser, usually up no later than six thirty, and I can rise and shine with the best of them, but CeCe's definitely got me beat.

As I take one last look around the apartment, I secretly hope I get to spend a lot more time here, and then I open the door and walk down the stairs.

When I make the turn at the bottom of the staircase, into the coffee shop, there's a vision in front of me. CeCe has a fresh bun on top of her head, exposing the creamy skin of her neck, and she's wearing the cutest fucking apron as she hums to herself—prepping coffee and filling the case with baked goods.

Good fucking morning to me.

"Hey," she says, popping up and swiping a strand of fallen hair behind her ear. "Didn't hear you come down the stairs."

I smirk, uncross my arms and stalk toward her. "I'm kind of a ninja. It's a secret I don't really tell many people…you always get those nosey ass questions, like *what turtle are you—*"

She throws her head back and laughs, a full-belly laugh, and I can't help leaning forward and capitalizing on the opportunity to get my lips on that gorgeous neck.

"Hey," she scolds, glancing toward the door and back at me. "I'm expecting my first customer any time, so there's no time for…that." She points her finger around my face, but her eyes stay locked on mine. There's a war going on here between what she wants and what she knows she doesn't have time for, so I save her by pressing a chaste kiss to her lips and stepping back.

"I've gotta run anyway," I tell her, walking around to the other side of the counter. "I'm meeting Mav at a new property this morning."

"Oh?" she asks, turning her back to me to finish what she was working on before I interrupted.

"Yeah, new place over on St. Ann. Really cool, old building, but it needs a lot of work. We're meeting with the current owner to see if it's something we can turn a profit on or not. Mav is chomping at the bit to get his hands on it, but I want to see the bottom line first."

Turning around, she sets a hot cup of coffee down in front of me and places a lid on top. "Y'all make a really good team," she says, pulling out a piece of wax paper and holding it up. "Croissant?"

"Danish?" I counter and she smiles, reaching into the case to get my breakfast of choice. What I'd really like is her, but I know she's busy and there's just something about thinking about her all damn day that makes finally having her that much more rewarding. So, I can wait.

Until tonight.

"Let me take you to dinner tonight," I tell her.

"I don't close shop until eight," she says. "That's kind of late for going out."

I shrug, not caring if it was midnight. I'd still want to see her. "I'll call Micah and see about a late reservation at Lagniappe."

The slow, easy smile she gives is enough to drive me crazy. "Is that a yes?" I ask, easing my craving with a bite of danish, instead of a bite of her.

"Okay."

"Good," I say around the flaky pastry. "It's a date."

Her smile drops a little, but she recovers quickly and replies. "It's a date."

The morning goes by quickly.

Maverick and I meet up and walk through the building, which I'm happy to report is very structurally sound. However, the deciding factor in any business decision is: return on investment. Can we make money?

Fortunately, this particular seller has had the building on the market for quite a while and is ready to sell…cheap.

So, we'll be signing the deal on Thursday.

Now, we're headed to a tux shop a few streets over to have our tuxes altered for the wedding and I decide to take this opportunity to talk to him about CeCe and the intense feelings I've been having.

I know he's not the biggest fan of our marriage, but I don't know who else to talk to. He has always been my go-to for anything and everything, so I take the chance.

"I've been wanting to talk to you," I tell him, squinting into the sun as we cross the street.

"What about?" Maverick asks as we both jog the rest of the way to the curb. These narrow streets can get a little sketchy. Plus, you just never know who's been drinking in this city, regardless of the time of day.

"CeCe."

Maverick stops in the middle of the sidewalk and a few people shoulder their way past us, but he doesn't seem to care he's taking up real estate. "What about her?" His hackles are already up and normally that'd piss me off, but something changes as we're standing there. No longer am I pissed at him for thinking the worst of me. Instead, I'm happy he cares so much about my girl to have her back, even with his best friend.

I think my respect for him just went up and I didn't even know that was possible.

"How did you know?" I ask, unable to say the word, because it still feels so foreign on my tongue—love—such a simple word, but when you go your entire life without saying it or having it said to you, you don't really know what to do with it.

His brows pull together and he cocks his head. "Know what?"

"About Carys…how did you *know*?" I raise my brows in hopes that he'll get it.

A sly smile takes over his perplexed expression and he lets out a heavy breath. "Fuck, man." He shakes his head, like he's in disbelief. "You're really falling for her, aren't you? This isn't a game or a business agreement."

That last part isn't a question, it's a statement and I'm relieved that he finally gets it…and that he believes me. "No, not in the slightest."

Slapping my shoulder, he levels me with his stare. "The fact you're asking me how tells me you've already figured it out…you just need to give your head time to catch up with your heart."

Leave it to Maverick to go and get all poetic and shit. That's probably one of those lines his grandfather wrote in the journal he left him. He's always pulling deep, meaningful shit out of it and spouting it off at random times.

But I've got to be honest, I wish I had something like that—anything to help me know what the fuck I'm doing—because I'm in uncharted territory and it's scary as shit.

Walking into the tux shop, although I've never been here before, it feels like home. Two things Maverick and I are well-versed in—suits and tuxedos. We've spent the majority of our lives dressed like CEOs. Our fathers are cut from the same cloth and believed in grooming us to take over one day.

Funny thing though, the longer I'm in New Orleans, the more I find myself enjoying the casual side of life. Sure, I'll always love a great suit. I love the confidence and power I feel when I wear one, but it's not necessary any longer. The power struggle I've been in my entire life is over.

I'm only worried about *my*self, *my* business, and *my* wife.

"How does this feel, sir?" the older gentleman asks as he sticks a pin at my shoulder, making a small adjustment along the seam.

Stretching my shoulders, I pull my arms forward to test it out. "Feels great."

As I watch him finish—meticulous in every detail and exhibiting care for the expensive fabric—Maverick calls out from behind the curtain where he's changing. "Forgot to tell you I got some info on Duval."

My ears perk up.

"Name and location," he continues. "He's in Houston. Seems as though he dabbles in real estate, mostly housing. One of my old contacts from Kensington Properties is a mutual friend, says the guy is a little underhanded." Maverick's tone turns serious. "I don't like the sound of it."

Me either. As a matter of fact, I fucking hate the sound of it. Sounds like Theo is a money-hungry dick who's found out he might have a stake in CeCe's business and isn't above fighting the system to stake a claim.

Over my dead body.

Reaching over for my phone, I pull up CeCe's name and hit the call button. It rings a few times before she picks up. "Hello?"

"CeCe?" Her connection sounds weak, so I press the phone closer to my ear and repeat her name again, "CeCe?"

"I'm here," she finally says. "Sorry, I've got a shitty reception."

"Where are you?"

There's a pause and I pull my phone back to make sure the call didn't drop, when I see it's still connected. "Hello?"

She's a little out of breath when she speaks up again, a little clearer this time. "Hey, sorry…I came outside, sometimes it's a little better out here. Can you hear me now?"

"Yeah, where are you?"

"Home. I came to find my missing pieces."

I pause for a second, not recognizing the feeling that hits me in my gut. She just left the city and didn't feel the need to tell me? I'm not going to lie, that doesn't sit well with me. "You drove to your mom's house?"

"Yeah, Paige is watching the shop this afternoon, but don't worry, I'll be back by eight. We're still on for dinner."

Well, that's good, but I'm still not happy she left without telling me. I know she still thinks this marriage is an arrangement and not a real marriage, but that's not the case anymore, at least not for me.

"Shep?"

"I'm here."

"Everything okay?"

I swallow down my initial reply—*no, everything's not fucking okay*—and settle on my second. "You should've told me you needed to go home. I would've taken you."

CeCe

"WHO WAS THAT?" MY MAMA ASKS, WALKING OUTSIDE where I'm standing on the front porch staring at my phone.

"Uh, a…" Every lie dies on my tongue. There's no way I can call Shep a friend, he's feeling like more than that every day. But I wasn't planning on telling her about the arrangement…marriage…whatever. Actually, I planned on her being at work while I slid in, found what I came for, and left.

Sounds shitty of me, but it was the easiest thing I could think of.

However, she came home early due to her hours being cut, so that spoiled my plan.

"A what?" she asks, suspicion creasing her forehead. "Friend? I could've sworn I heard you mention dinner. Are you dating someone?"

Now, there's a layer of hope tossed in for good measure and I inwardly cringe, not wanting to talk about this. Not with her. Not today.

As I turn around, I shield my eyes and my mama frowns, taking a step closer and reaching out to grab my hand. My left hand. The one with a gold band on a very important finger.

"What's this?"

Shit.

"Is there something you'd like to tell me?" she asks, her eyes snapping from my hand to my eyes.

"It's not what you think," I tell her, immediately feeling guilty, but not for the obvious reason. I should feel guilty about getting married without telling my mother, but instead, I feel guilty for downplaying my relationship with Shep, especially after the call I got from him and how disappointed he sounded that I came home and didn't invite him.

Honestly, the thought never crossed my mind…or maybe it did, but I shot it down like a rogue missile.

It's one thing for him to take me home to Dallas. But for me to bring him here, that's entirely different. However, the thought of Shep standing in the middle of my mother's double-wide trailer isn't as foreign as it would've been a month ago, especially after last night. I expected him to seem out of place in my small apartment, too large for my life, but somehow, he fit, and that made me both happy and scared. Happy because I love having him in my life and scared because I don't know what will happen when he's not.

She lets my hand go and takes a step back, turning to walk inside. "I think you've lost your mind…am I close?"

Huffing out a laugh, I roll my eyes and follow her back in the house. "It's complicated."

Much, much more complicated than I ever dreamed it would be.

"I was hoping you were going to tell me it's a ring out of a Cracker Jack box you decided to wear to keep men from hitting on you at the bar."

For some reason, her response makes me go on the defensive. "Again, it's not what you think it is." I know it's definitely not what I thought it was going to be, that's for sure.

"Why don't you help me understand," she says with a lot more snark than I've heard from her in years, if ever.

Sighing, I sit down at the kitchen table and continue flipping through the papers I dug out of the spare bedroom. She swears the original hand-written will is in here somewhere with a letter from my uncle dated just a week before his passing. If I could find both, they'd be great pieces of evidence in my case against Theo.

"It's temporary," I finally tell her, hoping it'll end this conversation and I can take care of business and get back to the city in time for dinner…with Shep…my temporary husband. "His name is Shepard Rhys-Jones and he's best friends with Maverick. He needed someone to marry and I volunteered."

Her mouth drops and she stands to pace the small kitchen. "Is he…paying you? Like a hooker or something?"

"No, Mama!" I exclaim. "It's nothing like that." Rubbing my temples, I curse myself for not remembering to take my wedding band off. It was very foolish and reckless of me. "It's a mutual agreement between two consenting adults." I don't even mention the money because it does make the agreement sound more tawdry than it is.

Actually, it's probably good she's grilling me on this. I need a good dose of reality because the last week or so has felt a lot like a fairytale—me married to Shep and actually enjoying our time spent together…forgetting we're only in this for a short time. Last night, and the one before that, felt very real and raw and like something I could get used to.

But when I really start to think about it, my stomach drops and my palms get sweaty.

How can I allow myself to fall for someone like Shep?

How can I allow myself to fall for anyone? Period.

"You really did a number on me when it comes to relationships, you know," I mutter, feeling the weight of my emotions come crashing down. I turn to her as I brush the hair out of my face and cross my arms. I feel like a petulant child, but I'm frustrated over the entire situation and she's going to get the brunt of it for now. "You never gave me advice on boys…or men." Her expression is stoic as she waits for me to finish. "I feel like I'm driving blindfolded," I confess.

"I raised you to be capable enough to take care of yourself so you wouldn't have to worry about marrying a man," she confesses. "I didn't prepare you for marriage because there's no guarantee in it. I prepared you for yourself... I made you strong and confident and capable. I never wanted you to grow up and be attached to a man, look where it got me."

I remember exactly where it got her.

My mom was a pathetic mess when my father left. I took care of Rory and the house for weeks while she moped around and felt sorry for herself. We were all sad for a long time, but if I had to guess, she still is.

"How temporary are we talking?" she asks, pulling me out of my memories.

"A year."

She laughs, but it holds no humor. "A year? Well, I hope he doesn't break your heart and crush your dreams before time runs out."

"He won't," I tell her, but I'm not so sure about that. I was in the beginning. I had no plans of getting attached and giving him that kind of power over me, but I feel myself slipping with every passing moment.

Too many more nights like last night and I'll be a goner.

Looking up, I see the hard set of her eyes—eyes that have been there and done that, eyes that see my deadbeat dad in every man—and that protective streak over Shep rears its head and I balk at her disapproval. "He's not Dad."

"A lot of men seem great until their feet are put to the fire, and then they run. It's in their DNA."

"You don't know him," I defend. "He's...good."

When she rolls her eyes, I turn back to my stack of papers. I've got to find what I'm looking for and get back to New Orleans before we both say things we'll have a hard time coming back from.

As I thumb past an old receipt for car repair, I stop on the next piece of paper. It's a letter with an old, battered envelope stapled to the top. "What's this?" I ask, pulling it from the stack and flipping it over.

The envelope was addressed to a Cynthia Rawlings and there's a return to sender stamp on the front, along with a few notes from the post office. Switching back over to the front, I start to read the letter as my mama comes up behind me, reading over my shoulder.

"Oh, yeah," she mumbles. "I forgot about this…Cynthia is Theo's mother. When I was going through his papers that were in the safety deposit box, this was in it."

"And you didn't think it might be important?" I ask incredulously. My mama is a smart lady, but sometimes she just doesn't use all of her brain.

Going back to the letter it's stapled to, I read that Uncle Teddy tried to contact Cynthia to get in touch with Theo sometime after he turned eighteen. He thought since he was now an adult, he'd like to meet his father.

There's another letter behind the first one that's from Cynthia and her reply is that Theo didn't want to meet Uncle Teddy and he asked her to return the letter.

"You've never opened the letter?" I flip the envelope over and sure enough, it's still sealed.

"I told you, I forgot this was even here," she defends. "At the time I found it, I thought it was none of my business. Your Uncle Teddy had just passed away and it all felt too fresh and like an invasion of privacy. This was the only thing he ever kept to himself. He and I were alike in a lot of ways," she says thoughtfully, more to herself than me. "After Cynthia, he never loved again, and I think Theo not wanting anything to do with him hurt more than he ever wanted to admit."

Holding the unopened letter in my hand feels like more like a grenade with the pin pulled.

What if this is something stating how Uncle Teddy wanted Theo to have the building and shop?

Will this trump his handwritten will?

What does all of this mean?

Why does my life suddenly feel much too complicated?

It's all too much and I feel the urge to get the hell out of here, leaving all of this for another day. Worrying about things that are out of my control is a constant battle in my mind. I can easily take an average issue and flip, turn it, and reverse it—thinking about every scenario: good, bad, and everything in between.

Exhaling loudly, I set the letter and unopened envelope to the side, deciding to open it later.

Maybe I should talk to Jules first and see what he thinks? He might be able to shed some light and give me some advice on whether or not it can hurt or help our case—*my case*, because let's face it, when all of this is said and done, it all falls on me.

No one else.

That's how it's been my entire life.

Why would this be any different?

Shep

THIS ALL FEELS SO FAMILIAR, LIKE DÉJÀ VU, EXCEPT CeCe isn't standing across from me, she's entirely too far away—on the other side of Carys, while Carys and Maverick say their vows.

"Do you, Maverick Kensington, take Carys Matthews as your bride? To have and to hold from this day forward?" the minister asks, looking up at Maverick expectantly.

When I glance over at CeCe and catch her gaze, I can't help but smile while my heart squeezes in my chest. The feeling is overwhelming as I stand there, realizing if, given the chance, I'd marry her again today…and the next. And all the days after that.

This realization has me feeling like I want to shout my feelings for her from the rooftops again. If we weren't standing in the middle of our best friends' wedding, I might do just that.

I need to talk to her. I need her to know what I'm feeling, and I need to know she's feeling the same way—that this is real. We're no longer faking or pretending, and I have zero intentions of letting her go at the end of a year.

She's mine.

To have and to hold from this day forward.

She must be feeling at least a fraction of what I am because *I* feel it—every time she kisses me or touches me or fucks me. The same intensity coursing through my veins is reflected back through her actions.

Then there's the way she looks at me, like right now. She can't take her eyes off me and I fucking love it.

When she swipes her fingers under her eye and blinks up to the heavens, I realize she's crying and I want to go to her. Even if they are happy tears, I want to be there for them. Every tear she ever sheds, I'll be there to wipe them away. I want to carry her burdens and make her life easier and I never want her to feel like she has to do everything on her own ever again.

I love that she's strong and brave…tenacious and stubborn…so, so stubborn. And I never want her to change, but I do want her to let me be by her side along the way.

"I now pronounce you husband and wife," the minister announces. "You may kiss the bride."

The small group of friends and family cheer louder than a stadium full of fans as Maverick dips Carys deep and kisses the shit out of her. She wraps her arms around his neck and falls into it and for a minute, I think I'm going to have to break it up and tell them to get a fucking room, but Maverick stands, bringing her with him, but not letting her go.

The smile on his face when he turns to look at all of us is huge. I've never seen my best friend as happy as he is today, and it might sound sappy, but it makes me fucking happy too. And it makes me want what he has…true, unconditional love.

I think it's what I always wanted; I just didn't know it. I'd never had a taste so I didn't know what I was missing out on. But now, I have CeCe and there's something evolving between the two of us that I can't describe any other way.

After Maverick and Carys make their way down the makeshift

aisle in the middle of the courtyard, CeCe and I follow suit. She smiles at me again, making my chest feel tight. "Hey," I say, my voice sounding weird even to my own ears, so I clear my voice and try again. "You're stunning…it's actually frowned upon to outshine the bride… very rude of you."

"Shut up," she says with a soft giggle, swatting at me with her bouquet, and I don't miss the faint blush on her cheeks.

Leaning over, I nuzzle her neck and make her squeal. That particular sound goes straight to my dick. Thankfully, I'm saved from an impending hard on by Jules throwing himself at us, pulling us both into a tearful hug. "I'm just so fucking happy that all my bitches are happy."

CeCe gives into the hug and I slip my way out of the mix and over to the bar, pouring myself a drink. Before I can even get two sips, I'm ripped away from the bourbon and forced into the streets of New Orleans in, apparently, what's called a second line.

Jules yells, "Condragulations," as instruments begin to play and a hankie is thrust into my hand.

Where the fuck is the first line?

That's a question I'll have to consider later, because right now, all I can do is fall in line and be in the moment. When I turn to look at CeCe, she's holding a white parasol and smiling from ear to ear, her dark hair a bit of a mess in the humid New Orleans day. Somehow, I don't notice the heat or the humidity, even though I'm in a fucking tuxedo. I just notice *her* and how beautiful she looks. The way the sun hits her hair and shows all the hidden hues of brown.

As a brass band plays, everyone dances their way down the street, newcomers joining as we make our way to St. Louis Cathedral, around Jackson Square, and finally ending at Come Again.

We're all hot, sweaty messes, but there's not one person who doesn't look like they just had the time of their life, my wife included. She turns to me, obviously caught up in the moment, and wraps her arms around my neck, kissing me with everything she's got.

I lift her off the ground and hold her to me, giving it all back.

When she breaks the kiss, our eyes meet for a second and something passes between us that I can't quite read. As she slips down my body, she swallows and bites down on her bottom lip, but doesn't say a word, just takes my hand and leads me into the bar where there's enough food and drink being served to feed an army…or half the city of New Orleans.

"Look at you," Avery says, beaming at Carys with a hand resting on her overly-large belly. A belly that's entirely too big for her petite frame. From behind, you'd never know she's pregnant, but then she turns around and it's like BAM. Pregnant. "Married…both of you," she says, reaching across for CeCe's hand.

CeCe glances over at me, that same peculiar expression on her face from earlier. I can't help but hold her stare, wanting to know what it means and make sure she's okay. I can't tell and I don't like it.

When the women go back to gushing over Carys and then Carys and CeCe turn their attention to Avery and her belly, I excuse myself to find another drink.

Maverick walks over to the bar, meeting me there as we wait on Paulie to hook us up. "Who'd have thought the two of us would be in a bar in New Orleans, both married?"

"Life's crazy, man," I agree. "But I have zero regrets." Glancing back over to where I left CeCe, I have an overwhelming desire to sweep her up into my arms and carry her to my townhouse and remind her why this is a good arrangement…why she wants to be married to me and why we make a good fit.

He turns around, leaning against the bar. "I can't think of a fucking place I'd rather be…best day of my damn life."

"I'm happy for you," I tell him, slapping his shoulder as Paulie sets our bourbon down on the bar.

"Congratulations, Maverick," he says. "Poured y'all the good stuff. Nothing but the best on your wedding day."

"Thanks, Paulie." Mav smiles and we both lift our glass, clinking them together before taking a healthy drink and letting the warmth slide down as we both let our new lives sink into our souls.

I've never really considered myself lucky. It's always seemed like a falsehood. My father raised me to believe we all make our own luck and with enough money, anything can be bought. But standing here, in the middle of Come Again with all the important people in my life and a beautiful woman to call my own, I feel pretty damn lucky, and money didn't play one fucking part in any of it.

CeCe

When my phone chimes with an incoming text message, I don't look at it. I know it's Shep. I've been avoiding him the past week and he doesn't like it.

Truth is, neither do I, but I've been in a state of mental overdrive the past couple of weeks. Between my trip home, my mother's words lingering, and Maverick and Carys's wedding, I haven't had time to get a grip.

My heart is falling for Shepard Rhys-Jones, but my brain is doing what it does best and scrambling for the nearest exit.

There's been an unsettled feeling in the pit of my stomach and I can't shake it. It feels a lot like doubt and distrust and I know it stems from my mama's reaction to me being married, mixed with my own stupid fight or flight mechanism.

I thought I could do this—be married to Shep, help him out, make it a year, and get out.

I thought I could keep my emotions and feelings out of it, but I was wrong.

If Shep had turned out to be what everyone expects—a spoiled rich guy who never has to answer for his actions—I would've stood a chance.

But he's nothing like that. He's caring and thoughtful. He's protective and chivalrous. He goes out of his way for people who have nothing to give him in return. And he doesn't expect it. Actually, he shies away from praise, even though he comes off like a cocky bastard. The outside is chiseled features and perfection. The inside is soft and flawed. And that's the part I love the most.

Yeah, I said it.

I. Love. Shep.

Like that overwhelming, all-consuming love you only read about or see in cheesy romance movies.

And I haven't the slightest clue what to do with that.

Even though the shop is closed, I don't startle when I hear the chimes come alive as the door opens. "Hey, Jules," I call out. The man is punctual, if nothing else.

"Hey." He walks over and props a hip on the counter beside me. "What are you doing standing in the dark all by your lonesome?" he asks. "And I don't mean to go all mama bear on you, but you really should lock up when you're here alone. You just never know what kind of riff-raff will walk in."

Leveling me with his stare, he pauses and examines me intently. When I don't give him anything, he continues. "Besides, it's very film noir of you and it's not becoming. You're light and color, hunty, so wipe that solemn look off your pretty little face and let's get going."

I smirk, unable to hide my chuckle. Leave it to Jules to pull me out of my lovesick funk.

"Let's go. Maybe we can beat Mr. Terrell to the restaurant and have a drink before he gets there," I tell him, walking to the door and holding it open for him. "Ladies first."

He smiles, moving past me and waiting while I set the alarm and lock the deadbolt.

We're meeting my uncle's lawyer at Lagniappe tonight to go over the documentation I have and papers that need to be filed before we can get a court date. I decided to go with him because he already knows the history of Neutral Grounds and that at least cuts out some of the bullshit.

Have I mentioned how much I hate the complicated turn my life has taken? So much. If I could wiggle my nose and go back a few months when my biggest concern was the impending New Orleans summer, I would.

Wouldn't I?

If that meant no Shep, would I still go back?

"You're thinking too much," Jules says. "What's got you all twisted up tonight? I thought since you were getting regular dick you wouldn't be so stressed." He bumps me with his shoulder and I give him a pity chuckle.

The regular dick, as he puts it, is definitely not my problem.

"The dick is good," I reply.

"Then what's the problem?" he asks, stepping in front of me to open the door to Lagniappe. "Age before beauty."

Rolling my eyes, I walk into the restaurant and my mouth immediately starts to drool, just like it does every time I walk through the doors. Actually, my mouth begins to drool every time someone even mentions Lagniappe. It's like a Pavlovian response.

"Hey, y'all," Micah greets, grabbing a few menus from the hostess stand. "Is Shep joining you?"

Shep's name is another Pavlovian trigger—desire, lust, need, want, and confusion. So much confusion.

"No," I tell him, glancing around the place for an older man with white hair. "We're meeting a *Mr. Terrell*. Is he here yet?"

"Not that I know of, but I have your table ready in the back."

Jules and I follow Micah and he leads us to the same table we sat at the night Shep and I came to an agreement to marry. Has it really only been a month? How has he worked his way so deep under my skin? How did I let him do that?

"Can I get y'all something from the bar?" Micah asks, interrupting my thoughts…or more like saving me from them—from myself.

"Vodka and club soda," I tell him. "With a lime. And make it a double."

"I want that fruity drink with rum in it…the one you stole from Shaw," Jules says with a wide smile, appreciating the view that is Micah Landry.

Jules has no shame in his game and I love that about him.

"Double vodka and club soda with a lime and a Come Again," Micah repeats our order with a smirk. "And we didn't steal it. We're borrowing it…with Shaw's blessing."

Jules hums his approval as Micah turns toward the bar. "Speaking of coming again…" he mutters under his breath. "Mmm."

"Jules," I hiss, swatting his arm.

He laughs, turning back to me. "What? You can't tell me you're so dickmatized you no longer recognize a Grade A piece of meat when it's right in front of you." His massive eye roll is audible. "That man is more than a snack, he's a whole fucking meal. I swear, I've gotta find me some more single bitches. All this monogamy is bringing me down."

My expression falls at the mention of monogamy and Jules notices. I know he's just joking around, but he played right into my inner turmoil. "What's that look for?" he asks.

"Nothing," I say, seeing a waiter walking toward our table with a tray of drinks.

He lets it go, for the moment, but as soon as the waiter leaves, he's back like an attack dog. "Okay, before Mr. Terrell gets here, let's clear the air. It's stifling."

"I don't think I can do it," I confess, immediately bringing my glass to my lips and taking a drink, appreciating the burn of the vodka.

"What?" Jules asks. "This meeting? The court hearing? You'll have to help me out here, because sister friend has a few irons in the fire. What exactly do you think you can't do?"

It's a challenge. I see it in the way he quirks his perfect eyebrow and sips his drink.

"Everything, Jules." I sigh, taking another healthy drink. "This. The fight with Theo. Being married to Shep. All of it. I just want to go back to when I knew what was coming every day and I was ready for it. Lately, I've had this feeling in the pit of my stomach like I just jumped out of an airplane and I forgot my parachute."

He laughs. "Well, first, and I quote, you'd never jump out of a perfectly good airplane." He gives me a pointed stare, because, yeah… okay, I've said that before. "Two, if you did jump out of a perfectly good airplane, you'd have a back-up to your back-up parachute."

"Exactly!" I exclaim, the vodka obviously altering my normal volume. "And there's no fucking parachute. See, this isn't me. I should've never agreed to this—"

"Then, why did you?" he asks, cutting me off before I can begin to whine. Nobody likes a whiner, especially Jules. "And from the story I was told, you volunteered your fine ass before he could ask."

I drink on that for a minute. Sure, I know the answer, but it doesn't really make sense in my brain anymore, nothing does. "I did it because Shep needed someone and I…wanted…to…help him out," I finally say, as unsure as my words sound.

"So, this was a completely selfless act?" Jules asks, leaning his elbows on the table and leveling me with his stare. "There wasn't anything in it for CeCe? Well, besides the cool mil. Let's leave money out of it for now."

"It sounded easy," I tell him, my lines of communication loosening up as I finish the last dregs of my glass in record time. "What's a year, you know? And how bad could being married to Shep be?" I shrug. Even though I'm asking the questions out loud, they're more for me than Jules. "I knew I was attracted to him, but I thought it was lust… or unrequited feelings. Honestly, there was a part of me who thought if I could just have him for a short time, I'd get my fill and more than likely be so annoyed with him at the end of a year I'd be happy to give him a divorce."

"But?" Jules asks, prompting me to continue.

"But I don't see that happening."

We sit there quietly for a minute before Jules makes his final closing statement. "You love him."

Mr. Terrell saves me from facing the judge and jury by making his appearance. "Ms. Calhoun," he says, pulling out his chair. Jules and I both stand and we all shake hands.

"Hello, Mr. Terrell. Thank you for meeting me after hours."

"Oh, no problem," he says, waving it off. "I had a case that went late, so it's a nice change of scenery for me. Besides, if I would've gone home, I would've resorted to a cold sandwich."

I smile, feeling at ease with the older man immediately.

After easy conversation, a quick bite to eat, and another round of drinks, we dive into the real reason we're here and Mr. Terrell becomes all business. "I've looked over all of the documents you scanned in," he says, his wire-rimmed glasses perched on his nose. For an older gentleman, he's quite handsome…very distinguished. "Thanks for that, Jules." Jules nods and Mr. Terrell continues after a long, drawn-out exhale. "Mr. Duval does have a case and he's barely slid in under the five-year mark. If he would've contested the will just a few months later, it probably wouldn't have mattered. In the state of Louisiana, a will can be challenged within five years of going to probate. That window closes at the end of October, but I assume Mr. Duval knows that."

His annoyance with my so-called cousin is obvious.

"Listen, CeCe," he says, turning all of his attention on me and dropping the papers to the table. "You know and I know your uncle intended for you to have that building and run his business. He and I had a good working relationship and I have no doubt he would be mad as a hornet if he knew this greedy little bastard is coming back after this property after all this time."

"I did find a returned letter," I tell him, pulling it out of my bag. "It was in a stack of papers at my mama's house stapled to a letter from a *Cynthia Rawlings*. From what my mama told me, she's Theo's mother."

Mr. Terrell takes the envelope and quirks an eyebrow when he sees it's still sealed. "May I?"

"Yes," I tell him, glancing over at Jules. "I think I've just been waiting on someone else to do it. I didn't know if it was going to hurt or help and I've honestly been a nervous wreck thinking about it… like it's a ticking time bomb."

Mr. Terrell's eyes scan the paper as I hold my breath.

His eyebrows go up and down and occasionally he cocks his head and then nods in agreement.

"Well," he says after a few painful moments. "It's a letter from your Uncle Teddy to Theo, and it's basically his last-ditch effort to reach out to him." He hands it to me and I rip the bandaid off and read it for myself.

Theodore,

You turned twenty-five today and I want you to know I've thought about you every day for twenty-five years. There's not one that goes by that I don't wish things were different. And I'll admit, I've always hoped that when you were grown, you'd make the decision to come find me. Every attempt I've made in the past to form a relationship has been rejected and that's a lot for an old man like me to take.

I'm sending you this letter to let you know my door is always open. Even if it's another twenty-five years. If I'm still alive, and that's not a guilt trip, my old ticker ain't what it used to be…my door and my heart will always be open.

Teddy

My hand clutches my chest as I feel the pain from my Uncle Teddy's words bleed off the page. He wanted to know his son and I hurt for something he didn't get, because he was a good man and he deserved better than what he got.

"What will this mean in court?" I ask.

Mr. Terrell shakes his head. "Nothing, if we don't want to use it. The judge never has to know about this letter." He sighs, leaning back. "Off the record, I think this is a dig for gold. I've done a little digging myself and it seems as though Theo is in the real estate game and he's been losing lately. If I had to guess, he thought he could come back after all this time, contest the will, win because of his name and walk away with the spoils."

My heart drops to my stomach. "Will he be able to do that?"

"Sadly," Mr. Terrell says. "I've seen things like this go both ways. In all honesty, it could very well come down to the judge and how good his lawyers are."

"Do you know them?" I ask, pointing to the letterhead from the top of the original document I received in the mail.

"Yes," he says with another sigh and I don't like it one bit.

"And?"

"They're some of the best."

Fuck.

Shep

I'm over CeCe ignoring me. If there's something we need to talk about, I want to have it out and get past it. That's what married people do, right? They fight or argue—clear the air—and then have makeup sex.

That's what I want.

And I want it with CeCe.

I didn't even know I wanted that until her.

Just when I'm getting ready to pick up my phone and call her, there's a knock on my door.

Maybe she slipped away from the shop for a midday quickie. I did suggest it the other day when I stopped by to drop off her favorite muffalata from Central Grocery and she didn't seem completely opposed.

But even then, she was distracted.

Even when I kissed her, it's like there was a mental wall I couldn't get past. CeCe is always guarded, but the last week or so has been different.

Opening the door, I'm shocked, to say the least. "Finley?"

"Hey," he says, scratching the back of his head and looking unsure of himself, which isn't like him, especially not with me.

"What are you doing here?"

He shrugs, like he doesn't even know the answer to that himself. "I…well, your parents fired Maggie and she moved to Odessa to be with her sister. I didn't have a place to live and I didn't want to move to Odessa…so here I am."

There's a duffle bag and his saxophone case at his feet and if I had to guess, that's the extent of his belongings, but I'm still stuck on the part where he said my parents fired Maggie. "What do you mean they fired Maggie?"

"You didn't know?" he asks, a smidge of anger slipping through.

"Of course, I didn't know," I assure him, opening the door a little wider and reaching down for his bag, leaving the saxophone case to him. "Come in."

"I'm sorry to barge in on you like this, but when my grandma decided to leave, I had no choice but to leave too…and this was the only place I could think of coming."

"I'm glad you did," I tell him, giving his shoulder a tight squeeze. "I just can't believe they'd let her go…she's worked for them for so long. It doesn't make sense."

He barks a laugh and looks around the place. "Yeah, well, they're out to get you…any way they can. You know that, right?"

"What do you mean?" I ask, motioning for him to have a seat on the couch as I walk to the kitchen. "Beer?"

"Sure," he calls back. When I walk back in and hand him one, he's looking at me wearily. "Maggie was trying to keep quiet. You know she's loyal to your family…but she's more loyal to you than them."

I nod, cracking open my can and taking a drink. I feel like I'm going to need this to get through whatever bullshit he's going to dish.

"Well, she said she overheard your parents talking a couple of months ago about forcing you to marry Felicity Crawford," he says with a lift of his eyebrows as he opens his beer and takes a drink.

"Maggie knew you'd never go for it, but she didn't want to say anything when you were home because you had CeCe and she really likes her. She didn't want to cause trouble or make waves. It's not because she didn't want to warn you. Believe me, she did…but she needed her job."

"I know," I tell him. "I don't blame her. And my parents wanting to marry me off to Felicity Crawford doesn't surprise me one bit. But it doesn't really matter because I beat them at their game. Marrying CeCe was the best thing I ever did."

"I don't think your dad is going to stop trying to figure out a way to get his hands on your inheritance."

Leaning back in my seat, I chuckle darkly. "He can try, but he won't win."

"What if he tries to mess with you and CeCe?" he asks, worry evident on his face.

I sigh, running a hand through my hair. "Look, Finley, he can try, but it wouldn't matter. I think he's forgotten if I don't make it to a year, which I will…I plan on being married to CeCe for the rest of my life. But if it didn't work out, the one hundred million would go to charities. I've even thought about telling them to go ahead and make a donation. Over the past month, that money has become less and less important. Sure, it'd make business easier for me and Maverick. But we can make it without it." Taking another drink of my beer, I let my mind wander for a second before continuing. "I'm sorry Maggie lost her job, but truthfully, she's better off not being there. I won't have to worry about her as much. And if she needs money, I'll give it to her."

"She doesn't need money," Finley says quickly. "You've done enough. She's grateful and she wanted me to make sure you knew your father was plotting."

"Tell her thanks, but I'm going to be fine," I tell him confidently. Inheritance or no inheritance, I'll be fine. As long as I have CeCe, nothing else matters. She's the real prize in all of this. "What about you, though? You need a place to stay?"

He lets out a deep breath, resting his elbows on his knees. "I might," he admits. "I didn't really think it through, just hopped on the first bus out of Dallas and ended up here."

"You did the right thing," I tell him. "New Orleans is going to love you. And you can stay here as long as you need to."

"Thanks, man," Finley says. "For everything. I'm not sure where I'd be if it weren't for you."

That uncomfortable itch starts just like it does every time someone pays me an honest compliment and I blow it off. "Nah," I tell him, waving him off. "I just believed in you, that's all."

"It was more than anyone else had ever done."

CeCe

A VERY PREGNANT AVERY WADDLES INTO THE SHOP and my mood immediately lifts. "There's my baby mama," I call out, handing a customer their drink. "Thanks for coming in."

Avery gives me a weary smile when she makes it to the counter and I reach across to hold her hand. "You hanging in there?"

"No," she says, her voice quaking and I immediately hurry around the counter and pull her into a hug.

"Hey, hey," I soothe. "It's okay."

"Shaw won't let me go anywhere on my own," she cries into my shoulder. "Not that I want to go anywhere. It's hotter than forty hells and I'm as big as a whale. I mean, I'm surprised I fit in your door." Her cries grow louder and I give my lingering customers an apologetic smile, mouthing *pregnant women* over her shoulder. I would never let her see that. She cries about everything nowadays.

"Speaking of Shaw…" I glance out the window and see him wave at me before turning to walk back toward Come Again. I guess I'm on preggo duty, which is fine by me. I need the distraction. I need to think about something besides all of the crazy shit going on in my life right now.

"He dropped me off," Avery says, finally sniffling to dry up those tears. "Like I'm a little kid."

Pulling back, I take a look at her, smiling as I wipe under her eyes. "How about you have a seat and I'll make you a delicious smoothie."

"Fuck smoothies," she grumbles.

"A decaf iced cappuccino?"

She finally sits and crosses her arms over the beach ball she's toting around these days that holds my future godchild. I am going to be its godmother, even if I have to fight someone for the title. "A regular iced latte."

"Half caf," I counter.

"Deal."

Walking back around the counter, I get to work on making the best iced *fully decaffeinated* latte this pregnant woman has ever tasted. What she doesn't know won't hurt her.

Avery smiles up at me when I sit her drink down in front of her and sighs after the first sip. I leave her to it and go to help a few more customers before she finds her way back up to the counter. "Give me something to do," she demands. "If Shaw shows up to get me and I'm on my feet I'll never hear the end of it, but I have this crazy rush of energy…I feel like I need to clean something or organize something… *do something*. Maybe it's the espresso?"

I turn from her, hiding my lying smile.

"Man, I'm telling you, that stuff really is liquid gold," she continues. "I feel like a new woman."

Turning back around, I shake my head as I wipe down the counter. The foot traffic has slowed as the evening settles on the Square. At this time of day, most people are at the restaurants eating dinner or imbibing at the bars on Bourbon Street. I used to try and keep late hours, giving people somewhere to hang who didn't want to bar hop, but it wasn't very profitable for me and I ended up wearing myself out, burning the candle at both ends even more than normal.

"Here," I tell her, taking her the tray of coffee syrups and a warm towel, "wipe these down and make it quick. I don't want to be in trouble for letting a pregnant woman work."

She laughs, but she knows it's the truth. If we thought Shaw was protective before she got pregnant, we didn't know anything. He's fiercely protective and I honestly love it. No one deserves it more than Avery.

I'm crouched behind the counter taking inventory of paper goods when I hear the door open and the bell chime. My stomach does that weird flippy thing because this is the time of day Shep usually makes his appearance. I both love and hate it all at the same time.

I love it because there's no one I'd rather see at the end of the day and just the sight of him soothes my frayed edges.

I hate him for the same because I don't want to depend on him like that.

Temporary.

That's my word of the week. He's temporary. I'm trying to redirect my brain and my heart from the path they've been on lately, the one where Shep is the destination instead of a pit stop.

When I don't hear Avery greet anyone, I poke my head up to see a man in a suit, but not my man in a suit. "Hello, welcome to Neutral Grounds," I greet, wiping my hands down my apron and feeling every hour of the day weigh on my shoulders. Paige has been off for a few days to make up for all of the extra hours she's worked lately and I can tell.

Before her, the only other person who'd ever helped me was Avery, and that was only for a short time

Again, temporary.

Everyone is temporary.

"Can I get you something?" I finally ask when he doesn't approach the counter.

"Nice bones," he murmurs and I think I've for sure misunderstood him.

"I'm sorry?"

"Nice bones," he repeats, his eyes scanning the walls all the way up to the tall ceiling. "The building…it has nice bones, good structure." His tone is matter-of-fact, like he's confirming something he already knew and I cock my head in confusion. Don't get me wrong, I see my fair share of weirdos around here, but most of them are harmless. But this guy? He doesn't settle well with me.

I glance over at Avery who's now all ears, an eyebrow quirked in the man's direction.

"Yeah," I offer, glancing around at my shop…the metal shelving, odd and end merchandise, art I've hand-selected from local artists… everything about it is me and I find great pride in that.

"It'd make great apartments or office space," he adds. "That'd be a lot better use of this kind of square footage and layout."

Now, my hackles are up. How dare he come here and pick apart my coffee shop. The audacity of some people. "Well, I think my customers might disagree," I say, trying to keep a teasing edge to my voice, but I want to tell him to go fuck himself. That's the great part about being your own boss and the owner. You can do whatever you want. Sure, you'll reap the consequences, but they're all yours. "Can I get you an iced coffee or a pastry?" I ask, trying to shift the conversation to a safer topic.

"No," he says and I balk, crossing my arms over my chest in a defensive move.

"An ice water?" It's a last-ditch effort, but he doesn't bite. Instead, he smirks and takes a few steps closer and it's then I see the resemblance. I don't know how I missed it, but the nose and hairline are exactly like my Uncle Teddy's.

When he sticks out his hand, I hesitate for a moment. Not wanting to seem like a brat, I accept it and offer him a tight smile. "I'm Theodore Duval," he says expectantly, but I don't give him anything.

He's going to have to work for anything he gets, including my shop.

"CeCe Calhoun," I counter.

"I know." Stepping back, he shoves his hands in the pockets of his pants and he leans back on his heels as he continues to inspect the building, one I'm sure he has some sort of claim on. "Do you know who I am, CeCe?"

He's now verging on cocky and I don't like it. I know he's come here to intimidate me, but it's not going to work.

"I know exactly who you are," I reply calmly, coolly—taking a page out of Shep's handbook. Then I catch Avery's stare over Theo's shoulder. I feel her giving me a mental high five and I continue. "If you came here to see if I would back down, you've wasted your time, because I'm not going anywhere without a fight."

The condescending expression he turns on me makes me want to fly over this counter and pummel him. This guy has balls. I knew he did when I got that first letter. Anyone who'd come back to contest a will of his deceased father after never darkening his doors or even having the decency to attend his funeral, is more than ballsy. He's entitled and that's worse.

"I'll tell you what's going to happen here," he says, leaning his hands on my counter and forcing me to bite back a snarl that's begging to escape. "You're going to waste what little bit of savings you have on attorney fees and court costs and I'm still going to win, and you'll be left with nothing. Besides that, you'll be in debt and you won't have any choice but to go running back to your mama's double-wide."

He pauses and I seethe, my breath feeling like fire as it forcefully passes through my nose.

"So, how about you save us all this time and money and cut your losses?" We lock eyes and I know the second he sees the answer to that question. Lifting his hands off the counter, he backs away, a cynical laugh filling the quiet of the shop. The only other person in here is Avery and I'm thankful for her presence. I hate to admit it, but it gives me strength. "Suit yourself."

I'm so angry, I can't make my mouth work. My jaw is so tight, it's locked down, but I can't let him leave, thinking he got the last word. So, just before the door closes behind him, I call out.

"I'll see you in court!" Huffing, I blink a few times to get my bearings.

Avery stands and walks over to the counter, gripping my hand in hers. "Hey," she says, trying to get my attention but I can't look up at her. I'm too angry, and unfortunately, my anger often presents itself in the form of tears. "He's not going to win. Do you hear me?"

"I know," I say to the counter.

"And even if he does," she adds. "He'll still be the loser and you'll always have a place here."

Her words are both comforting and painful. I can't even let myself go there—me without this place. It's part of my identity. I'd hate having to walk by this building, one my Uncle Teddy worked so hard for and see it turned into some office building or whatever.

How sad.

How lifeless.

I have news for him, this place is mine—*my job, my livelihood, my business, my home*. Mine. My Uncle Teddy wanted me to have it and somehow, I'll prove it.

The door opens again and Shaw walks in. "What are you doing standing up?" he asks, more exasperated than angry as he walks up behind Avery and places his hands on her nonexistent waist, pulling her back into his chest.

"She's been sitting, I swear," I tell him, finally pulling my eyes up from the counter and trying to let go of the rush of emotions.

"What's wrong?" he asks, looking down at Avery and then back up at me.

I shake my head, smoothing my hair back. "Nothing, just an unwanted visitor."

Shaw's expression grows dark and he turns Avery around to get a good look at her.

"Nothing like you're thinking," she says, knowing to talk fast before he overreacts. He's good at that. "That dickwad who thinks he's going to take the shop from CeCe stopped by. You just missed him."

"What the fuck," he swears, running a hand through his hair, reminding me an awful lot of Shep.

I wish he was here.

I need him.

I want to sink into his warm embrace and forget the whole world exists…just for a while.

He's the only one who can do that for me. He's the only one I trust enough to let myself be so exposed and raw with. I know he'll take care of me.

When the bell rings on the door again, I don't even have to look, I just know.

"Hey," Shep says and I'm forced to meet his gaze, his voice is like a locator beacon for me. I have no choice but to heed the call.

"Hey," I say, my shoulders sinking in defeat. All the walls I've tried to erect between us over the past few weeks begin to crumble. I just can't do it tonight. I need him too much.

"We're going to go," Shaw says, drawing me away from Shep and back to the present. "You okay?"

"I'm fine," I tell him. "Make sure this one gets home and gets some rest."

Walking around the counter, I pull Avery into a hug.

"Don't let that asshole get to you," she whispers but Shep hears.

"What asshole?" he asks, looking from me to Shaw.

Shaw walks toward the door, ushering Avery ahead of him. I'm surprised he doesn't just swoop her up and carry her. Actually, he's probably tried, but that would never fly with her. "The asshole that's trying to contest the will."

"What?" Shep asks, eyes back on me—hard and angry. "He was here?"

"We'll see y'all later," Shaw calls out.

Avery adds, "Call you tomorrow."

Once the door shuts, I walk over and lock it, leaning my forehead against the weathered wood.

"Why didn't you call me?" Shep asks, that same hurt from the day he found out I went home and didn't invite him is back in his tone and it makes me feel horrible.

"He just left about five minutes before you walked in," I tell him, my attention still turned toward the dark sidewalk in front of the shop. "I don't really want to talk about it."

"What did he say?" he asks, persisting.

Groaning, I turn around and lean against the door. "He was just trying to scare me into rolling over and playing dead."

He closes his eyes and breathes out a fuck under his breath. "Son of a bitch."

"Literally, from what I hear," I say, trying to bring some levity to the situation, but Shep's not having it.

"I'm goin—"

"You're going to take me upstairs and help me forget this whole day," I say as I take a few steps toward him, reaching out to grip the hem of his shirt—untucked and totally un-Shep. At least, not like the Shep I met two years ago. But the Shep I know today is a different man…same, but different. He's lost the shiny persona and perfectly tailored suits. The real him is a little scruffy and unkempt in a white button-down shirt and jeans. He's not perfect. He's real.

And even more desirable.

His jaw is still set in a hard angle when I reach up on my tiptoes and kiss his neck, pausing momentarily to appreciate the feel of his scruff before moving up until my lips are on his. It doesn't take long for him to get on board and his arms come around my waist, pulling me to him.

When our mouths open, taking each other in, we both sigh in relief…gratitude…want.

It's been a while and it's obvious we both need this.

The kiss starts slow and languid—tasting, exploring, appreciating—but quickly turns desperate and needy. My stomach leaps into my throat when Shep's hands leave my back and grip my ass, picking me up and forcing me to latch onto him with my legs to keep from falling.

"Lights," I breathe out between kisses as we approach the stairs.

Shep stops briefly and swats at the light switch, bathing the shop in darkness and casting shadows over us. In the dimly lit staircase, Shep's lashes cast a shadow on his cheeks and I can't help but force his head down so I can kiss them.

The moment turns soft and meaningful as we share breaths in silence.

Words aren't spoken, but feelings are expressed.

I missed you.

I need you.

I want you.

Please.

Since the first time I had sex with Shep, he's always known what I wanted before I did, meeting my needs without me having to ask. This time is no different.

Pressing my back against the wall, he uses it to hold me in place while he rips my apron off and pulls my t-shirt over my head. His mouth immediately goes to my breasts—licking and sucking through my thin bra and making every cell in my body stand at attention.

Yes.

When I thread my hands through the strands of his hair, which is longer than usual, I press him closer. "More," I plead. "I need more."

Dropping my legs, he unfastens my jeans and pushes them down my legs.

"Step out," he instructs, his voice thick and gruff, sounding like liquid sex. I do as he asks and am immediately rewarded with his mouth on my sensitive flesh. There in the hallway of the shop, with a perfectly good bedroom just up the stairs, Shepard Rhys-Jones sends me to heaven with his tongue and brings me down to hell with his fingers.

"Shep," I call out when he's sucking my clit and pumping two fingers in tandem, playing my body like it's an instrument and he's the maestro. When my legs begin to shake under the intense tidal waves of pleasure, I pant his name and feel like crying and laughing all at the same time.

It shouldn't feel this good. Nothing should. It should be illegal.

"Come for me, CeCe," Shep says before slipping his tongue back between my folds.

With his words ringing in my ear and his fingers buried inside me—hitting just the right spot—I come hard. It hits me like a freight train and obliterates my body. I can't even focus as I quake from the aftershock, but do when I hear the unzipping of Shep's jeans. And then I feel his tight grip as he lifts me up and centers his cock at my entrance.

The tip grazes my overly sensitive flesh and I cry out—not in pain, but in pleasure—begging for it as he teases me, rubbing himself through my wetness. "Please… I need you."

"You have me," Shep says. "All of me. Anything you want."

When he thrusts inside, I exhale in relief. Even though I just had one of the best orgasms of my life, this is what I wanted. Skin to skin. Heat to heat. Me and him. A connection I can't even put into words, but it's there and it's real and it's us.

I might regret this in the morning, but for tonight, I'm going to take as much as he'll give me.

Shep

I WAKE EARLY WITH MORNING WOOD AND AN ARM I can't feel. CeCe is curled against me, naked and impossibly beautiful, especially in the pale light that leaks into her bedroom from the street lamps below. I'd love nothing more than to stay and make love to her again before we start our day, but I have something I need to do and there's reconnaissance to be done before I can make that happen.

Plus, I think she might fight me on my decision and I'd rather ask forgiveness than permission for my actions.

I'm still gunning for make-up sex.

Every other type of sex with CeCe has been out of this world, life changing. Whatever last night was set the bar high. Sure, we've had more erotic nights together, but last night had a level of emotion and need to it that made me want to open up my chest and allow her to climb inside.

She needed something from me and I hope I gave it to her. I meant it when I said I'd give her anything, including what I'm planning on doing today.

When I slip out of the bed, CeCe stirs and then her fucking alarm clock goes off.

Shit.

"Time to make the donuts," she mumbles before rolling over and searching the bed for me.

I can't help but chuckle. She's so fucking adorable in the morning with her raspy voice and sleep-mussed hair. The way it falls into her eyes, covering half her face is basically morning porn. It makes me want to flip her over and take her from behind, gripping that wild mane of hair in my fist.

Another day.

We'll have plenty of chances for that.

"Where are you going?" she asks, sitting up and letting the sheet fall to her waist, exposing the creamy white skin of her bare breasts and making my mouth water.

Clearing my throat, I shake my head and continue buttoning my shirt. "I forgot to tell you that Finley showed up yesterday."

"What?" she asks, rubbing her eyes and sweeping her hair out of her face, trying to get awake. "Here? Did you know he was coming?"

"No," I tell her, searching for my shoes and then remembering I kicked them off by the door. "I was actually on my way to see you when he knocked."

"Is he okay?" She's always so perceptive, always worried about other people. It's a shining quality in CeCe Calhoun, one I'd like to rub off on me. She makes me want to be a better human.

Turning to her, I kneel on the bed and cup her face in my hands, kissing her lips lightly, slowly. Neither of us have time for more, so I keep it as innocent as possible while still getting my morning dose of CeCe. "He's fine, but my parents fired Maggie," I say quietly. "He didn't have anywhere else to go and he also wanted to warn me about some plan my father claims to have."

She stiffens and I pull back to look at her. "What?" I ask.

"A plan…" she says, drifting off and climbing out of bed. With her pacing the bedroom naked, it takes everything in me to not go caveman on her—throwing her over my shoulder and taking her back to my lair. "He mentioned that the night we danced at our reception. I meant to tell you, but we flew back late and then…well, you know," she says, alluding to our night together at my house after Dallas.

That weekend and following night at my house pretty much sealed the deal for me that she's mine and she always will be.

"Everything has been such a whirlwind since…I kind of blocked your father from my mind. I needed that space for other things," she mutters absentmindedly. "What's his plan?"

Her eyes go to mine and they're wide and worried.

Walking over to her, I fold her in my arms, placing her head under my chin and holding her to me, loving the way her body fits against mine and the way she smells—part her, part me…wholly us. "Don't worry about it. I'm not," I assure her.

"Okay," she says, relaxing into me. "I have to get downstairs and get things going." Her tone is reluctant and her words don't match the tight grip she has on the back of my shirt.

"I do too," I mumble against her hair before kissing the top of her head. "But I'll be back later."

A bit of her walls seem to slide back into place when I step away and look back at her from the door. I assume she's overthinking my father's plan or worried about Maggie being fired, so I leave it alone. When she doesn't say anything, I tap the door frame. "Call me if you need me."

She nods, but her eyes don't meet mine and I don't like it.

"CeCe?" I ask, drawing her attention to me. "You okay?"

What I want to ask is are *we* okay? I hate when she pulls away from me like that, especially after nights like last night.

"I'm fine," she says, offering me a half smile. "I'll…I'll talk to you later."

When she turns to head into the bathroom to get ready for the day, I see myself out.

I spent the better part of the day using mine and Maverick's connections around town to locate Theo Duval. He actually wasn't that hard to find. Mav made a call to Hotel Monteleone, and after kissing a few people's asses, he found out Theo was scheduled to check out tomorrow morning, which means I need to act fast.

The sale on my house in Dallas closed a few days ago and the money hit my account this morning, which feels like perfect timing because I'm going to need the cash flow for what I have planned.

Hopping out of the cab, I slip the guy a twenty and adjust the cuffs of my suit. Lately, I've been living in jeans, but that won't cut it for this. I need to look the part and play up the Rhys-Jones name, using it to my advantage.

As I walk into the illustrious foyer, I glance around before heading to the Carousel Bar. This place has always puzzled me. The fact that the carousel literally spins as booze is served seems like it would be problematic. Yet, people flock here. Thankfully, today seems to be a slower one and I scan the place for a balding man in a three-piece suit.

Maverick's source said he'd be here.

With the bar turning, I wait for a full revolution before turning on my heels and deciding he's not there. I'm not leaving until I find the bastard, so I make my way over to a sitting area and wait.

People mill around, some are staying at the hotel, others are here to see the grandiose chandeliers and the sparkling lobby. There are women dressed to the nines and men checking them out. One, in particular, garners my attention and I know it's Theo.

He's stockier than he looked in his photo online, but aren't most people.

Social media is the worst thing that ever happened to our society.

"Mr. Duval," I say, standing as he goes to pass me.

His head swivels and he meets me with a squinted stare, obviously trying to place me. "I'm Shepard Rhys-Jones." I offer my hand and he shakes it, but the hold is too dainty for my liking and I have to force myself to not outwardly cringe. Get a fucking grip, man, literally.

You can't do business with a flimsy handshake.

A dead fish handshake—the ultimate faux pas in business.

"I don't believe we've met," he says, hesitantly looking around.

"No, we haven't, but I have a proposition for you."

When his eyebrows shoot up in interest, I know he's going to be an easy sell.

Too eager.

Too greedy.

I've known men like him my entire life. If there's one thing I can thank my father for, it's experience. By working my way up through our company, I've had the privilege of working with a variety of people from varying backgrounds.

Mr. Duval is your typical overachiever who doesn't have the right skills to master his craft.

If I had to guess, he had a few lucky deals in the beginning or some sort of windfall. Then, he got in too deep with no safety net. Now, he's pushing fifty and struggling to keep his head above water. On any given day, he's more than likely one deal short of bankruptcy.

"Let's have a seat." Motioning to a secluded seating area, I allow him to walk ahead.

Even though he has a good twenty years on me, I have more experience in my pinky than he has in his whole fucking body. I can tell by the way he's already eating out of the palm of my hand. A true businessman would never show their cards this early in the game.

"What's this about?" he asks as we both take a seat. "I'm a very busy man."

Sure you are, fucker.

"The commercial property on St. Louis Street," I tell him, cutting to the chase. There's no sense skirting the issue at hand. I'm also a very busy man. "How much would it take for you to walk away?"

His expression grows confused before turning skeptical.

"What do you know about that property?"

"Enough," I tell him, not wanting to give away any more than I have to.

Clearing his throat, he looks around and adjusts his suit coat over his protruding stomach as the tiny beads of sweat on his forehead multiply. "It's not mine to sell…yet, but when it is, I'd be willing to let go of it for one-point-five."

Inwardly, I smirk, because I would've paid him two million, but now he's going to accept one.

"I tell you what," I say, leaning back to present a more relaxed front. "I'll give you seven-fifty to walk away now."

He cocks his head back and I think he's going to actually stutter, but quickly collects himself and counters with, "What makes you think I'd walk away?"

"You're obviously desperate and it's going to cost you at least two-fifty in legal fees to see this thing through. So, I give you seven-fifty today, you walk and save yourself the headache of fighting a losing battle." When it fully registers what I'm offering and implying, his plump face turns a darker shade of red. "On the off chance you win," I add with a tilt of my head, expressing my doubt. "There will still be the painstaking process of putting it on the market and finding the right buyer. After you pay commission on a piece like that, you're looking at a profit of about a million dollars, give or take a couple hundred thousand. So, the way I see it, you take my offer, sign an agreement I'll have my lawyer send over, and be done with this whole mess."

We sit in silence for a moment, the tension so thick you could cut it with a knife, but I love it. I live for deals like this. It's kind of like a game of Monopoly, but with real money.

Let's make a fucking deal.

"One and a quarter," he counters.

With my arms stretched on the chair behind me, I lock eyes with him, begging him to break, wanting to see him squirm. When he does, I soak in the silent victory.

"One, and that's my final offer."

He sticks his hand across for me to shake, entirely too eager for my liking. If I was him, I'd have made one last-ditch effort to try and get closer to my asking price, which just goes to show he doesn't know what the fuck he's doing. But finally, I meet him halfway and accept the handshake.

When he holds on longer than is customary, I draw my brows together in question. For a second, I think he's going to tell me to go fuck myself, but instead, he asks, "What's in this for you?"

I shrug, trying to keep my cards close to my chest.

"So, you pay me a million to walk away, and then what?"

"Nothing."

He's confused again and I see his wheels turning. "What's she to you?"

"She's my wife." It comes out more lethal than I intended, but I hope it's enough of a warning. I hope he understands if he ever darkens her door again or thinks for a second about reneging on our deal, I'll come after him.

And next time, it'll be for blood.

Fuck the money.

Nobody messes with CeCe and gets away with it.

CeCe

I GOT THE CALL AN HOUR AGO FROM A FRANTIC Sarah, letting me know that Avery's water broke and Shaw was driving her to the hospital.

I called Paige and offered her double-time to cover for me on short notice and as soon as she got there, I ran to the Blue Bayou and Carys and I hopped in a cab. We've been pacing the waiting room, practically wearing the shine off the linoleum floor ever since.

Sarah and Paulie are keeping the bar and the cooking school running. Shaw is back with Avery. Maverick and Jules are taking care of the Blue Bayou until the baby gets here. And I'm not sure where Shep is. I called him once and texted twice.

Carys said he stopped by the hotel this morning but he and Maverick stayed locked in the office until he left.

I'm sure he'll call when he can.

After last night and this morning, I had every intention of telling him I want out.

It's too much.

I can't stay married to him only to have my heart decimated when things between us come to an end.

And they will. Of that, I'm sure.

But now, with Avery having the baby and needing her support system to be intact, I don't want to make waves.

I know my friends will support me, regardless of my decisions, but I want to break things off with Shep in a way that leaves the least damage. Part of me wants to hold onto as much of him as I can. I want the cliché. I want to still be friends. But the other part of me wants to run away and change my name, because I have no clue how I'll look at him and not crumble.

My hope is he'll move on, find someone else to marry, get his one hundred million dollars and be happy.

That's what I want, right?

I'm not sure anymore, but that's the story I've been telling myself. It's the only logical course of action. I even made a pros and cons list a few days ago.

Pros of divorcing Shep:

He's freed up to marry someone else who will play the part much better than me.

Everything can go back to normal, as soon as I figure out this business with the will contest and find a way to keep my life intact.

I'll be able to get back to basics—taking care of myself and my family.

He'll get back to his life.

I'll get my safety net firmly back in place.

Cons of divorcing Shep:

I'm going to miss him.

And there's a solid chance I'll never marry again.

And I'm going to miss that too.

But this temporary pain is worth it to avoid having it multiplied. If we were to continue in this agreement, I'd be so in love with him there would be nothing left of me when he walks away. I'm not that reckless or selfish. I'm not my mother. People depend on me and I can't let them down. If I did, where would that leave them?

"Avery Cole's family," a nurse calls out and Carys and I immediately turn for the door. "It's not quite time, but we're close. She's dilated to a nine and we're going to start pushing soon." She smiles. "I promised Avery I'd keep y'all updated."

"Thank you," we say in unison.

When she leaves, Carys turns and studies me. "What are you thinking about?"

She's always been able to read me like a book. There's no sense lying to her because I'm sure my inner turmoil is written all over my face. It's another reason I've been avoiding Shep like the plague.

I sigh, looking back to the door the nurse disappeared behind and think about lying, but I can't. "I'm thinking…" I pause, swallowing down the lump that forms every time I think about it, let alone say it. "I think I'm going to ask Shep for a divorce."

The confession is barely above a whisper, but Carys hears me loud and clear.

"What? Why?" she asks, her eyes growing wide as she walks closer to me. There's disappointment and sadness on her face that I didn't expect. I thought she'd sigh in relief or maybe tell me she was wondering when I'd come to my senses. "You're…well, you seem like you're getting along so well. And it's only been a couple of months. Don't you want to give it more time?"

Slowly lowering myself to a chair, I can't make eye contact with her so I keep my attention focused on the door. "I can't." It's the only thing I can manage. I feel the tears threatening to make their presence known.

"Is he that horrible to be married to?" she asks, sitting beside me and knocking her knee against mine, trying to get me to snap out of the melancholy, but it doesn't work.

"That's the problem," I admit. "He's really great to be married to. The best husband I've ever had." A soft, sad chuckle escapes and I wipe my thumb under my eye, trapping a lone tear.

"Oh, CeCe," Carys soothes, reaching over and grabbing my hand.

"Honey, what's wrong?"

"I can't do this, Carys. I thought I could, but I can't. I'm falling for him and I'm so freaking scared. I've tried to turn it off and force myself to think of this as the arrangement I agreed to, but I can't. Every day, it becomes more and more real. He's becoming...*everything*. And you know me, I don't work like that. I can't just give myself to him and wait to collect all the pieces when it's over at the end of a year."

"What if it doesn't have to be over?" Carys asks, voicing my deepest desire, one I haven't let myself even consider. "I think he might surprise you. He's surprised me." She smiles, shaking her head in dismay. "I've known Shep for a while and a year or so ago, I would've told you he was a perpetual bachelor, never getting married, but seeing the way he is with you changes my mind. You should talk to him about it. Don't you owe him that much?"

Chewing on my lip to keep from crying, I turn to her. "I don't know, Carys..." I try not to let her words give me false hope. She's such a hopeless romantic and I know she wants me to have what she has, but I'm afraid she's seeing it all wrong. "I think there's a part of Shep that would tell me anything I want to hear to keep me from leaving before he gets his inheritance. I don't blame him for it...it's a part of him he can't control. But I'm not stupid enough to believe this is anything more than what I signed up for."

Her hold on my hand tightens and I squeeze back.

"I...I feel like I'm jumping off a cliff without a parachute...and the ground is too close and there's no safety net...How can anyone feel this and not want to run the other way?"

She gives me a sad smile. "It's called falling in love."

"Maybe I'm not meant to? Maybe I'm destined to always be single? I think I'm wired differently than everyone else...there's obviously something fundamentally wrong with me."

There has to be, because no one in their right mind would walk away from Shepard Rhys-Jones.

He's definitely worth the fall.

An hour or so later, the nurse comes back to the waiting room and gives us a wide smile. "The baby is here," she says, motioning for us to follow her. "And the mama is asking for the two of you.

Carys and I give each other hopeful smiles, partly due to happiness for Avery and the bundle of joy…and partly due to our conversation. I push the latter to the back of my mind for now and focus my attention on my new godson…or daughter. The anticipation is killing me.

When the nurse opens the door to Avery's room, Carys and I both gasp but stay put in the doorway. Avery is sitting up in her bed, holding a tiny bundle, and it's the most natural and beautiful thing I've ever seen. I feel like, if we step inside, we'll burst the perfect bubble they're in so I'm completely content to stay here and watch from the sidelines. I assume Carys feels the same because she still hasn't moved either, except to brush my hand with hers and look at me with tears in her eyes, mirroring my own.

"Are you two gonna come and meet my son or what?" Avery finally asks, laughing. She looks so beautiful. That pregnancy glow she's been sporting has nothing on this.

"Are you sure it's okay?" Carys asks timidly.

"Of course, it is, silly! Just make sure you wash your hands first before you hold him."

That snaps us out of our trance and we both walk into the room quietly, but with great purpose. Carys and I agreed earlier I'd be the one to hold the baby first since I'll be the godmother, so I head to the sink to wash my hands while she sits in a chair by Avery's bed.

"Aww, he's so cute! Does he have a name yet?" Carys asks, peeking over Avery's shoulder and looking at the baby.

"He does. Ladies, meet Shae Brady O'Sullivan."

Avery hands Shae to me and when I look down at his precious, sleeping face, I absolutely melt. "Oh, Avery, he's the most beautiful baby I've ever seen." And, he is. Pink, chubby cheeks, pouty lips, and a dark smattering of hair, Shae is a perfect combination of his parents.

I can feel my ovaries warming up, but quickly push those thoughts out of my head. Just like I never thought I'd get married, I also have never thought much about having kids of my own. It always seems like something other women did, not me. But, now, I can't help but wonder what it'd be like to have a baby—Shep's baby—and I start tearing up again.

Gah, I'm all over the place today. One minute, I'm plotting to divorce him and the next, I'm wanting a baby with him.

Fuck.

Thankfully, I can play off my watery eyes by turning my attention back to the angel in my arms. "Uh, Avery, is something wrong with his eyes? He looks like he's already had his first fistfight."

"Yeah, about that…see, he was coming *fast* and I was having major contractions," she says, reaching over for her cup of ice chips. "Those things really do hurt like hell, by the way…don't let anyone ever tell you they don't…it's bullshit." Smoothing her hair away from her face, she continues. "Anyway, Shaw was about to lose his shit, so the doctor allowed me to get an epidural, but it didn't stop the pain. So, I was given another dose and then, later, another and then I was so numb, I couldn't feel anything from the waist down."

She pauses, slightly out of breath, and Carys and I share a look that says maybe we'll opt for c-sections when it's our turn to push a baby out of our vaginas.

"Seriously, I couldn't feel my legs. I still can't! When it came time to push, Shae was already crowning so I didn't have to work very hard. Poor thing, he went through the birth canal so fast, he gave himself black eyes!"

I look back down at the baby, hoping my giggles aren't bothering him, but he's still sleeping soundly. "Already a bruiser, huh, Shae? Don't worry, you'll be a lover, not a fighter. I'll make sure of it."

"Speaking of Shaw," Carys starts, "where is he? I'm surprised he's not here hogging the baby already."

"Right?" Avery laughs and it makes me so happy to see her like this. It was a tough road for her and Shaw, but it's obvious it was worth it. "He went to get cigars for everyone but should be back soon."

"Well, we brought you something to help celebrate but it's totally cool if you want to wait before having it," Carys says, walking back to the door and grabbing the small cooler she brought with her.

"What is it?" Avery eyes the cooler, looking equal parts excited and worried.

"We brought you sushi and a small box of wine because you can now have them again!"

"You guys are so great! Thank you!" Avery wipes her eyes and laughs. "Ugh, stupid hormones. My nurse said it'll still be a while before they get back to normal, much to Shaw's dismay."

"Don't worry, we'll be here to help in any way we can," I assure her.

After a few minutes, I pass Shae off to Carys so she can have a turn and then pull another chair up beside Avery. "That baby looks good on you," I tell her, feeling her happiness radiate all over the room. It's kind of rubbing off on me.

"He's the best thing I've ever done or will ever do," she says, looking over at him with so much love it makes my chest ache.

The second Shaw is back in the room, he immediately steals Shae and snuggles in on the edge of Avery's bed. He kind of consumes the room and it's obvious we're no longer needed.

"We'll let y'all rest," Carys says. "Don't forget about your contraband sushi and wine."

Shaw's eyebrows shoot up in question and I roll my eyes.

"She's no longer with child, let the woman have her reward."

"Besides," Carys adds, "we don't smoke cigars, so give us a break on the sushi and wine."

We kiss Avery goodbye, promising to return the next day and making them promise in return that they'll call us if they need anything.

"I'll check with Sarah and make sure their meals are covered for the next week or so," I tell Carys as we ride down the elevator.

"Sounds good," she says. "Let me know if I need to make something. I'm sure Mary wouldn't mind either."

When we make it to the parking lot to wait on our cab, I check my phone to see if Shep ever called or texted me back. Sure enough, I have a text waiting.

Shep: Call me.

"Shep?" Carys asks, eyeing my phone.

"Yeah."

"What are you going to do?"

"I don't know." And that's the truth. One second, I'm dead set on ending it and moving on with my life, and the next, I'm thinking about forever and wondering if I could possibly have that with Shep.

Instead of calling him, I text him once we're in the cab and let him know that Shae is here and he's a boy and he's healthy. He immediately replies back that he'll meet me at the shop and I try to keep my heart from beating out of my chest with indecision.

"You gonna be okay?" Carys asks as we stand outside of the Blue Bayou.

"I'll be fine," I assure her.

"Call me if you need me."

I give her a quick wave, turning and heading toward Neutral Grounds. I'm still a good hundred feet away when I spot Shep's tall frame and blond hair standing outside the shop.

Even dressed down, he's stunning. When he turns toward me and smiles, my resolve crumbles a little.

"So, you're a new godmother," he states with a proud smile.

"I am," I confirm. "Even if I have to fight Sarah over it. That baby is mine."

He laughs and it's throaty and deep and everything good in the world.

"I have some more good news for you," he says, walking over to the bench that faces the shop.

Sitting down, he pats the spot beside him and I hesitantly sit, feeling the nerves and uncertainty coming back in full force. "What's the news?"

"I had a talk with Theo today."

"What?" I ask. "Why?"

Shep shrugs. "We talked…business."

My stomach drops, just like it always does when I think about Theo Duval and the threat he poses to me and my life as I know it. "Wh—what kind of business?"

"Let's just say I made him an offer he couldn't refuse and you won't be hearing from him again."

My stomach that was at my feet is now in my throat. "You what?"

Confusion paints his expression as he takes in my obvious state of duress. "I offered him a million dollars to walk away. Being the greedy bastard he is, he took it."

Everything feels like it's spinning…and in slow motion. I'm struggling to get a grip on exactly what he's telling me. "You paid him off…" It's not a question. It's a statement. Shep's news is starting to come in loud and clear. He fucking paid Theo off. "Why would you do that?"

I'm now standing, pacing the pavement in front of the bench where Shep is still sitting, staring at me like I'm a ticking time bomb. I might be. My heart is racing in my chest and my mind is reeling.

"I did it for you," Shep says like it's the simplest explanation in the world. "I wanted to make things easier on you and there was no fucking way I was letting someone swoop in and steal your business out from under you. Not on my watch."

Now he sounds mad, angry that I'm not understanding him.

"Except now, you basically own my shop…you own my life!" My words sound crazy to my own ears, so I know they sound crazy to him. People are staring, I feel their eyes on me, but I don't care. For today, I'll be another sideshow on the square. "This is my shop…my life. I'll either make it or break it, but I do it on my own."

"I don't want anything from you," Shep grounds out. "All I want is for you to be happy. Can't you see there's no ulterior motive here? I saw a problem and I fixed it, end of story."

"You should've asked me first!" I yell, feeling like my head is about to explode. "You can't go behind my back like that."

He gets a guilty look on his face and I really start to see red.

"You knew," I seethe. "You knew I wouldn't want you to do that, but you did it anyway. Is this some sick, twisted way to make sure I stay married to you for the rest of the year? An insurance policy for your inheritance?"

"No!" He throws his hands up and then runs one through his hair.

We're quite the pair, both of us up in arms and yelling like a couple of lunatics.

"What happens after this arrangement is over?" I ask, needing to get down to the root of the problem. It's time to lay it all out in the open. "What then?"

"I'm in this," he says, but his back is turned to me and I need to see his face to really know what he's thinking and how he's feeling. "I'm all in."

"For how long, Shep?" My palms slap my thighs as I try to get his attention, but he continues to give me his back and all I can figure is he doesn't want to lie to my face.

"No one is ever permanent in your life. I've heard it all these years from you…and Maverick. Why would I be any different? Your track record speaks for itself. So, sure, you're in it now, but for how long? Because, you know what? I don't want to be around when you decide you've got your hundred mil and you don't want to be married anymore. It'll be too late for me then, because I'm already falling… and I know if I were to let myself fall completely, when you walk away, it'll kill me. I'll be just like my mother, but I won't have a ten-year-old daughter to pick up the pieces for me and keep my life going. So, no…I don't want this. Find somebody else. There are plenty of people who would be more than willing to marry you for far less than a million dollars."

When he doesn't turn around or reply, I take that as my answer and walk into the shop and straight up the stairs.

I'm done.

Shep

Fuck.

I stand with my back to the shop, to CeCe, trying to get a grip on the anger I feel churning in my gut. When I hear her footsteps depart, there's a pull to go after her, but I fight the urge because I have no fucking clue what just happened or how to fix it.

When I finally turn back around, my eyes go to the window, looking for a glimpse of her, but she's nowhere to be seen and instead I find Paige, staring out the window with a confused look on her face.

What the fuck just happened?

Rubbing at my chest, I realize my heart is pounding like I just ran a few miles, and my mind is spinning. The thought crossed my mind that she'd be a little pissed, but I never dreamed she'd lose her shit like that. Kicking the bench, I growl out my frustration and then brace my hands on my knees, trying to get a fucking grip.

Leave it to me, the man with zero relationship experience, to fuck all of this up so spectacularly.

What I had intended on being a grand gesture ended up being an epic failure.

As I rake my hand through my hair, I turn to look out over Jackson Square and then back to the shop, considering going in there and demanding she talk to me. She can't just walk away from me like that...we're married. That's not how this works.

I want to fight it out with her.

I want to somehow make her understand I did this for her and I have no intentions of staking a claim on Neutral Grounds or her building. I don't want anything out of this, except for her and her happiness. But I have no idea how to do that.

Her words come back to haunt me—*I don't want this. Find somebody else.*

She can't really mean that, right?

Surely she doesn't really mean that. There was that part about her falling for me...but if she was really falling, why would she walk away? Why would she push me away?

As I begin to aimlessly walk around the square, I try to imagine how I'd feel if she were to follow through and move on without me. The pain in my chest is immediate. The mere thought of CeCe with someone else—loving someone else, spending her life with someone else—has me wincing.

No way.

Now that I've had her and know what it's like to be with her, there's no way I can even entertain the thought of being with someone else... or her being with someone else. Just the idea makes my stomach roll and my blood pump even faster.

At some point, I eventually stop walking and take my eyes off the pavement in front of me to see I'm standing in front of Come Again. Thankfully, the universe got something right today by leading me here. I could use some liquid courage to deal with this onslaught of emotions and feelings, because I have no fucking clue how to handle them on my own.

Pushing my way into the bar, I immediately feel a small sense of comfort. In my short stint as a resident of New Orleans, this place has become a familiar fixture, always being the central location for happy occasions. I don't want to taint it today with my fucked-up mood, but I don't know where else to go.

Sure, I could go to the hotel and unload on Maverick. He's never turned me away before, but for some reason, it doesn't feel right. Carys is CeCe's best friend and Maverick cares for her like a sister. And right now, I just need an unobjective ear—someone who's not going to berate me for messing everything up.

And I need booze.

"Hey, Shep," Paulie greets as I slide into a seat at the end of the bar. "You look like shit," he declares as he goes about his job of making drinks.

My only response is a sigh as I run a hand down my face and back up into my hair.

That's all I've got.

I don't have it in me to speak or make a request, but a few minutes later, three fingers of bourbon show up in front of me. "Drink that and then we'll talk."

Doing as he instructed, I take healthy sips of the amber liquid, letting its warmth soothe the fragments of my psyche, hoping for clarity. But by the time I get to the bottom of the glass, my mind is still a muddled mess.

Once a few of the patrons clear the bar, Paulie walks over, tossing a towel down and bracing his hands on the weathered wood in front of me. "So, how bad did you screw up?"

Smirking sardonically, I shake my head and push my glass toward him. While he gives me another pour, I begin with, "Pretty fucking bad, apparently."

"Apparently?" he asks, giving me a chuckle. "You don't know?"

"Fuck me." I groan, giving my face another rough scrub down. "No, I don't know. I thought I was helping, but I'm pretty sure that's not what she wanted. And now…"

"You're fucked?"

Accepting the full glass, I take another drink before answering, "Thoroughly."

"Tell me about it," he says, making himself comfortable as he leans against the bar behind him, another bartender taking over his duties. So, I do. I fill in the bits and pieces of the backstory with Theo that Paulie didn't already know. Then I tell him about meeting up with him and paying him off, forcing him into signing an agreement stating he won't have any further contact with CeCe and will drop the will contest.

At that, Paulie's brows go up and I know right then I'm the only person on the face of the planet that thought it was a good idea. When he whistles, I inwardly cringe.

"That bad, huh?" I ask, finishing off my second glass.

He pushes off the bar and shakes his head. "I don't know CeCe as well as everyone else, but I'm a little…observant, I guess you could say. Occupational hazard. I watch people and read people." He pauses, glancing across the bar and then back to me. "One thing I've always noticed about her is she takes care of other people, but no one ever takes care of her. She's self-reliant to a fault. So, my guess is that you coming in like a fucking knight in shining armor and treating her like a damsel in distress was too much for her to handle. Not to mention, you fucked with her business and like everyone else around here, that's personal. These people—Shaw, Carys, CeCe—see their business like a member of the family. And you don't mess with family."

"I know she's not the kind of woman who can be bought and I swear that's not what I was doing. I honestly thought I was taking out the trash…removing the shit from her life so she wouldn't have to worry about it anymore…I thought I was helping," I grit out, my frustration growing with each passing second. I feel like I'm speaking a foreign language and no one understands me. "How is me paying off Theo to get him off her back wrong? Help me understand, because right now, I feel like I'm losing my goddamn mind!"

"CeCe is a different breed," Paulie says in a calm, even tone, not even responding to my outburst. "You're going to have to go after her in a different way. Buying her affection won't work. Interfering with her business will definitely not work. She sees it as a threat…like she's now in debt to you with a million dollars standing between her and her livelihood. You're going to have to find a different way to help her see that you're in this for good." He pauses for a second, giving me time to process what he's saying, before he asks, "You *are* in this for good, right?"

The way he stares at me with his hard, no-nonsense expression makes me sit back, putting a little distance between us as I think before I speak. "I want to be," I tell him honestly. "I want to be married to her more than I want… anything."

"Then find a way to show her…and not with your fucking trust fund."

How the fuck do I do that?

Later, on my walk home, I go back to Neutral Grounds, maybe to torture myself that I can't go up and crawl into bed with her or maybe I was hoping her light would be on and I'd text her…and she'd tell me to come up and we'd talk it out and have that makeup sex I've been meaning to have.

But none of that happens.

The entire building is dark, just like the street. It's late and the only people who are still out at this time of night are drunk, like me.

Actually, I'm not quite there, even though I wanted to be, Paulie cut me off after a few glasses, telling me it was for my own good. And fuck if I don't have a little more respect for the man after tonight. He helped me think through some of the shit going on in my head and he shed a little light on a part of CeCe I hadn't really taken the time to notice.

She's so good at helping others but she fucking sucks at accepting it in return.

I don't hate anything about CeCe, but if I did, it'd be that, because I want to be able to help her…I want to be there for her and fucking show up. We all need someone in our corner. Isn't that what being in a relationship is all about?

I'm really asking, because fuck if I know.

Standing in the middle of the broad sidewalk, I look up at CeCe's window, wishing I could rewind everything and go back to a few nights ago when I was wrapped around her.

Eventually, I keep fucking walking, letting the sultry night air soak into my bones. I don't take a direct path home...I basically wander, until I see a familiar building and cut down a back alley that I know ends up across from my townhouse. Thankfully, there's an old street light that illuminates the path, but even with it, I almost fall on my face after I stumble over an old crate. Steadying myself on a filthy dumpster, I wipe my hands on my jeans and glance around out of habit. It's not like anyone is watching me at this time of night, and who the fuck cares if they are.

When I turn back around, something catches my eye. There's a huge butterfly painted on the side of the old brick building. Its wings are vivid shades of greens and blues. Even in the dim light, I can see there's so much detail.

I walk closer to run my hand over the rough surface and notice words wrapping around one of the wings. *If you love it, set it free.*

I've never been one to believe in fate, but something about this fucking butterfly in a dirty, abandoned back alley of New Orleans is speaking to my soul, the one I've often questioned whether it even existed.

I've spent the better part of the last few days doing exactly this: staring out of the window in my office, the one that faces the direction of Neutral Grounds, trying to make sense out of the cacophony of conflicting thoughts running through my head.

Whoever said being in love was easy was a lying bastard.

It's fucking hard. Don't get me wrong, loving CeCe is easy. It's easier than breathing. But figuring out a way to help her understand that what I'm feeling is real and I have no intention of walking away... that's the hard part.

How do I force someone to take a chance on me?

I don't.

I can't.

And I know I have my answer, but it doesn't mean I have to like it.

Setting CeCe free will be the hardest thing I've ever had to do, but I'll do it for her.

As I'm getting ready to head out the door to meet Maverick and a prospective buyer for one of our properties, my phone rings. "This is Shep."

"Shepard." My father's voice catches me off guard and I pull the phone back to check the number. Sure enough, it's him, not that I could mistake his tone for anyone else's, but I wasn't expecting to hear from him.

"Father," I greet in a tone that matches his—cool, cold, and calculated.

Clearing his throat, I can almost picture him unbuttoning his suit jacket and leaning back in his office chair, like he's the fucking king of the world. "I expected to see you back in Dallas by now, but since it seems as though you're making New Orleans a more permanent location, I'm resolved to a phone call."

If this is supposed to be a guilt trip for me selling my house without telling him, he's barking up the wrong tree. Selling that house is the best thing I've done in a while, even if it did give me the cash flow to make the biggest mistake of my life, I find it hard to feel regret. Bottom line, even if CeCe and I are over, I no longer have to worry about her losing the building and everything she's worked so hard for. Over the past few days, I've been making peace with my decisions, facing the consequences, and trying to move forward.

"And to what do I owe this honor?" There's more sarcasm dripping off that question than an ice cream cone on a hot summer day and I hope he hears every last drop. I'm still not over the bullshit he pulled with CeCe, and if I had to guess, this phone call is part of his *plan*. So, let's see what the fuck he has up his sleeve.

"It's time to cut the shit," he barks out.

"Losing patience so soon?" I ask, goading him. He shouldn't fall for it though. I learned it from him. "How very uncharacteristic of you."

He exhales loudly before stating more calmly, "This little charade you've been playing is over. It's time for you to stop being an entitled asshole and come home. I'm tired of carrying the burden for this family just so you can reap the benefits when I'm dead and gone."

"And what charade am I playing?" I ask, knowing what he's referring to, or who, but forcing him to spell it out for me. It's time we clear the fucking air. I knew when my grandfather left his entire estate to me that it would force my father's hand. If anyone is entitled in this family, it's him.

"Put an end to this sham of a marriage, for starters."

I chuckle lowly. "What does my marriage have to do with anything?"

"It's not part of the fucking plan," he states, anger lacing his tone. I can hear his fist connect with his desk and then a whoosh of papers, among other things hitting the floor. "You're fucking up everything!"

"Enlighten me," I challenge. "Please, tell me how me marrying CeCe is fucking with your plan. Last I checked, this is the fucking twenty-first century and I can marry who the fuck I want, when the fuck I want."

"You know you only married her to gain the inheritance," he spits out.

"So what if I did?" I volley.

We're both yelling now and I briefly consider the thickness of my walls, hoping like hell they're soundproof.

"It's not even your fucking money!"

I bark out a laugh, pacing the length of my office. "Now we're fucking getting somewhere. Go ahead, tell me how that money is supposed to be yours. You're pissed, right? Fucking furious! Well, guess what, there's not a fucking thing you can do about it, old man.

For once, this is something that's completely out of your control."

"Like hell it is," he seethes. "Everything is in my control."

His words sound lethal, but it doesn't scare me.

Not much does these days.

There's a long pause and I have a feeling it's for dramatic effect, but his theatrics won't work on me. I couldn't give two shits what he has to say from here on out. He could tell me the sky is falling and it still wouldn't make me agree to divorce CeCe.

"Stay married to that gold-digging whore—" he starts and I immediately cut him off.

"She's my wife!" My body is literally vibrating with anger. "I know the term means nothing to you, you sorry-ass excuse for a man." I want nothing more than to reach through this phone and shed blood. I pause, needing to breathe before I literally come apart and explode into a million pieces. "Never speak about CeCe like that again. As a matter-of-fact, keep her name out of your *fucking* mouth."

"Divorce her or you'll be cut-off. You have a week to decide. I'll be waiting to hear from you."

"What's your angle?" I ask, needing all of the details before he hangs up, because after today, I never want to speak to him again.

"Marry Felicity Crawford," he says matter-of-factly. "Assume your role in this family and get back to being a contributing factor instead of a liability. Then we'll talk about leaving your trust fund intact. Until then, consider yourself disinherited."

I bet it would please him immensely to know my predicament.

Divorce CeCe, which is what she asked me to do, and marry Felicity to gain my inheritance *and* keep my trust fund or refuse CeCe the divorce and lose both…and possibly her when it's all said and done.

Either way, I'm fucked.

CeCe

I JUST FINISHED CLEANING FOR THE NIGHT AND AM about to turn off the lights and set the alarm when a commotion outside the window catches my attention. A very brightly colored commotion, to be exact, which can only mean one thing.

Jules.

Sure enough, as I approach the door, he's standing there, dressed in a bright purple suit and wrapped in a neon pink feather boa, holding up a large bag of… I don't know what.

"Jules…" I'm speaking through the pane of glass but I have no doubt he can still hear the whine in my voice.

"No, ma'am," he says while wagging his perfectly manicured finger in my face. "No. Ma'am. You are going to let me in right this second. We have business to conduct and it's an *emergency*."

The seriousness in his voice plus his use of the words "business" and "emergency" have me unlocking and opening the door against my better judgment. I know Shep said he paid off Theo but I'm still scared he's going to come back, so Jules's surprise visit has me worried.

He steps inside—no, he *shantays*—with what can only be described as flourish. If I had to guess, he worked the early shift at Club Revelry, or took off early to come here. As I'm locking the door behind him, out of the corner of my eye, I see him make a full spin before stopping back in front of me. Jules is always a bit extra, but Jules after a shift at the drag club is next level and probably exactly what I need tonight.

"Whoa," he declares. When I turn to face him fully, his expression grows serious and concerned. "This is worse than I thought."

"What? What's worse?" I ask, bracing myself on the door behind me. "Did you hear something… about Theo?"

"Theo?" He frowns and waves me off with his boa, littering my floor with pink feathers.

Great, I just swept.

"No, I haven't heard anything about that piece of trash," he scoffs. "I'm talking about you, sis."

My chest deflates with a relieved gush of air. I've been on pins and needles the last couple of weeks, waiting for the shoe to drop—waiting for Shep to back out of the deal and follow through with my demands—expecting the worst. So, it takes a few seconds for the second part of his statement to register. "Wait, what about me?"

"No tea, no shade, darlin, but you look like utter shit. I mean, if ragamuffin was the look you were going for today, then you nailed it."

I glance down at myself—jeans, worn t-shirt, and a dirty apron. There's not much to see here, I'll admit. "Gee, thanks. You sure know how to make a girl feel good about herself," I deadpan.

Since I ended things with Shep, I just can't be bothered to put forth much of an effort. I bathe and brush my teeth and I never forget deodorant, so that's a win in my book.

"Oh, don't even start with me. You know I love you but it's time to face facts. You, my dear, have let yourself go and I'm here to help you find yourself again. We are gonna scrub, exfoliate, smooth, detox and depuff your skin for the gods. And then, we'll kiki the house down!"

"Good lord, Jules," I groan, kicking off the door and walking toward the stairs. "I swear I need a drag glossary every time you speak.

I have no idea what you said or what I'm agreeing to."

"But you're agreeing," he says with a waggle of his eyebrows and a wide, knowing smile. "And you won't regret it."

He grabs my hand, pulling me halfway up the stairs. "Do not fret. Mama Jules is gonna take care of you and all you have to do is sit still and drink wine. Think you can handle that?"

I know it's no use to refuse Jules. Besides, as much as I may not want to admit it, I'm sure he's right in his assessment. Self-care has been the least of my worries over the last couple of weeks, to be sure.

"Come on. It'll be mostly painless, I swear. I'm speaking to myself, of course. You, on the other hand, better start praying for deliverance."

Laughing, for the first time in what feels like forever, I follow him into my apartment, still unsure of what's in store, but going along with it if for nothing else than a distraction. Anything to keep me from another night alone with too much time to think.

Jules pops a bottle of wine in the freezer to chill and his iPhone on my dock, turning on a playlist, immediately setting the mood. Taking my hand, he drags me into the bathroom and forces me to sit on the counter. I don't ask questions—and he offers no explanations—I just let him do his thing.

The wine helps pass the time and helps me not care about…well, anything. But my butt is starting to get numb and I've decided the wallpaper in here is hideous. Plus, I'm pretty sure my legs have fallen asleep.

"There's a good chance I won't be able to walk out of here," I mumble, closing my eyes and giving over to mind-numbing pampering. "You might have to carry me to bed."

Jules ignored my complaints, only humming to himself as he works with the intensity of a starving artist.

After a few more minutes, he spritzes my face with some kind of concoction that smells delicious, then wipes his brow before giving what I hope is his final assessment. I watch as he moves his eyes over every inch of my face. It's a bit unnerving to be studied in this way, but it's Jules, and I trust him.

Finally, he brings his palms together in front of his face, as if he's praying, and closes his eyes. "You did it, Jules. You just performed the biggest miracle of your life!" After congratulating himself, he opens his eyes and smiles. "You've officially achieved goddess status once again. Praise be!"

"Can I look in the mirror now?" I ask, curious what he's managed to accomplish while I've been losing feeling in my extremities.

"You certainly may." He helps me stand and thankfully, my legs come back to life, holding my weight. But, when I see my reflection, they weaken a bit, because the difference between CeCe from this morning and CeCe now is nothing short of incredible. I look rested, refreshed, and could almost pass for happy, if I needed to.

Fake it until you make it, right?

"Wow, Jules," I gush, turning my face one way and then the other, truly impressed at his abilities. "I knew you gave good face masks, but I didn't know you could do *this*. I look…human again." I turn toward him and throw my arms around his neck. "Thank you."

"Oh, hush. You know I love a challenge," he says, pulling me back and giving me a wink. "Now, let's go pig out on ice cream and dish."

Jules and I collect two tubs of ice cream and two spoons from the kitchen, then grab my thick, woven blanket off the back of the couch and cuddle up.

This is exactly what I needed. Not just the facial and pampering, but this—human contact. It might sound crazy because I'm surrounded by people all day, but they're strangers, and even though there is conversation and interaction, it never goes below the surface.

I miss closeness, having another person in my space. I thought I'd never say that, but it's true. And while Jules is a good substitute, he can't give me everything I'm missing, but I don't want to dwell on that right now.

"So, not to beat a dead horse or anything, do you really think Theo is gone for good?" I ask, after a few therapeutic bites of Rocky Road. "I mean, I know Shep paid him off, but what if he decides he wants Shep's money *and* the building?"

"According to Mr. Terrel, he's most definitely gone. The will contest has been dropped. That greedy bastard was only after the money, and the quicker the better, so I don't think you have anything to worry about. Besides, that agreement your man made him sign is airtight—very legit and *very* legal—so if he ever did try to sniff around again, you can sue his ass."

"That's great news," I say, keeping my attention on the television. *The Golden Girls* is on, just like every night. It's the only thing that brings me comfort while I'm trying to wind down and go to sleep. Just the opening song alone makes me feel like I just got a much-needed hug. "But you know Shep's not my man, Jules. He never really was."

"Have y'all divorced?"

"No." I'm actually surprised and confused as to why I haven't been served divorce papers by now. I assumed Shep would act fast, wanting to end things between us so he could move on. The longer he waits, the longer it will be until he gets his inheritance.

Even though it's been two weeks since our fight, my heart still aches every time I think about it—about him. I miss him.

"Well, then, he's still your man," Jules declares. "Whether you like it or not, as long as you're married, you're stuck with him. That's kind of how it works. And, I have a feeling you do like it…or you would if you allowed yourself to be honest with him…and yourself."

"I was completely honest with him," I say, ignoring the other part of that statement. "I told him I was falling for him and you know what he did? Nothing. Absofuckinglutely nothing. He wouldn't even look at me." My voice quivers but I don't try to hide it. Jules has officially seen me at my worst, what's a few tears going to matter at this point?

"Do you need me to knock some sense into him?" Jules asks, wrapping an arm around my shoulder and pulling me against him. "You want me to kick his ass? You tell me and I'll do it."

I snicker and wipe at my eyes. "I know you would, and I love you for it."

We sit like that for a few minutes before we trade tubs of ice cream. "Have you seen him?"

Jules sighs. "He's been by the hotel a few times, but he and Maverick are usually in the office."

"How does he…I don't know…look? Seem?" I ask, not wanting to snoop or seem desperate for information about Shep, but dammit, I am. I can't help it.

"You want me to tell you he looks like death?" Jules asks and my stomach drops as an ache forms in my chest. "Like someone ran over his puppy and stole his ice cream…or like his wife just told him she wants a divorce?"

I don't respond to that. I can't. There is part of me that was hoping he'd tell me Shep looks like I feel—confused, torn, and full of regret. But the other part of me, the part that knows it's in love with Shep—the good, the bad, and the overbearing—hopes he's doing okay, because that part can't wish ill will on him even if it wanted to.

"I will tell you this," Jules says, throwing me a bone. "He's been pouring himself into work and taking Maverick with him. Carys was complaining the other day that she saw her husband more before he was her husband."

"I guess it's good that they're leaving soon for their honeymoon," I tell him, remembering what Carys said when she stopped by the other day.

We leave it at that for the rest of the night, keeping our conversation on Rose, Blanche, Dorothy, and Sophia. It's easier to pick apart other people's lives when yours isn't going like you want it.

Which leads me to the question: how do I want it?

If this isn't it, then what is?

Letting Shep go and getting Theo to go away, those two things were supposed to make my life go back to normal. But what the heck is normal? I don't feel normal. I definitely don't feel like myself. I feel…sad and tired, and tired of being sad…and bored, if I'm being completely honest.

Without the threat of losing Neutral Grounds and my home and job, and without my agreement with Shep still intact, I was supposed to feel safe, right? That's what I wanted. I wanted my safety net back. I wanted to know my exit strategy, but now that I have all of that, I feel like there's something missing.

Or someone.

But I don't think I'm ready to admit that.

Or the fact that it might've been too late to end things with Shep. I might've been too far gone. I still might be and I don't know what to do with that. I keep telling myself I didn't fall in love with Shep overnight, so I can't expect myself to fall out of love with him so quickly.

I keep waiting to get divorce papers, thinking that would make it real and force me to face the facts that it's over. But they never come.

I also keep waiting to hear the news that Shep's moved on…that he's dating someone…or fucking someone. But that hasn't come either.

"Hey," Carys says, walking up to the counter.

"Hey," I reply, giving her a warm smile. "I thought you were supposed to be leaving on a fancy honeymoon with your husband." Why does that hurt to say? It shouldn't. I'm happy for my friend and the love that she's found.

My inner voice says I'm also jealous of all that. I'm envious of the realness of her relationship with Maverick and how palpable the love is between them.

"So, how's…everything?" she asks, walking around behind the counter and making herself at home while I work. "I haven't seen Paige around much."

"School is back in session," I tell her. "I've been kind of letting her make her own hours."

Carys laughs. "Sounds about right…which means you're back to working ungodly hours every day, if I have to guess."

"It's what I do," I say with a shrug, handing a drink to a customer. "Thanks for coming in," I call out as they leave. Turning back to Carys, I add, "it's not like I have anything else to do. Besides, I'm used to it… but I have thought about hiring another employee. Having someone to delegate to hasn't been the worst thing in the world. And business has been good, so I could financially support another employee."

She smiles, but it doesn't reach her eyes. "You should do that," she says. "I liked seeing you take some time off…you deserve it. We all need a break from time to time…and it's nice to have someone to share the load with."

We both know she's talking about Shep. I can tell she's feeling me out, but I can't force myself to ask her about him. I know she would tell me anything I want to know, but I can't do it—I can't ask—even though it's right on the tip of my tongue.

When I don't reply, she takes it as her cue to leave, not offering up any information probably in an effort to save my feelings.

"Guess I better go," she says, leaning over and pulling me into a hug. "Promise me you'll take care of yourself while I'm gone."

"I promise," I tell her, holding on a little tighter than usual. "Promise me you'll have the best honeymoon ever." *Do it for me*. "And bring me back something super cheesy."

She laughs, pulling back. "A t-shirt or a coffee mug?"

"Coffee mug, duh," I deadpan, motioning to our surroundings.

One last goodbye and she's out the door, heading home to her husband and letting him whisk her away to somewhere tropical. She's chasing her happily ever after and not holding anything back or sitting around waiting for the worst-case scenario to happen. She's been through that and lived to tell about it. My past experiences don't hold a candle to what Carys has been through, so why can't I be free like that? What's wrong with me?

Gah, this isn't how it was supposed to be.

I feel more confused and out of control than I did a month ago. That safety net I was trying so desperately to reinstall doesn't feel so great anymore. It feels lonely and solitary. I used to be good with that, but now that I've had a taste of the other side—the married, in a relationship side—I don't know if I can go back.

Jules is great, but he's not mine. One of these days, he will make a man very happy and I will be happy for him.

Carys has Maverick.

Avery has Shaw and the baby.

Everybody has someone.

Except me.

And Shep.

And I'll be damned if that doesn't make me even sadder than my own loneliness. When I think about his shitty family and that he doesn't have anyone to rely on either, besides Maverick…who has Carys…I want to go to him and tell him to forget everything I said and stay married to me forever.

But then there's that lingering, nagging thought that I'm not marriage material. I'll always be a control freak. I'll always need to feel in charge of my own destiny. That part of me will never change or go away.

I decided to walk to Avery's house today to see her and the baby, it wasn't until I was about half way here that it dawned on me I'll be next door to Shep, or at least his house, and closer to him than I've been in over three weeks.

Carys and Maverick get back from their honeymoon today and Avery wants to plan a get together for everyone to catch up and see the baby. I'm trying to be happy about it, about everything, but nothing feels right anymore, even more so now than before…

Before I let myself get in the way of my own happiness.

Was it really so bad that Shep paid Theo off? No, but I used it as an excuse.

It did make me feel threatened, but not in the same way Theo did. It's different. I felt like my self-reliance was being threatened, like somehow Shep was buying him out to lord it over me. Yet, here we are, almost a month down the road and he's yet to throw it in my face or demand anything in return.

He hasn't even darkened my doorstep.

No texts.

No calls.

And it hits me—I've been ghosted again.

It's definitely worse the second time around. Now, I'm not just missing his body and the things he can do to mine. I'm missing him—late-night spaghetti dinners, someone to ask me about my day, hearing him talk passionately about things that interest him, the banter, and the recognition. He saw me for what I was and never asked me to be anything different.

I'm the one who pushed him away because I didn't want to hang around and see what happened in the end. Now, I'm wondering if it wouldn't have ended badly after all. Maybe he was feeling the same things I was, but instead of being a coward, he embraced it.

But I ruined all of it by pushing him away.

As I approach the colorful houses that mark the area Shaw and Avery, and now Shep, live in, my heart starts to beat faster. Maybe I should just walk up to his door and knock. If he turns me away, at least I'll be able to look at myself in the mirror tomorrow without regret, knowing I tried.

Just as I'm getting ready to cross the street, I see Shep's door open and I freeze. Two seconds ago, I was all in, but now that I'm being faced with the idea of seeing him again for the first time in weeks, I don't know what to do with myself.

My palms are sweaty.

My breaths are short.

I swallow.

And then, disappointment settles my nerves.

It's just Finley. Well, not *just* Finley. I like Finley. But he's not Shep. No one is.

"Hey, man," he says, his phone pressed to his ear as he turns to lock the door and I hide behind the bushes that separate the two walkways.

Why am I hiding behind the bushes?

What the heck is wrong with me?

"Hahaha," he laughs into the phone sarcastically. "Very funny. No, I'm not having ragers at your pad. Don't worry."

He starts to walk away and I stand, seeing he's headed down the sidewalk.

"How's Dallas?"

Dallas?

Shep. He has to be talking to Shep. Shep's in Dallas.

"Sounds great, man. I'll call you if anything changes here. Thanks again for letting me have a place to crash. I'm looking for my own place, but it's kind of slim pickings…"

The further he walks down the sidewalk, the less I can make out from his conversation, but I heard enough and my stomach is now sitting at my feet…along with my heart.

Shep went back to Dallas and I guess I have my answer—it's really over.

CeCe

"Hello?" Avery's voice is entirely too chipper for this early in the morning, but when I texted her a few minutes ago and told her to call me when she was awake, she replied back with "*Already awake. Living on baby time!*"

A second later, she texted me to call her, probably assuming I was up early with the chickens to make coffee. *I wish.*

"Hey," I groan, speaking into my phone that's lodged between me and my pillow.

"Oh, no," she drawls. "What's wrong? You sound horrible."

"All I said was hey," I reply, trying to sound human but failing miserably.

"Just a sec," she says, shuffling some things around, probably laying Shae down so she can have her hands free. My godson is the best thing since sliced bread and his mama is one of the best I've ever seen. She's so patient and gentle. I love watching the two of them together, but it does make my ovaries ache. I never thought I had a biological clock—or if I did, it was broken—until Shae was born.

Now, it ticks loudly.

"Sorry, I'm back," she whispers. "What's wrong? Are you sick?"

"Yes." My distaste for my current state of health is obvious in my tone. I hate being sick. Actually, I've never been this sick...at least not in the last five years. If it wasn't for Paige, who thankfully replied immediately to my SOS call for help, I would have to close the shop today, which is unheard of and completely out of the question. I'm not sure what I would have done without her, but I would've figured something out. Thank goodness we started training a new girl last week, so at least she'll have some help later today. "I just wanted you to know that I have some sort of plague...or flu...I don't know. My whole body aches and I can't keep anything down. It's horrible and I want to die, but more importantly, I wanted to make sure I didn't give anything to Shae."

I held him for over two hours yesterday, unable to stop inhaling his sweet baby scent—even though he did poop on me...twice—and feeling his soft baby hands. It was the happiest two hours I've had in a while, but now I'm worried I passed horrible germs to my godson.

"He's fine," Avery coos, probably to me and to Shae, or maybe she just talks to everyone in that soothing, motherly tone these days. "Don't worry...I'll keep an eye on him, but babies are very resilient and you washed your hands and used hand sanitizer a million times. Do you think it could've been something you ate?"

I sigh, trying to roll over in bed and then regretting it immediately. "No...maybe. I don't know. I mean, I felt fine yesterday evening after I got home." It was Sunday and I've started closing the shop on Sundays to give myself and everyone else a day off, so after my visit with Avery and Shae, I took the long way back home, thinking mostly about what I overheard from Finley. "I didn't even know I was sick until I woke up around three o'clock this morning and I had to make a run for the bathroom."

"Awww, I'm so sorry. Do you need me to send Shaw over?" Avery's offer of sending her brooding fiancé over to check on me is laughable, but I can't laugh. I can't do anything right now.

"No," I tell her. "I'll be fine. Just keep an eye on my baby, okay?"

She laughs lightly and lets out a sigh. "I will, but you have to promise to call me if you need anything and if I call you, you better answer your phone or I'm sending first responders to your apartment, presuming you're in a coma or something."

"Fine."

After I hang up the phone, I try to go to the kitchen and make a mug of tea, but I can't do it. My legs are so weak, the only thing I can manage is a glass of water and that feels like an extreme feat.

Making it as far as the couch, I pull my blanket off the back, wrap up in it, and promptly fall back asleep. My dreams are fitful and weird. Shep makes an appearance as usual, but he's not there in his usual capacity and they aren't my usual dreams. He's just walking…and walking…never making it to a destination.

I have no idea how long I sleep, but at some point, I wake up to a brown paper bag sitting on the coffee table in front of me and a cup from downstairs that smells like peppermint tea. With zero recollection of anyone coming into my apartment, I assume it was Paige and hope to God she didn't touch me or anything in here. The last thing I need is for my help to get sick.

Managing a few sips, I decide that's as much as I can and should do, just in case it decides to make a reappearance. When I roll over to place it back on the table, I notice a trash can at my side and a folded-up washcloth…it's still damp, so I apply it to my forehead and fall back asleep.

The next time I wake, it's dark outside, but my television is on and *The Golden Girls* is playing.

Dorothy is eating cheesecake and just the thought makes my stomach roll, so I close my eyes, trying to block it out. I usually tend to agree with them that cheesecake fixes everything, but not tonight. Cheesecake will definitely not fix this.

My door shutting is what wakes me up the next time and I sit up, startled someone was in my apartment, and again I didn't even know. I swear, I've never been this out of it. My head swims with the quick movement and I think about laying back down but my bed sounds like a nice change, so I try to make it there.

Thankfully, my legs still work, so I make a quick side trip to the bathroom and survey the area. I can't remember much, but it looks cleaner than the last time I was here, whenever that was.

Stripping off my t-shirt and shorts, I pull a clean nightgown out of my drawer and throw it on, appreciating the clean cotton against my skin. As I climb into bed, I pick up my phone from the nightstand and see a few missed messages from Avery, Carys, Paige, and Jules.

That explains the ninja coming in and out of my apartment.

Avery warned me she'd send in the cavalry if I didn't answer. I hate that I worried her, but I'm grateful to know she wouldn't let me just die here *alone*.

That's comforting.

Avery: Are you alive?

Avery: Hello?

Avery: I'm sending Jules over. Carys said we can use him as a sacrifice.

Jules: Do you like chicken soup?

Jules: Can you eat soup?

Jules: I'm bringing tea and a bagel.

Carys: Hi honey. How are you?

Carys: Text me.

Paige: If you heard that loud bang, don't worry. It was a rambunctious kid running around and he knocked over a shelf. Nothing's broken. But I told his parents I was giving him espresso if it happened again.

Paige: It happened again.

Paige: And something's broken.

Paige: But it's not the kid and I have it under control.

Again, at four-thirty this morning…

Paige: I tried calling you last night but you didn't pick up. I have to go to class today for a few hours to take a test. Any ideas who I could call to work the shop???

That gets my heart pumping and I'm coherent enough to pull myself back up into a sitting position.

What time is it?

Rubbing my eyes, I focus in on the time at the top of my phone.

Ten. In the morning, obviously, because the sun is out.

Pushing out of bed, I go back into the bathroom and turn on the shower. After rummaging around in the medicine cabinet, I find a thermometer and take my temperature. Ninety-nine. That's close enough. If I'm not running a fever, I'm not contagious, right?

After I let the warm water run over my skin, bringing me back to the present, I take inventory of the rest of my body.

The nausea is basically gone.

My bones no longer feel like they're being put through a trash compactor.

My muscles still ache, but more like I just went for a short jog and not a marathon.

I'm not one hundred percent, but I don't feel like I'm knocking on death's door either, so I think I can swing working for a few hours.

Fifteen minutes later, I'm dried off and dressed in jeans and a t-shirt with my damp hair pulled up in a bun. One look at myself in the mirror has me cringing. The dark circles under my eyes tell a different story than the lie I'm feeding myself, but I don't have time to worry about that.

It's not until I bend down to put my shoes on that I really regret this decision, but what choice do I have? None. When you're the owner, manager, and CFO, you pull your shit together and get it done.

Or, at least, that's the pep talk I give to myself on my way to the door.

You can do this.

Taking a deep breath, I brace myself for the smell of coffee and baked goods and pray to God I'm able to push through.

Gingerly, I make my way down the steps, somewhat comforted by the familiar sounds of customers chatter, faint music coming from the speakers, and a fresh pot of coffee brewing. I can't help but smile. Apparently, the world doesn't end if I'm incapacitated, imagine that.

But it's the sight I see when I make the corner into the shop that really gets my attention…I mean, my full fucking attention, because Shepard Rhys-Jones is handing a customer their order and he's wearing an apron—*my apron*—over his starched white shirt and jeans.

With a pencil behind his ear and his hair a disheveled mess, he looks…delectable and utterly comfortable in his environment—*my environment.*

I'm frozen in place, afraid if I move or make a sound it will all disappear…*he'll* disappear. Maybe I'm hallucinating. This could very well be a side effect from being sick. I could still be dreaming.

Then, the door swings open and Paige comes hurrying into the shop. "I'm here," she calls out, running around the counter and tossing her backpack in the corner. "Thanks for covering! Sorry I'm late!"

Shep takes the apron off and tosses it to her, like this is the most normal thing in the entire universe. He never once looks my way, which I honestly don't mind, because I look like shit and I'm happy just to see him.

Yeah, I said it. I'm happy to see him.

Like, ridiculously happy to see him.

Whatever lingering symptoms I might've had feel alleviated with his presence.

*Him…in my shop…*I'm speechless.

"Call me if you need me," he tells Paige. "I've got to run. Maverick is expecting me in twenty minutes." The next thing I know, he's walking out the door.

Dazed and a bit confused, I walk out of the doorway where I've been lurking and into the shop where Paige spots me right away.

"What are you doing out of bed? Are you feeling better?" she asks, multitasking as she fills a cup of ice for an iced coffee and then pops a croissant into the toaster oven.

"What was he doing here?" I ask, my eyes still on the door where Shep exited only moments ago. I think I can still smell his scent lingering in the air and I can't help but inhale deeply. I might even close my eyes.

"Do you need to sit?" she asks me warily.

Popping my eyes open, I shake my head and look back at her. "No, I…I'm fine. I think. But what was he doing here?" I ask again, pointing toward the door.

"Oh, Shep?" she asks, like there was another *he* here…he's the only he at the moment. The only he that matters, anyway. "He stopped by earlier to check on you and I told him I needed to go to class to take my test…did you get my text?"

"Yeah."

"Right, well, he stopped by and offered to help out, so I gave him a crash course and he told me he could handle it."

Looking around, I see everything is still standing, even the shelf Paige had mentioned in her text messages. The place looks intact. Nothing is burning. The customers are happy. Paige is watching me…

"What?" I ask.

"Are you sure you're feeling well enough to be down here? Because if you're not, you can go back to bed. I'm fine. Alex will be here in thirty minutes.

"Shep worked here…by himself?" I ask, stuck on that piece of information.

"Well, I think Carys came over to help him out for a while, but she had to go back and cover the desk at Blue Bayou because Jules is sick."

"What?"

"Yeah, we were sending him up to check on you and I think he caught what you had." She winces.

I groan, rubbing my head. It's a lot to wrap my tired, foggy brain around. "What day is it?"

"Wednesday," she offers, passing an order across the counter. "Can I get you anything else?" she asks the man and woman, who tell her no, offering us both a smile and wave as they take their coffees back out into the sunshine. I don't blame them, that actually sounds really nice.

"I've been out for three days?" I ask.

"Yeah, I was really getting worried about you," she says with a sigh. "You sure you're feeling okay?"

"I'm better. I promise." Still trying to put all the pieces of this bizarre puzzle together, I ask, "I thought Shep went back to Dallas?"

"Oh, he did," she replies, leaning against the counter. "He had some business to attend to. He sold his house," she offers, like it's common knowledge, but I didn't know that. "And since it sold so fast, he had everything put into storage. So, he had to go and figure out what he wanted to bring to here and what he wanted to sell. Then, he finalized the sale on the property he and Maverick have been working on…oh, and he drove the Porsche back."

In typical Paige fashion, she rambles on and I let her go because she's a wealth of information.

"So, he didn't move?" I ask, needing to clear up that misunderstanding.

She frowns and shakes her head. "No, why would you think that?"

"No reason," I mutter, glancing back out the window of the shop like I might be able to still catch a glimpse of him. "I didn't know he sold his house."

I didn't know a lot of things, apparently.

"Oh," she says, pushing off of the counter and walking to the register, pulling out an envelope. "He did say to give you this when you were feeling better."

I take the envelope and turn it over. There's no writing on the outside. It's just a plain, small envelope and for a second, I think it's a card or something, but instead, when I open it up, I find a worn

Monopoly card—*Tennessee Avenue*—and just like that, I'm transported back in time.

Dear CeCe,

Someone wise once told me it's not about how expensive the property is. It was you, you're the wise one. And how appropriate that we connected over a game of Drunk Monopoly? I knew then you couldn't be bought, which is why I cheated my way to a kiss...and to a weekend with you, one that stuck with me every day that followed. I'd like to make it up to you and give you what you won, fair and square.

Your Silly, Sexy, Shep.

Monopoly card—Tennessee Avenue—and just like that I'm [illegible] back in time.

[illegible]

Shep

PACING THE CONCRETE FLOORS OF THE EMPTY building, I check my watch.

She said she'd be here and I know she will be, but it doesn't stop me from counting the seconds and minutes. Shit, I've been counting since I got her text message last night. I thought about calling her back instead of sending her a text, needing to hear her voice, but I'm trying to stay true to the promise I made myself—give her space and set her free.

A few weeks ago, when my father called and gave me an ultimatum, initially, I felt like I was stuck between a rock and a hard place. There was no way I would walk away from CeCe for all the money in the world and I knew there was a chance our marriage was over, which left me completely cut out of both my grandfather's will and my father's trust fund. But over the past few weeks, I've done a lot of thinking and I came to the conclusion that my father actually freed me.

What felt like no choice became the easiest one I've ever made.

I choose her.

For better or worse.

For richer or poorer.

When the door creaks, I turn to see her and I can't help the way my heart speeds up. It's been the longest fucking month of my life and not knowing how today will go is putting me on edge, but I need to hold my shit together and get through this.

"I thought you might stand me up," I tease, only semi-joking.

She gives me a half smile, trying to hide it. "I considered it, but then again, you did go to all that trouble to leave me a Monopoly card."

"I stole it," I confess, taking a step closer.

"So, you're a thief and a cheater." She quirks an eyebrow and it's then I notice the dark circles under her eyes from being sick. It makes me want to sweep her up and carry her to bed. When I heard that she was too sick to work, I knew it had to be bad, which is what made me go to the shop. I didn't really think I'd end up slinging coffee, but there's a first time for everything and I was happy to help.

Actually, I fucking loved it.

I'd do it again…anything for her.

"I hear you also know how to make a mean cup of coffee," she says, her expression softening. "Thank you for helping out while I was sick. That was—"

"My pleasure," I say, cutting her off. "I was happy to do it."

"Well, it means a lot to me."

Paulie's advice about finding a way to show her I'm in this for good comes back to me. I'd work in her shop until I'm old and grey if it was enough to prove my feelings for her. Honestly, there's not much I wouldn't do, which brings me to why I asked her to come here today.

Walking over to the lone table in the middle of the room, I brace my hands on either side of two stacks of papers. "A while back, you told me you didn't want this—to be married to me," I start, forcing my voice to stay calm and collected. It's a gift, really. Something I've learned over the years of business deals. Glancing up, I see that she's stone-faced and I'm worried this won't end in my favor. "After a talk with Carys a few weeks ago, she helped me understand you haven't been given a lot of choices in your life, so I'd like to change that. But first, I need you to know a few things."

She swallows and tucks her arms around her body, hugging herself, and I wish I could see inside her head, know what she's thinking…feeling. It would make this so much easier, but I promised myself that today, I'd lay all my cards on the table and walk out of here with no regrets.

"I did cheat in that game of Monopoly. You won, fair and square. But it was the best damn game I've ever played in my life because it led me to you." I pause for a moment and take her in, memorizing this moment and the way she looks, just in case it's the last time I see her while she's still mine. "But this hasn't been a game for a long time, at least not for me. I love you, CeCe. I love everything about you, even your exit strategies and safety nets. I'm sorry for buying Theo out and not talking to you about it first. I can't say I regret it because I would do anything to make your life better, but I get it now. I know I overstepped—"

"Shep," she starts to interrupt, taking a step closer until the only thing separating us is the table.

"Let me finish…please." She huffs and cocks her head, giving me the most beautiful stubborn expression and I'd love nothing more than to kiss it off her face, but she's letting me finish, so I continue. "I know you're never going to be the woman who needs saving, and I'm okay with that. I just want to be the man who gets to walk by your side…and be your shoulder to lean on from time to time." Sliding one set of papers around to face her, I look up and lock onto those gorgeous brown eyes. "This is the deed to this property we're on right now…the one that's been rightfully yours for the last two years. I want you to have it, regardless of any other decision you make tonight."

She goes to speak, but again, I stop her, needing to finish what I came here to say.

"These," I tell her, pushing the other stack of papers toward her, "are the papers for our divorce. But, before you make your choice, I need you to know this isn't a fake marriage, not to me, and if we get divorced, that won't be fake either. It will be real, just like my love for you."

Walking around the table, I use every ounce of strength I have to not force her into giving me an answer right here, right now, and instead, lean down and press my lips to her forehead. For a second, I allow myself to just inhale and trust in fate and this crazy journey we've been on together.

I keep telling myself there's no way all of this is for nothing.

Setting the keys to the building on the table, I breathe. "I'll be waiting for your decision…and whatever it may be, I'll support it."

I hope she reads between the lines—*I'll support you…I'm here for you…it's me and you forever, if you'll have me.*

"WHERE'S MY WIFE?"

I felt him before I heard him. It's strange, but now that I've given myself over to him so completely, it's like the cells in my body are connected to his. And it's not scary, it's the best feeling in the world.

"I think she's in the kitchen," Avery replies. "Who wants to hold a baby while I pour us all a glass of wine?"

The entire living room erupts with offers, but I hear Shaw dominate the bidding pool. "I haven't seen him in six hours," he says gruffly, but I know his actions are quite the opposite. Even being a daddy hasn't softened all of his edges, but when he's holding Shae, he's a different human being. He melts, just like the rest of us. "You greedy bastards wait your turn."

"Language!" Avery calls from behind me. "I swear, I never dreamed he'd be like this." Her laugh tells me she loves every second of it and every bit of that man and the baby he's hogging.

"Really?" I ask. "You didn't dream that Shaw O'Sullivan would be a protective, possessive, dominating daddy?" I scoff and shake my head as I continue to slice vegetables.

We're finally getting around to having the get together Avery wanted. It took us a while to get everyone together. With all of our hectic schedules and new projects flying around, it's a miracle we managed it at all.

"I'm just kidding," Avery says, checking me with her hip as she saddles up beside me. "Your cocky…uppity…smug husband is looking for you." She giggles, taking a sip of wine.

"How many glasses have you had?"

"Two," she says flatly. "I'm a cheap, easy drunk, what can I say?"

I thought I'd never get used to hearing Shep being referred to as my husband, or me as his wife, but somehow, over the past few months, I have. Every time he's in the room, it's like I'm wearing my favorite tattered sweatshirt while listening to Otis Redding on my record player, drinking a glass of wine on a Saturday night…while *The Golden Girls* reruns play in the background.

He's all of my favorite things rolled into one fantastic man…that's all mine. Any time of day. Whenever I want. He's there for me. He did something no one else has ever stopped and taken the time to do…he gave me a choice.

And I chose him.

Avery and I collect the platters of appetizers and carry them into her and Shaw's large, open great room. Sometimes, when the weather is nice, we take things outside and open up the gate Shep and Shaw installed between the two small backyards. But tonight, it's raining, and that's just as well, because I love seeing everyone together—Carys, Maverick, Jules, Avery, Shaw, Shae, Sarah, Paulie…even Micah and Dani and Cami and Deacon joined us tonight.

Cami is opening her new art gallery soon and they've been staying at the Blue Bayou quite a bit during the week to keep them from driving back and forth to French Settlement every night. Sometimes, they have their adorable kids with them and sometimes it's just the two of them. Tonight, it's adults only, except for Shae.

We all crowd around the long table, passing food and wine and banter.

When Shep catches my eye as I pass a bowl of pasta and gives me a wink, before leaning in for a kiss on the cheek, I feel my entire body heat up, just the way it does every time he's near.

This life isn't perfect. There are always ups and downs and risks and rewards, but at the end of it, as long as we're with the ones we love, that's all that matters.

Later, after I've helped Avery clean up the kitchen and tucked my godson into bed, I make my way next door. It's no longer Shep's house…it's our house.

Finley moved into my old apartment above the coffee shop and he keeps an eye on things for me, while enjoying really cheap rent.

And, every morning, Shep walks me to Neutral Grounds and comes in for a cup of coffee to get his day started…and sometimes a little lagniappe…not the restaurant, but the kind only I can give him.

When I shut the door behind me, he calls out from the office. "Get your ass in here."

"If you're telling me what to do, you better be naked."

I smirk as I kick off my shoes by the door and hang up my raincoat on the hook. Shortly after I ripped up the divorce papers and signed my name to the deed for the building next door, Shep and I negotiated new ground rules, not for an arrangement, but for our marriage.

Number one: We discuss any and all business dealings before they happen.

Number two: We live under the same roof.

Number three: I don't try to do everything on my own.

Number four: He doesn't tell me what to do…unless he's naked, then, anything is fair game.

When I walk into his office, he's sitting in his chair with his back to me. I stand in the doorway and rest against the frame, waiting. As I clear my voice, he swivels in his chair and I have to bite back a laugh… and a groan.

"What are you doing?" I ask, trying to keep my eyes on his, but failing miserably. When a piece of art like Shepard Rhys-Jones is sitting in front of you, in a leather chair that probably cost more than some cars, wearing only a tie…and a very, very cocky smile…it's hard to maintain any level of decorum.

"Strip," he says, clasping his hands in front of him, with everything else unabashedly on display. When I continue to stand there, he raises an eyebrow. "CeCe..."

My heart rate triples as my body begins to respond. *Right... clothes...off.* With Shep's intense gaze following my every move, I discard every article of clothing down to the black satin panties he bought me last week...just because.

That's another concession I've had to make. Shepard is going to buy me gifts and it doesn't mean he's trying to buy *me*. It's just who he is and how he's made. When I chose him, I chose him flaws and all. There's nothing about him I want to change, because I love every piece of him—his good heart, his smug confidence, the way he commands a room...even his bossiness and bravado.

"I've been imagining you out of those clothes all fucking day."

I swallow. "Really?" I ask, wanting to hear more about what he's been imagining...or better yet, maybe he could show me.

One thing Shep has gotten really good at is showing me how much he loves me...thoroughly, erasing all doubts and insecurities. When it's just me and him and all of our walls disappear, I love the Shep only I get to see. Under the well-tailored suits and expensive shirts—which he doesn't wear as much these days, but still plays the part when necessary—is someone who's real and vulnerable and desires to be loved and to love in return.

I plan on giving him exactly that, every day, as long as we both shall live.

"Come here," he demands, crooking his finger. "Let me show you."

Walking further into the office, I can't help the smile that spreads across my face as I indulge my senses. Everything about this office is so him—the woodsy, masculine scent, the dark woods—it's intoxicating.

As I step closer, he reaches out and wraps his hand around my waist, pulling me forward until I'm straddling his lap, inches away from bringing us both the satisfaction we desire...being one, our bodies melding together.

When our eyes meet, I can't help the overwhelming emotions that flood me, every time we're like this. He's mine. My husband...*my silly, sexy, Shep.*

Acknowledgments

And now for the part where we say thank you, which seems entirely insignificant because everyone we mention plays such a big part in this process.

To the VIPs in our lives—our kiddos, family, friends, and readers. What is life without amazing people to share it with? Every Jiffy Kate book has an element of family, whether it's the family our characters are born with or the family they create for themselves. Family is important to us, which is why it plays such a big part of our stories. And we wouldn't be where we are today without ours.

We'd also like to thank Pamela Stephenson for being our beta reader! She's always there from the beginning, watching and reading as the story takes shape. Thanks for being you, Pamela!!

Nichole Strauss, our editor, thank you for always approaching every new story we throw at you with an insightful eye. You've taught us better sentence structure and kept us from the pitfalls of repetitive words. Thank you for teaching us to be better writers!

Our proofreader, Janice Owen, thank you for taking us on at such short notice!

We'd also like to thank our cover designer and formatter, Julianna. Thank you for the creativity and time you put into every cover.

Also, a huge shout-out to our pimp team—Pamela, Lynette, Megan, Shannon, Candace, Stefanie, Laura, Kat, Debbie, Polly, Letica. Thank you for always putting your two-cents worth in and giving us a safe place to bounce ideas! We love y'all!

Thank you to all of our readers and everyone in Jiffy Kate's Southern Belles. All of you make our days better. We always say it takes a village and we're so glad all of you are in ours.

Until next time,
Jiffy Kate

About The Authors

Jiffy Kate is the joint pen name for Jiff Simpson and Jenny Kate Altman. They're co-writing besties who share a brain and a love of cute boys, good coffee, and a fun time.

Together, they've written over twenty stories. Their first published book, Finding Focus, was released in November 2015. Since then, they've continued to write what they know—southern settings full of swoony heroes and strong heroines.

You can find them on most social media outlets at @jiffykate, @ jiffykatewrites, or @jiffsimpson and @jennykate77.

CPSIA information can be obtained
at www.ICGtesting.com
Printed in the USA
BVHW042122291019
562449BV00007B/122/P